MIKE ASHLEY is a full-time writer, editor and researcher who has compiled over one hundred books, from studies including *The Seven Wonders of the World* and *The British Monarchy* to such specialist works as *Starlight Man*, the biography of Algernon Blackwood, and *The Mammoth Book of King Arthur*. With William Contento he compiled *The Supernatural Index*. He has also edited two companion volumes to *Sisters in Crime* for Peter Owen: *The Darker Sex: Tales of the Supernatural and Macabre by Victorian Women Writers* and *The Dreaming Sex: Early Tales of Scientific Imagination by Women*. He lives in Kent with his wife and three cats.

D1165986

THE FIGURE STILL WENT IN FRONT OF ME . . .
from 'The Warder of the Door' by L.T. Meade

SISTERS IN
CRIME

Also edited by Mike Ashley and published by Peter Owen

The Darker Sex:
Tales of the Supernatural and Macabre by Victorian Women Writers

The Dreaming Sex:
Early Tales of Scientific Imagination by Women

SISTERS IN CRIME

Early Detective and Mystery Stories by Women

Edited by
MIKE ASHLEY

PETER OWEN
London and Chicago

PETER OWEN PUBLISHERS
81 Ridge Road, London N8 9NP

Peter Owen books are distributed in the USA by
the Independent Publishers Group,
814 North Franklin Street,
Chicago, IL 60610, USA

This collection first published in Great Britain 2013 by
Peter Owen Publishers

Selection and Introduction © Mike Ashley 2013

All Rights Reserved.
No part of this publication may be reproduced in any form or by any
means without the written permission of the publishers.

ISBN 978-0-7206-1516-6

A catalogue record for this book is available from the British Library

Typeset by Octavo Smith Ltd in
Baskerville MT 10/13

Printed and bound in the UK by
CPI Group (UK) Ltd, Croydon, CR0 4YY

SOURCES AND ACKNOWLEDGEMENTS

Stories

'Levison's Victim' by Mary E. Braddon, first published in *Belgravia*,
January 1870

'Going Through the Tunnel' by Mrs Henry Wood, first published in
The Argosy, February 1869

'Mr Furbush' by Harriet E. Prescott, first published in *Harper's New Monthly
Magazine*, April 1865

'Traces of Crime' by Mary Fortune, first published in *Australian Journal*,
2 December 1865

'The House of Clocks' by Anna Katharine Green, first published in
The Golden Slipper (Putnam, 1915)

'The Polish Refugee' by Elizabeth Corbett, first published in *Secrets of a
Private Enquiry Office* (Routledge, 1891)

'The Long Arm' by Mary Wilkins Freeman, first published in *Chapman's
Magazine*, August 1895

'The Redhill Sisterhood' by C.L. Pirkis, first published in *The Ludgate*, April
1893

'The Villa of Simpkins' by Arabella Kenealy, first published in *The Ludgate*,
August 1896

'The Warder of the Door' by L.T. Meade, first published in *Cassell's Family
Magazine*, July 1897

'The Tragedy of a Doll' by Lucy G. Moberly, first published in *The Lady's
Magazine*, October 1903

'A Point of Testimony' by Carolyn Wells, first published in *Adventure*,
October 1911

Pictures

From 'The Redhill Sisterhood', Bernard Higham (*The Ludgate*,
April 1893)

From 'The Villa of Simpkins', R. Savage (*The Ludgate*, August 1896)

From 'The Warder of the Door', John H. Bacon (*Cassell's Family Magazine*,
July 1897)

CONTENTS

Introduction 13

Mary E. Braddon Levison's Victim 15

Ellen Wood Going Through the Tunnel 33

Harriet E. Prescott Mr Furbush 54

Mary Fortune Traces of Crime 64

Anna Katharine Green The House of Clocks 77

Elizabeth Corbett The Polish Refugee 113

Mary E. Wilkins The Long Arm 126

C.L. Pirkis The Redhill Sisterhood 161

Arabella Kenealy The Villa of Simpkins 187

L.T. Meade The Warder of the Door 205

Lucy G. Moberly The Tragedy of a Doll 223

Carolyn Wells A Point of Testimony 234

INTRODUCTION

In my previous two anthologies in this series, *The Darker Sex* (2009) and *The Dreaming Sex* (2010), I presented examples of works by women writers that contributed to the development and popularization of the supernatural story and science fiction respectively. For this third volume I have turned to crime and mystery fiction.

Women have long been regarded as major contributors and innovators when it comes to crime fiction – one has only to think of Agatha Christie, Dorothy L. Sayers, Margery Allingham, P.D. James, Ruth Rendell, Patricia Cornwell, Sara Paretsky, Kathy Reichs (and on and on and on) to show what a force women are in the field. But their forebears do not always get the same recognition. When charting the growth of crime fiction during the Victorian period the names of Edgar Allan Poe, Wilkie Collins, Charles Dickens and, of course, Arthur Conan Doyle will come readily to mind, but among women writers perhaps only Mary E. Braddon will get a grudging recognition, as will Anna Katharine Green, who is, at least, called the 'mother of the detective novel'.

As for Catherine Pirkis or Mary Fortune or Arabella Kenealy or Lucy Moberly – who remembers them? Yet their roles in popularizing the genre are every bit as important. Mary Fortune was the most prolific writer of crime stories during the Victorian period, but because her work appeared only in Australian newspapers she has long been forgotten.

So for this anthology I have brought together just a few of these excellent writers. There are many more – I could have filled this book ten times over without repeating any authors. All of the stories feature a crime or a mystery, and many of them are also detective stories. What struck me in putting together this collection is that the women rose as equally to the challenge as men in creating fascinating puzzles and bizarre mysteries, but they added an extra depth of character. You will find believable people in these stories who understand the problems of others and are determined to fight injustice. That is because many of these writers had experienced their own sufferings and privations and had struggled to survive against long odds.

All the stories are, of course, written in the style of their day, and it is interesting to compare the earliest, from 1865 with the most recent (!) from 1915. The stories are presented more or less in chronological order so that you can follow the development of the field, and I have provided backgrounds on all of the authors in an introduction to each story. You will find a far more relaxing style compared with much of today's fiction. These are stories to curl up with and wind down to at the end of the day. And they are a remarkable window on the past. So prepare to be transported to those wonderful gaslit days of mystery and escape the present, just for a while.

Mike Ashley
May 2013

Mary E. Braddon

LEVISON'S VICTIM

Mary E. Braddon (1835–1915) was one of the most popular and bestselling novelists of the Victorian period, as well as one of the most notorious. After a challenging childhood – raised and educated by her mother after her father deserted them and going on to the stage in her early twenties to support her mother – Braddon found, by 1860, her gift for writing. After several short stories and a blood-and-thunder novel Three Times Dead *(1860) she struck gold with* Lady Audley's Secret *(1862), which became the sensation of the decade. It tells of an attractive but devious woman who, though now respectably married, discovers that her first husband (who had previously deserted her) is still alive and likely to cause problems, so she attempts to murder him. Braddon followed this with the equally sensational* Aurora Floyd *(1863), with more bigamy and murder. The popularity of her work – and she would go on to write over eighty novels – allowed her to survive public reaction to her own sensational life which, in Victorian England, would have ruined a lesser woman. Braddon had moved in with and had children by her publisher, John Maxwell, who was still married, though his wife was in an Irish asylum for the insane. Braddon married Maxwell only after his wife died in 1874.*

The following story was written during a particularly difficult time. Her mother and sister had died within a month of each other at the end of 1868, and soon after Braddon gave birth to a daughter and fell into a state of both physical and nervous collapse, aggravated by puerperal fever. She had by then written twenty novels in less than ten years and had been editing the magazine Belgravia. *This story, which was published in* Belgravia *in January 1870, with its profound sense of loss and recovery, may well have helped her get over her depression.*

Levison's Victim

'HAVE YOU SEEN Horace Wynward?'

'No. You don't mean to say that he is here?'

'He is indeed. I saw him last night; and I think I never saw a man so much changed in so short a time.'

'For the worse?'

'Infinitely for the worse. I should scarcely have recognized him but for that peculiar look in his eyes, which I dare say you remember.'

'Yes; deep-set grey eyes, with an earnest penetrating look that seems to read one's most hidden thoughts. I'm very sorry to hear of this change in him. We were at Oxford together, you know, and his place is near my father's in Buckinghamshire. We have been fast friends for a long time; but I lost sight of him about two years ago, before I went on my Spanish rambles, and I've heard nothing of him since. Do you think he has been leading a dissipated life – going the pace a little too violently?'

'I don't know what he has been doing; but I fancy he must have been travelling during the last year or two, for I've never come across him in London.'

'Did you speak to him last night?'

'No; I wanted very much to get hold of him for a few minutes' chat but couldn't manage it. It was in one of the gambling-rooms I saw him, on the opposite side of the table. The room was crowded. He was standing looking on at the game over the heads of the players. You know how tall he is, and what a conspicuous figure anywhere. I saw him one minute, and in the next he had disappeared. I left the rooms in search of him, but he was not to be seen anywhere.'

'I shall try and hunt him up tomorrow. He must be stopping at one of the hotels. There can't be much difficulty in finding him.'

The speakers were two young Englishmen; the scene a lamplit grove of trees outside the Kursaal of a German spa. The elder, George Theobald, was a barrister of the Inner Temple; the younger, Francis Lorrimore, was the son and heir of a Buckinghamshire squire, and a gentleman at large.

'What was the change that struck you so painfully, George?' Lorrimore asked between the puffs of his cigar. 'You couldn't have seen much of Wynward in that look across the gaming-table.'

'I saw quite enough. His face has a worn, haggard expression, he looks like a man who never sleeps; and there's a fierceness about the eyes – a contraction of the brows, a kind of restless searching look – as if he were on the watch for someone or something. In short, the poor fellow seemed to me altogether queer – the sort of man one would expect to hear of as being shut up in a madhouse, or committing suicide, or something bad of that kind.'

'I shall certainly hunt him out, George.'

'It would be only a kindness to do so, old fellow, as you and he have been intimate. Stay!' exclaimed Mr Theobald, pointing suddenly to a figure in the distance. 'Do you see that tall man under the trees yonder? I've a notion it's the very man we're talking of.'

They rose from the bench on which they had been sitting smoking their cigars for the last half-hour, and walked in the direction of the tall figure pacing slowly under the pine trees. There was no mistaking that muscular frame – six feet two, if an inch – and the peculiar carriage of the head. Frank Lorrimore touched his friend lightly on the shoulder, and he turned around suddenly and faced the two young men, staring at them blankly without a sign of recognition.

Yes, it was indeed a haggard face, with a latent fierceness in the deep-set grey eyes overshadowed by strongly marked black brows, but a face which, seen at its best, must needs have been very handsome.

'Wynward,' said Frank, 'don't you know me?'

Lorrimore held out both his hands. Wynward took one of them slowly, looking at him like a man suddenly awakened from sleep.

'Yes,' he said, 'I know you well enough now, Frank, but you startled me just this moment. I was thinking. How well you're looking, old fellow! What, you here, too, Theobald?'

'Yes; I saw you in the rooms last night,' answered Theobald as they shook hands, 'but you were gone before I could get a chance of speaking to you. Where are you staying?'

'At the Hotel des Étrangers. I shall be off tomorrow.'

'Don't run away in such a hurry, Horace,' said Frank. 'It looks as if you wanted to cut us.'

'I'm not very good company just now; you'd scarcely care to see much of me.'

'You are not looking very well, Horace, certainly. Have you been ill?'

'No, I am never ill; I am made of iron, you know.'

'But there's something wrong, I'm afraid.'

'There is something wrong, but nothing that sympathy or friendship can mend.'

'Don't say that, my dear fellow. Come to breakfast with me tomorrow and tell me your troubles.'

'It's a common story enough; I shall only bore you.'

'I think you ought to know me better than that.'

'Well, I'll come, if you like,' Horace Wynward answered in a softer tone. 'I'm not very much given to confide in friendship, but you were once a kind of younger brother of mine, Frank. Yes, I'll come. How long have you been here?'

'I only came yesterday. I am at the Couronne d'Or, where I discovered my friend Theobald, happily for me, at the *table d'hôte*. I am going back to Buckinghamshire next week. Have you been at Crofton lately?'

'No. Crofton has been shut up for the last two years. The old housekeeper is there, of course, and there are men to keep the gardens in order – I shouldn't like the idea of my mother's flower-garden being neglected – but I doubt if I shall ever live at Crofton.'

'Not when you marry, Horace?'

'Marry? Yes, when that event occurs I may change my mind,' he answered with a scornful laugh.

'Ah, Horace, I see there is a woman at the bottom of your trouble!'

Wynward took no notice of this remark and began to talk of indifferent subjects.

The three young men walked for some time under the pines, smoking and talking in a fragmentary manner. Horace Wynward had an absent-minded way, which was not calculated to promote a lively style of conversation; but the others indulged his humour and did not demand much from him. It was late when they shook hands and separated.

'At ten o'clock tomorrow, Horace?' said Frank.

'I shall be with you at ten. Good-night.'

* * *

Mr Lorrimore ordered an excellent breakfast, and a little before ten o'clock awaited his friend in a pretty sitting-room overlooking the gardens of the hotel. He had been dreaming of Horace all night and was thinking of him as he walked up and down the room waiting his arrival. As the little clock on the mantelpiece struck the hour, Mr Wynward was announced. His clothes were dusty, and he had a tired look even at that early hour. Frank welcomed him heartily.

'You look as if you had been walking, Horace,' he said, as they sat down to breakfast.

'I have been on the hills since five o'clock this morning.'

'So early?'

'Yes; I am a bad sleeper. It is better to walk than to lie tossing about hour after hour, thinking the same thoughts with maddening repetition.'

'My dear boy, you will make yourself ill with this kind of life.'

'Don't I tell you that I am never ill? I never had a day's illness in my life. I suppose when I die I shall go down at a shot – apoplexy or heart disease. Men of my build generally do.'

'I hope you may have a long life.'

'Yes, a long life of emptiness.'

'Why shouldn't it be a useful, happy life, Horace?'

'Because it was shipwrecked two years ago. I set sail for a given port, Frank, with a fair wind in my favour; and my ship went down in sight of land, on a summer's day, without a moment's warning. I can't rig another boat and make for another harbour as some men can. All my world's wealth was adventured in this one argosy. That sounds tall talk, doesn't it? but you see there is such a thing as passion in the world, and I've so much faith in your sympathy that I'm not ashamed to tell you what a fool I have been – and still am. You were such a romantic fellow five years ago, Frank, and I used to laugh at your sentimental notions.'

'Yes, I was obliged to stand a good deal of ridicule from you.'

'Let those laugh who win. It was in my last long vacation that I went to read at a quiet little village on the Sussex coast, with a retired tutor, an eccentric old fellow, but a miracle of learning. He had three daughters, the eldest of them, to my mind, the loveliest girl that ever the sun shone upon. I'm not going to make a long story of it. I think it was a case of love at first sight. I know that before I had been a week in the humdrum sea-coast village I was over head and ears in love with Laura Daventry; and at the end of a month I was happy in the belief that my love was returned. She was the dearest, brightest of girls, with a sunshiny disposition that won her friends in every direction, and a man must have had a dull soul who could have withstood the charm of her society. I was free to make my own choice, rich enough to marry a penniless girl, and before I went back to Oxford I made her an offer. It was accepted, and I returned to the university the happiest of men.'

He drank a cup of coffee and rose from the table to walk up and down the room.

'Well, Frank, you would imagine that nothing could arise to interfere with our happiness after this. In worldly circumstances I was what would be considered an excellent match for Miss Daventry, and I had every reason to believe that she loved me. She was very young, not quite eighteen, and I was the first man who had ever proposed to her. I left her with the most entire confidence in her good faith, and to this hour I believe in her.'

There was a pause, and then he went on again.

'We corresponded, of course. Laura's letters were charming, and I had no greater delight than in receiving and replying to them. I had promised her to work hard for my degree, and for her sake I kept my promise and won it. My first thought was to carry her the news of my success; and directly the examinations were over I ran down to Sussex. I found the cottage empty. Mr Daventry was in London; the two younger girls had gone to Devonshire, to an aunt who kept a school there. About Miss Daventry the neighbours could give me no positive information. She had left a few days before her father, but no one knew where she had gone. When I pressed them more closely they told me that it was rumoured in the village that she had gone away to be married. A gentleman from the Spanish colonies, a Mr Levison, had been staying at the cottage for some weeks and had disappeared about the same time as Miss Laura.'

'And you believe that she had eloped with him?'

'To this day I am ignorant as to the manner of her leaving. Her last letters were only a week old. She had told me of this Mr Levison's residence in their household. He was a wealthy merchant, a distant relation of her father's, and was staying in Sussex for his health. This was all she had said of him. Of their approaching departure she had not given me the slightest hint. No one in the village could tell me Mr Daventry's London address. The cottage, a furnished one, had been given up to the landlord and every debt paid. I went to the post office, but the people there had received no directions as to the forwarding of letters, nor had any come as yet for Mr Daventry.'

'The girls in Devonshire – you applied to them, I suppose?'

'I did, but they could tell me nothing. I wrote to Emily, the elder girl, begging her to send me her sister's address. She answered my letter immediately. Laura had left home with her father's full knowledge and consent, she said, but had not told her sisters where she was going. She had seemed very unhappy. The whole affair had been sudden, and her father had also appeared much distressed in mind. This was all I could ascertain. I put an advertisement in *The Times* addressed to Mr Daventry, begging him to let me know his whereabouts, but nothing came of it. I employed a man to hunt London for him, and hunted myself, but without avail. I wasted months in this futile search, now on one false track, now on another.'

'And you have long ago given up all hope, I suppose?' Lorrimore said as Wynward paused, walking up and down the room with a moody face.

'Given up all hope of seeing Laura Levison alive? Yes; but not of tracking her destroyer.'

'Laura Levison! Then you think she married the Spanish merchant?'

'I am sure of it. I had been more than six months on the look-out for Mr Daventry, and had begun to despair of finding him, when the man I employed came to me and told me that he had found the registry of a marriage between Michael Levison and Laura Daventry at an obscure church in the City, where he had occasion to make researches for another client. The date of the marriage was within a few days of Laura's departure from Sussex.'

'Strange!'

'Yes, strange that a woman could be so fickle, you would say. I felt convinced that there had been something more than girlish inconstancy at work in this business – some motive power, strong enough to induce this girl to sacrifice herself in a loveless marriage. I was confirmed in this belief when, within a very short time of the discovery of the registry, I came suddenly upon old Daventry in the street. He would willingly have avoided me, but I insisted on a conversation with him, and he reluctantly allowed me to accompany him to his lodging, a wretched place in Southwark. He was very ill, with the stamp of death upon his face, and had a craven look that convinced me it was to him I was indebted for my sorrow. I told him that I knew of his daughter's marriage, when and where it had taken place and boldly accused him of having brought it about.'

'How did he take your accusation?'

'Like a beaten hound. He whimpered piteously and told me that the marriage had been no wish of his. But Levison had possession of secrets which made him the veriest slave. Little by little I wrung from him the nature of these secrets. They related to forged bills of exchange in which the old man had made free with his kinsman's name. It was a transaction of many years ago; but Levison had used this power in order to induce Laura to marry him, and the girl, to save her father from disgrace and ruin, as she believed, had consented to become his wife. Levison had promised to do great things for the old man but had left England immediately after his marriage without settling a shilling on his father-in-law. It was altogether a dastardly business: the girl had been sacrificed to her father's weakness and folly. I asked him why he had not appealed to me, who could no doubt have extricated him from his difficulty, but he could give me no clear answer. He evidently had an overpowering dread of Michael Levison. I left him, utterly disgusted with his imbecility and selfishness; but, for Laura's sake, I took care that he wanted for nothing during the remainder of his life. He did not trouble me long.'

'And Mrs Levison?'

'The old man told me that the Levisons had gone to Switzerland. I followed post-haste and traced them from place to place, closely questioning the people at all the hotels. The accounts I heard were by no means encouraging. The lady did not seem happy. The gentleman looked old enough to be her father and was peevish and fretful in his manner, never letting his wife out of his sight and evidently suffering agonies of jealousy on account of the admiration which her beauty won for her from every one they met. I traced them stage by stage, through Switzerland into Italy, and then suddenly lost the track. I concluded that they had returned to England by some other route, but all my attempts to discover traces of their return were useless. Neither by land nor by sea passage could I hear of the yellow-faced trader and his beautiful young wife. They were not a couple to be overlooked easily; and this puzzled me. Disheartened and dispirited, I halted in Paris where I spent a couple of months in hopeless idleness – a state of utter stagnation from which I was aroused abruptly by a communication from my agent, a private detective, a very clever fellow in his way and well in with the police of civilized Europe. He sent me a cutting from a German newspaper which described the discovery of a corpse in the Tyrol. It was supposed, from the style of the dress, to be the body of an Englishwoman, but no indication of a name or address had been found to give a clue to identity. Whether the dead woman had been the victim of foul play, or whether she had met her death from an accidental fall, no one had been able to decide. The body had been found at the bottom of a mountain gorge, the face disfigured by the fall from the height above. Had the victim been a native of the district it might have been easily supposed that she had lost her footing on the mountain path; but that a stranger should have travelled alone by so unfrequented a route seemed highly improbable. The spot at which the body was found lay within a mile of a small village; but it was a place rarely visited by travellers of any description.'

'Had your agent any reason to identify this woman with Mrs Levison?'

'None, except the fact that Mrs Levison was missing and his natural habit of suspecting the very worst. The paragraph was nearly a month old when it reached me. I set off at once for the place named, saw the village authorities and visited the Englishwoman's grave. They showed me the dress she had worn: a black silk, very simply made. Her face had been too much disfigured by the fall and the passage of time that had occurred before the finding of the body for my informants to give me any minute description of her appearance. They could only tell me that her hair was dark auburn, the colour of Laura's, thick and long, and that her figure was that of a young woman.

'After exhausting every possible enquiry, I pushed on to the next village and there received confirmation of my worst fears. A gentleman and his wife – the man of foreign appearance but talking English, the woman young and beautiful – had stopped for a night at the chief inn of the place and had left the next morning without a guide. The gentleman, who spoke German perfectly, told the landlady that his travelling carriage and servants were to meet him at the nearest stage on the home journey. He knew every inch of the country and wished to walk across the mountain in order to show his wife a prospect which had struck him particularly upon his last expedition a few years before. The landlady remembered that, just before setting out, he asked his wife some question about her watch, took it from her to regulate it and then, after some peevish exclamation about her carelessness in leaving it unwound, put it into his waistcoat pocket. The lady was very pale and quiet and seemed unhappy. The description which the landlady gave me was only too like the woman I was looking for.'

'And you believe there had been foul play?'

'As certainly as I believe in my own existence. This man Levison had grown tired of a wife whose affection had never been his; nay, more, I have reason to know that his unresting jealousy had intensified into a kind of hatred of her some time before the end. From the village in the Tyrol, which they left together on the bright October morning, I tracked their footsteps stage by stage back to the point at which I had lost them on the Italian frontier. In the course of my wanderings I met with a young Austrian officer who had seen them at Milan and had ventured to pay the lady some harmless attentions. He told me that he had never seen anything so appalling as Levison's jealousy; not an open fury but a concentrated silent rage, which gave an almost devilish expression to the man's parchment face. He watched his wife like a lynx and did not allow her a moment's freedom from his presence. Everyone who met them pitied the beautiful girlish wife, whose misery was so evident; every one loathed her tyrant. I found that the story of the servants and the travelling carriage was a lie. The Levisons had been attended by no servants at any of the hotels where I heard of them and had travelled always in public or in hired vehicles. The ultimate result of my enquiries left me little doubt that the dead woman was Laura Levison; and from that hour to this I have been employed, more or less, in the endeavour to find the man who murdered her.'

'And you have not been able to discover his whereabouts?' asked Frank Lorrimore.

'Not yet. I am looking for him.'

'A useless quest, Horace. What would be the result of your finding him? You have no proof to offer of his guilt. You would not take the law into your own hands?'

'By the Heaven above me, I would!' answered the other, fiercely. 'I would shoot that man down with as little compunction as I would kill a mad dog.'

'I hope you may never meet him,' said Frank solemnly.

Horace Wynward gave a short impatient sigh and paced the room for some time in silence. His share in the breakfast had been a mere pretence. He had emptied his coffee-cup but had eaten nothing.

'I am going back to London this afternoon, Frank.'

'On the hunt for this man?'

'Yes. My agent sent me a description of a man calling himself Lewis, a bill-discounter, who has lately set up an office in the City and whom I believe to be Michael Levison.'

* * *

The office occupied by Mr Lewis, the bill-discounter, was a dismal enough place, consisting of a second floor in a narrow alley called St Guinevere's Lane. Horace Wynward presented himself at this office about a week after his arrival in London, in the character of a gentleman in difficulties.

He found Mr Lewis exactly the kind of man he expected to see: a man of about fifty with small crafty black eyes shining out of a sallow visage that was as dull and lifeless as a parchment mask, thin lips and a heavy jaw and bony chin that betokened no small amount of power for evil.

Mr Wynward presented himself under his own name. On hearing which the bill-discounter looked up at him suddenly with an exclamation of surprise.

'You know my name?' said Horace.

'Yes. I have heard your name before. I thought you were a rich man.'

'I have a good estate, but I have been rather imprudent and am short of ready money. Where and when did you hear my name, Mr Lewis?'

'I don't remember that. The name sounds familiar to me, that is all.'

'But you have heard of me as a rich man, you say?'

'I had an impression to that effect. But the circumstances under which I heard the name have quite escaped my memory.'

Horace pushed the question no further. He played his cards very carefully, leading the usurer to believe that he had secured a profitable prey. The preliminaries of a loan were discussed but nothing fully settled. Before leaving the money-lender's office Horace Wynward invited Mr Lewis to dine with him at his lodgings in the neighbourhood of Piccadilly on the following evening. After a few minutes' reflection Lewis accepted the invitation.

He made his appearance at the appointed hour, dressed in a suit of shabby black in which his sallow complexion looked more than usually parchment-like and ghastly. The door was opened by Horace Wynward in person, and the money-lender was surprised to find himself in an almost empty house.

In the hall and on the staircase there were no signs of occupation whatever; but, in the dining-room, to which Horace immediately ushered his guest, there was a table ready laid for dinner, a couple of chairs and a dumb-waiter loaded with the appliances of the meal. The dishes and sauce tureens were on a hot plate in the fender. The room was dimly lighted by four wax candles in a tarnished candelabrum.

Mr Lewis, the money-lender, looked around him with a shudder; there was something sinister in the aspect of the room.

'It's rather a dreary-looking place, I'm afraid,' said Horace Wynward. 'I've only just taken the house, you see, and have had in a few sticks of hired furniture to keep me going till I make arrangements with an upholsterer. But you'll excuse all shortcomings, I'm sure – bachelor fare, you know.'

'I thought you said you were in lodgings, Mr Wynward.'

'Did I?' asked the other, absently. 'A mere slip of the tongue. I took this house on lease a week ago and am going to furnish it as soon as I am in funds.'

'And are you positively alone here?' enquired Mr Lewis, rather suspiciously.

'Well, very nearly so. There is a charwoman somewhere in the depths below, as deaf as a post and almost as useless. But you needn't be frightened about your dinner; I ordered it in from a confectioner in Piccadilly. We must wait upon ourselves, you know, in a free and easy way, for that dirty old woman would take away our appetites.'

He lifted the cover of the soup tureen as he spoke. The visitor seated himself at the table with rather a nervous air and glanced more than once in the direction of the shutters, which were closely fastened with heavy bars. He began to think there was something alarmingly eccentric in the conduct and manner of his host, and was inclined to repent having accepted the invitation, profitable as his new client promised to be.

The dinner was excellent, the wines of the finest quality; and, after drinking somewhat freely, Mr Lewis began to be better reconciled to his position. He was a little disconcerted, however, on perceiving that his host scarcely touched either the viands or the wine, and that those deep-set grey eyes were lifted every now and then to his face with a strangely observant look. When dinner was over, Mr Wynward heaped the dishes on the dumb-waiter, wheeled it into the next room with his own hands and came back to his seat at the table opposite the bill-discounter, who sat meditatively sipping his claret.

Horace filled his glass but remained for some time silent, without once lifting it to his lips. His companion watched him nervously, every moment more impressed with the belief that there was something wrong in his new client's mind and bent on making a speedy escape. He finished his claret, looked at his watch and rose hastily.

'I think I must wish you good-night, Mr Wynward. I am a man of early habits and have some distance to go. My lodgings are at Brompton, nearly an hour's ride from here.'

'Stay,' said Horace. 'We have not begun business yet. It's only nine o'clock. I want an hour's quiet talk with you, Mr Levison.'

The bill-discounter's face changed. It was almost impossible for that pallid mask of parchment to grow paler, but a sudden ghastliness came over the man's evil countenance.

'My name is Lewis,' he said, with an artificial grin.

'Lewis, or Levison. Men of your trade have as many names as they please. When you were travelling in Switzerland two years ago your name was Levison; when you married Laura Daventry your name was Levison.'

'You are under some absurd mistake, sir. The name of Levison is strange to me.'

'Is the name of Daventry strange to you, too? You recognized my name yesterday. When you first heard it, I was a happy man, Michael Levison. The blight upon me is your work. Oh, I know you well enough and am provided with ample means for your identification. I have followed you step by step upon your travels – tracked you to the inn from which you set out one October morning nearly a year ago with a companion who was never seen alive by mortal eyes after that date. You are a good German scholar, Mr Levison. Read that.'

Horace Wynward took out of his pocket-book the paragraph cut from the German paper and laid it before his visitor. The bill-discounter pushed it away after a hasty glance at its contents.

'What has this to do with me?' he asked.

'A great deal, Mr Levison. The hapless woman described in that paragraph was once your wife: Laura Daventry, the girl I loved and who returned my love; the girl whom you basely stole from me by trading on her natural affection for a weak, unworthy father and whose life you made wretched until it was foully ended by your own cruel hand. If I had stood behind you upon that lonely mountain pathway in the Tyrol and had seen you hurl your victim to destruction I could not be more convinced than I am that your hand did the deed; but such crimes as these are difficult – in this case perhaps impossible – to prove, and I fear you will escape the gallows. There are other circumstances in your life, however, more easily brought to light; and by the aid of a clever detective I have made myself master of some curious secrets in your past existence. I know the name you bore some fifteen years ago, before you settled in Trinidad as a merchant. You were at that time called Michael Lucas, and you fled from this country with a large sum of money embezzled from your employers, Messrs Hardwell and Oliphant, sugar-brokers in Nicholas Lane. You have been "wanted" a long time, Mr Levison; but you would most likely have gone scot-free to the end had I not set my agent to hunt you and your antecedents.'

Michael Levison rose from his seat hastily, trembling in every limb.

Horace rose at the same moment, and the two men stood face to face – one the very image of craven fear, the other cool and self-possessed.

'This is a tissue of lies!' gasped Levison, wiping his lips nervously with a handkerchief that fluttered in his tremulous fingers. 'Have you brought me here to insult me with this madman's talk?'

'I have brought you here to your doom. There was a time when I thought that if you and I ever stood face to face I should shoot you down like a dog, but I have changed my mind. Such carrion dogs as you are not worth the stain of blood upon an honest man's hand. It is useless to tell you how I loved the girl you murdered. Your savage nature would not comprehend any but the basest and most selfish passion. Don't stir another step – I have a loaded revolver within reach and shall make an end of you if you attempt to quit this room. The police are on the watch for you outside, and you will leave this place for a jail. Hark! what is that?'

It was the sound of a footstep on the stairs outside, a woman's light footstep, and the rustling of a silk dress. The dining-room door was ajar, and the sounds were distinctly audible in the empty house. Michael Levison made for the door, availing himself of this momentary diversion, with some vague hope of escape; but, within a few paces of the threshold, he recoiled suddenly with a hoarse gasping cry.

The door was pushed wide open by a light hand, and a figure stood upon the threshold – a girlish figure dressed in black silk, a pale sad face framed by dark auburn hair.

'The dead returned to life!' cried Levison. 'Hide her, hide her! I can't face her! Let me go!'

He made for the other door, leading into the inner room, but found it locked, and then sank cowering down into a chair, covering his eyes with his skinny hands. The girl came softly into the room and stood by Horace Wynward.

'You have forgotten me, Mr Levison,' she said, 'and you take me for my sister's ghost. I was always like her, and they say I have grown more so within the last two years. We had a letter from you a month ago, posted from Trinidad, telling us that my sister Laura was well and happy there with you; yet you mistake me for the shadow of the dead!'

The frightened wretch did not look up. He had not yet recovered from the shock produced by his sister-in-law's sudden appearance. The handkerchief which he held to his lips was stained with blood. Horace Wynward went quietly to the outer door and opened it, returning presently with two men who came softly into the room and approached Levison. He made no attempt to resist them as they slipped a pair of handcuffs on his bony wrists and led him away. There was a cab standing outside, ready to convey him to prison.

Emily Daventry sank into a chair as he was taken from the room.

'Oh, Mr Wynward,' she said, 'I think there can be little doubt of my sister's wretched fate. The experiment which you proposed has succeeded only too well.'

Horace had been down to Devonshire to question the two girls about their sister. He had been struck by Emily's likeness to his lost love and had persuaded her aunt to bring her up to London in order to identify Levison by her means and to test the effect which her appearance might produce upon the nerves of the suspected assassin.

The police were furnished with a complicated mass of evidence against Levison in his character of clerk, merchant and bill-discounter, but the business was of a nature that entailed much delay, and after several adjourned examinations the prisoner fell desperately ill of heart disease from which he had suffered for years but which grew much worse during his imprisonment. Finding his death certain, he sent for Horace Wynward and to him confessed his crime, boasting of his wife's death with a fiendish delight in the deed, which he called an act of vengeance against his rival.

'I knew you well enough when you came home, Horace Wynward,' he said, 'and I thought it would be my happy lot to compass your ruin. You trapped me, but to the last you have the worst of it. The girl you loved is dead. She dared to tell me that she loved you; defied my anger; told me that she had sold herself to me to save her father from disgrace and confessed that she hated me and had always hated me. From that hour she was doomed. Her white face was a constant reproach to me. I was goaded to madness by her tears. She used to mutter your name in her sleep. I wonder I did not cut her throat as she lay there with the name upon her lips. But I must have swung for that. So I was patient and waited until I could have her alone with me upon the mountains. It was only a push, and she was gone. I came home alone, free from the worry and fever of her presence – except in my dreams. She has haunted those ever since, with her pale face – yes, by Heaven, I have hardly known what it is to sleep, from that hour to this, without seeing her white face and hearing the one long shriek that went up to the sky as she fell.'

He died within a few days of this interview and before his trial could take place. Time, that heals almost all griefs, brought peace by and by to Horace Wynward. He furnished the house in Mayfair and for some time led a misanthropical life there; but on paying a second visit to Devonshire, where the two Daventry girls lived their simple industrious life in their aunt's school, he discovered that Emily's likeness to her sister made her very dear to him, and in the following year he brought a mistress to Crofton in the person of that young lady. Together they paid a mournful visit to that lonely spot in the Tyrol where Laura Levison had perished and stayed there while a white marble cross was erected above her grave.

Ellen Wood

GOING THROUGH THE TUNNEL

Though the life of Ellen Wood (1814–1887) was not as sensational as that of Mary E. Braddon, her novel East Lynne *(1861) helped, with its adulterous and scheming heroine, to establish the vogue for novels of sensation. Wood may well have inspired Braddon, and it may be worth noting that one of the male villains of* East Lynne *has the surname Levison, which might just have inspired Braddon to choose that for her own villain. Until 1856 Ellen Wood's life had been fairly comfortable, though curvature of the spine in her childhood had left her partially handicapped and fragile; she stood barely five feet tall and could rarely carry anything heavier than a book – though, remarkably, she bore five children. But in 1856 her husband, Henry Wood, suffered financial failure, and the family returned to England from their home in France. Ellen had started to sell stories anonymously in 1851 and now turned to writing full time to support the family, though it was not until the publication of* Danesbury House *in 1860 that her name became well known and, with* East Lynne, *her reputation and financial security assured. When not publishing anonymously she always used the name Mrs Henry Wood, even after her husband's death in 1866. In 1867 she bought the magazine* The Argosy *and edited it for the rest of her life, assisted by her son Charles. For* The Argosy, *starting in 1868, she wrote, anonymously, a long series of stories related by Johnny Ludlow, of which the following is one. Ellen was delighted that the Ludlow series received high critical acclaim from those unaware they were the work of Mrs Henry Wood, whose other books the same critics snobbishly discredited. Ludlow himself is an orphan adopted by Squire Todhetley of Dyke Manor in Worcestershire, the county in which Ellen, then Ellen Price, had spent her childhood, and there is a quaint nostalgia in the homely recounting of these tales.*

Most of the Ludlow stories, over eighty episodes of which were produced, feature some crime or mystery that either Ludlow himself or his adopted family seek to resolve. They include child abduction, blackmail, theft, disappearances, even hauntings. The following story, from the February 1869 edition of The Argosy *— and included in the first of six volumes of Ludlow's accounts — is one of the more light-hearted ones.*

Going Through the Tunnel

WE HAD TO make a rush for it. And making a rush did not suit the Squire any more than it does other people who have come to an age when the body's heavy and the breath nowhere. He reached the train, pushed head-foremost into a carriage and then remembered the tickets. 'Bless my heart!' he exclaimed as he jumped out again and nearly upset a lady who had a little dog in her arms and a mass of fashionable hair on her head that the Squire, in his hurry, mistook for tow.

'Plenty of time, sir,' said a guard who was passing. 'Three minutes to spare.'

Instead of saying he was obliged to the man for his civility, or relieved to find the tickets might still be had, the Squire snatched out his old watch and began abusing the railway clocks for being slow. Had Tod been there he would have told him to his face that the watch was fast, braving all retort, for the Squire believed in his watch as he did in himself and would rather have been told that *he* could go wrong than that the watch could. But there was only me, and I wouldn't have said it for anything.

'Keep two back-seats there, Johnny,' said the Squire.

I put my coat on the corner furthest from the door and the rug on the one next to it and followed him into the station. When the Squire was late in starting, he was apt to get into the greatest flurry conceivable, and the first thing I saw was himself blocking up the ticket place and undoing his pocket-book with nervous fingers. He had some loose gold about him, silver, too, but the pocket-book came to his hand first, so he pulled it out. These flurried moments of the Squire's amused Tod beyond everything; he was so cool himself.

'Can you change this?' said the Squire, drawing out one from a roll of five-pound notes.

'No, I can't,' was the answer in the surly tones put on by ticket clerks.

How the Squire crumpled up the note again and searched in his breeches pocket for gold and came away with the two tickets and the change, I'm sure he never knew. A crowd had gathered round, wanting to take their tickets in turn, and knowing that he was keeping them flurried him all the more. He stood at the back a moment, put the roll of notes into his case, fastened it and returned it to the breast of his overcoat, sent the change down into another pocket without counting it and went out with the tickets in hand. Not to the carriage but to stare at the big clock in front.

'Don't you see, Johnny? exactly four minutes and a half difference,' he cried, holding out his watch to me. 'It is a strange thing they can't keep these railway clocks in order.'

'My watch keeps good time, sir, and mine is with the railway. I think it is right.'

'Hold your tongue, Johnny. How dare you! Right? You send your watch to be regulated the first opportunity, sir. Don't *you* get into the habit of being too late or too early.'

When we finally went to the carriage there were some people in it, but our seats were left for us. Squire Todhetley sat down by the further door and settled himself and his coats and his things comfortably, which he had been too flurried to do before. Cool as a cucumber was he now the bustle was over; cool as Tod could have been. At the other door, with his face to the engine, sat a dark, gentleman-like man of forty, who had made room for us to pass as we got in. He had a large signet-ring on one hand and a lavender glove on the other. The other three seats opposite to us were vacant. Next to me sat a little man with a fresh colour and gold spectacles, who was already reading, and beyond him, in the corner, face to face with the dark man, was a lunatic. That's to mention him politely. Of all the restless, fidgety, worrying, hot-tempered passengers that ever put themselves into a carriage to travel with people in their senses, he was the worst. In fifteen moments he had made as many darts – now after his hat-box and things above his head, now calling the guard and the porters to ask senseless questions about his luggage, now treading on our toes and trying the corner seat opposite the Squire and then darting back to his own. He wore a wig of a decided green tinge, the effect of keeping, perhaps, and his skin was dry and shrivelled as an Egyptian mummy's.

A servant, in undress livery, came to the door and touched his hat, which had a cockade on it, as he spoke to the dark man.

'Your ticket, my lord.'

Lords are not travelled with every day, and some of us looked up. The gentleman took the ticket from the man's hand and slipped it into his waistcoat pocket.

'You can get me a newspaper, Wilkins. *The Times* if it is to be had.'

'Yes, my lord.'

'Yes, there's room here, ma'am,' interrupted the guard, sending the door back for a lady who stood at it. 'Make haste, please.'

The lady who stepped in was the same the Squire had bolted against. She sat down in the seat opposite me and looked at every one of us by turns. There was a sort of violet bloom on her face and some soft white powder, seen plain enough through her veil. She took the longest gaze at the dark gentleman, bending a little forward to do it; for, as he was in a line with her and also had his head turned from her, her curiosity could only catch a view of his side-face. Mrs Todhetley might have said she had not put on her company manners. In the midst of this, the manservant came back again.

'*The Times* is not here yet, my lord. They are expecting the papers in by the next down-train.'

'Never mind, then. You can get me one at the next station, Wilkins.'

'Very well, my lord.'

Wilkins must certainly have had to scramble for his carriage, for we started before he had well left the door. It was not an express train, and we should have to stop at several stations. Where the Squire and I had been staying does not matter; it has nothing to do with what I have to tell. It was a long way from our own home, and that's saying enough.

'Would you mind changing seats with me, sir?'

I looked up to find the lady's face close to mine; she had spoken in a half-whisper. The Squire, who carried his old-fashioned notions of politeness with him when he went travelling, at once got up to offer her the corner. But she declined it, saying she was subject to face-ache and did not care to be next the window. So she took my seat, and I sat down on the one opposite Mr Todhetley.

'Which of the peers is that?' I heard her ask him in a loud whisper as the lord put his head out at his window.

'Don't know at all, ma'am,' said the Squire. 'Don't know many of the peers myself, except those of my own county: Lyttleton and Beauchamp, and –'

Of all snarling barks, the worst was given that moment in the Squire's face, suddenly ending the list. The little dog, an ugly, hairy, vile-tempered Scotch terrier, had been kept concealed under the lady's jacket and now struggled itself free. The Squire's look of consternation was good! He had not known any animal was there.

'Be quiet, Wasp. How dare you bark at the gentleman? He will not bite, sir: he –'

'Who has a dog in the carriage?' shrieked the lunatic, starting up in a passion. 'Dogs don't travel with passengers. Here! Guard! Guard!'

To call out for the guard when a train is going at full speed is generally useless. The lunatic had to sit down again, and the lady defied him, so to say, coolly avowing that she had hidden the dog from the guard on purpose, staring him in the face while she said it.

After this there was a lull, and we went speeding along, the lady talking now and again to the Squire. She seemed to want to grow confidential with him, but the Squire did not seem to care for it, though he was quite civil. She held the dog huddled up in her lap so that nothing but his head peeped out.

'Halloa! How dare they be so negligent? There's no lamp in this carriage.'

It was the lunatic again, and we all looked at the lamp. It had no light in it, but that it *had* when we first reached the carriage was certain for, as the Squire went stumbling in, his head nearly touched the lamp, and I had noticed the flame. It seems the Squire had also.

'They must have put it out while we were getting our tickets,' he said.

'I'll know the reason why when we stop,' cried the lunatic fiercely. 'After passing the next station, we dash into the long tunnel. The idea of going through it in pitch darkness! It would not be safe.'

'Especially with a dog in the carriage,' spoke the lord, in a chaffing kind of tone but with a good-natured smile. 'We will have the lamp lighted, however.'

As if to reward him for interfering, the dog barked up loudly and tried to make a spring at him, upon which the lady smothered the animal up, head and all.

Another minute or two, and the train began to slacken speed. It was only an insignificant station, one not likely to be halted at for above a minute. The lunatic twisted his body out of the window and shouted for the guard long before we were at a standstill.

'Allow me to manage this,' said the lord, quietly putting him down. 'They know me on the line. Wilkins!'

The man came rushing up at the call. He must have been out already, though we were not quite at a standstill yet.

'Is it for *The Times*, my lord? I am going for it.'

'Never mind *The Times*. This lamp is not lighted, Wilkins. See the guard, and *get it done*. At once.'

'And ask him what the mischief he means by his carelessness,' roared out the lunatic after Wilkins, who went flying off. 'Sending us on our road without a light! And that dangerous tunnel close at hand.'

The authority laid upon the words 'get it done' made it seem that the speaker was accustomed to be obeyed, and would be this time. For once the lunatic sat quiet, watching the lamp and for the light that was to be dropped into it from the top; and so did I, and so did the lady. We were all deceived, however, and the train went puffing on. The lunatic shrieked, the lord put his head out of the carriage and shouted for Wilkins.

No good. Shouting after a train is off never is much good. The lord sat down on his seat again, an angry frown crossing his face, and the lunatic got up and danced with rage.

'I do not know where the blame lies,' observed the lord. 'Not with my servant, I think. He is attentive and has been with me some years.'

'I'll know where it lies,' retorted the lunatic. 'I am a director on the line, though I don't often travel on it. This *is* management, this is! A few minutes more and we shall be in the dark tunnel.'

'Of course it would have been satisfactory to have a light, but it is not of so much consequence,' said the nobleman, wishing to soothe him. 'There's no danger in the dark.'

'No danger! No danger, sir! I think there is danger. Who's to know that dog won't spring out and bite us? Who's to know there won't be an accident in the tunnel? A light is a protection against having our pockets picked, if it's a protection against nothing else.'

'I fancy our pockets are pretty safe today,' said the lord, glancing around at us with a good-natured smile, as much as to say that none of us looked like thieves. 'And I certainly trust we shall get through the tunnel safely.'

'And I'll take care the dog does not bite you in the dark,' spoke up the lady, pushing her head forward to give the lunatic a nod or two that you'd hardly have matched for defying impudence.

'You'll be good, won't you, Wasp? But I should like the lamp lighted myself. You will perhaps be so kind, my lord, as to see that there's no mistake made about it at the next station!'

He slightly raised his hat to her and bowed in answer but did not speak. The lunatic buttoned up his coat with fingers that were either nervous or angry and then disturbed the little gentleman next him – who had read his big book throughout the whole commotion without once lifting his eyes – by hunting everywhere for his pocket handkerchief.

'Here's the tunnel!' he cried out resentfully, as we dashed with a shriek into pitch darkness.

It was all very well for her to say she would take care of the dog, but the first thing the young beast did was to make a spring at me and then at the Squire, barking and yelping frightfully. The Squire pushed it away in a commotion. Though well accustomed to dogs, he always fought shy of strange ones. The lady chattered and laughed and did not seem to try to get hold of him, but we couldn't see, you know.

The Squire hissed at him, the dog snarled and growled. Altogether there was noise enough to deafen anything but a tunnel.

'Pitch him out of the window,' cried the lunatic.

'Pitch yourself out,' answered the lady. And whether she propelled the dog or whether he went of his own accord, the beast sprang to the other end of the carriage and was seized upon by the nobleman.

'I think, madam, you had better put him under your mantle and keep him there,' said he, bringing the dog back to her and speaking quite civilly but in the same tone of authority he had used to his servant about the lamp. 'I have not the slightest objection to dogs myself, but many people have, and it is not altogether pleasant to have them loose in a railway carriage. I beg your pardon. I cannot see. Is this your hand?'

It was her hand, I suppose, for the dog was left with her, and he went back to his seat again. When we emerged out of the tunnel into daylight, the lunatic's face was blue.

'Ma'am, if that miserable brute had laid hold of me by so much as the corner of my greatcoat tail I'd have had the law on you. It is perfectly monstrous that anyone, putting themselves into a first-class carriage, should attempt to outrage railway laws and upset the comfort of travellers with impunity. I shall complain to the guard.'

'He does not bite, sir. He never bites,' she answered softly, as if sorry for the escapade and wishing to conciliate him. 'The poor little bijou is frightened of the darkness and leaped from my arms unawares. There! I'll promise that you shall neither see nor hear him again.'

She had tucked the dog so completely out of sight that no one could have suspected one was there, just as it had been on first entering. The train was drawn up to the next station. When it stopped the servant came and opened the carriage door for his master to get out.

'Did you understand me, Wilkins, when I told you to get this lamp lighted?'

'My lord, I'm very sorry. I understood your lordship perfectly, but I couldn't see the guard,' answered Wilkins. 'I caught sight of him running up to his van door at the last moment, but the train began to move off and I had to jump in myself or else be left behind.'

The guard passed as he was explaining this, and the nobleman drew his attention to the lamp, curtly ordering him to 'light it instantly'. Lifting his hat to us by way of farewell, he disappeared, and the lunatic began upon the guard as if he were commencing a lecture to a deaf audience. The guard seemed not to hear it, so lost was he in astonishment at there being no light.

'Why, what can have douted it?' he cried aloud, staring up at the lamp. And the Squire smiled at the familiar word, so common in our ears at home, and had a great mind to ask the guard where he came from.

'I lighted all these here lamps myself afore we started, and I see 'em all burning,' said he. There was no mistaking the home accent now, and the Squire looked down the carriage with a beaming face.

'You are from Worcestershire, my man.'

'From Worcester itself, sir. Leastways from St John's, which is the same thing.'

'Whether you are from Worcester or whether you are from Jericho, I'll let you know that you can't put empty lamps into first-class carriages on this line without being made to answer for it!' roared the lunatic. 'What's your name? I am a director.'

'My name is Thomas Brooks, sir,' replied the man, respectfully touching his cap. 'But I declare to you, sir, that I've told the truth in saying the lamps were all right when we started. How this one can have got douted, I can't think. There's not a guard on the line, sir, more particular in seeing to the lamps than I am.'

'Well, light it now. Don't waste time excusing yourself,' growled the lunatic. But he said nothing about the dog, which was surprising.

In a twinkling the lamp was lighted, and we were off again. The lady and her dog were quiet now. He was out of sight; she leaned back to go to sleep. The Squire lodged his head against the curtain, and shut his eyes to do the same; the little man, as before, never looked off his book; and the lunatic frantically shifted himself every two minutes between his own seat and that of the opposite corner. There were no more tunnels, and we went smoothly on to the next station. Five minutes allowed there.

The little man, putting his book in his pocket, took down a black leather bag from above his head and got out; the lady, her dog hidden still, prepared to follow him, wishing the Squire and me, and even the lunatic, with a forgiving smile, a polite good-morning. I had moved to that end and was watching the lady's wonderful back hair as she stepped out when all in a moment the Squire sprang up with a shout and, jumping out nearly upon her, called out that he had been robbed. She dropped the dog, and I thought he must have caught the lunatic's disorder and become frantic.

It is of no use attempting to describe exactly what followed. The lady, snatching up her dog, shrieked out that perhaps she had been robbed, too; she laid hold of the Squire's arm and went with him into the station-master's room. And there we were, us three and the guard and the station-master and the lunatic, who had come pouncing out, too, at the Squire's cry. The man in spectacles had disappeared for good.

The Squire's pocket-book was gone. He gave his name and address at once to the station-master, and the guard's face lighted with intelligence when he heard it, for he knew Squire Todhetley by reputation. The pocket-book had been safe just before we entered the tunnel; the Squire was certain of that, having felt it. He had sat in the carriage with his coat unbuttoned, rather thrown back, and nothing could have been easier than for a clever thief to draw it out under cover of the darkness.

'I had fifty pounds in it,' he said. 'Fifty pounds in five-pound notes. And some memoranda besides.'

'Fifty pounds!' cried the lady quickly. 'And you could travel with all that about you and not button up your coat! You ought to be rich!'

'Have you been in the habit of meeting thieves, madam, when travelling?' suddenly demanded the lunatic, turning upon her without warning, his coat whirling about on all sides with the rapidity of his movements.

'No, sir, I have not,' she answered in indignant tones. 'Have you?'

'I have not, madam. But then, you perceive I see no risk in travelling with a coat unbuttoned, though it may have bank notes in the pockets.'

She made no reply: was too much occupied in turning out her own pockets and purse to ascertain that they had not been rifled. Reassured on the point, she sat down on a low box against the wall, nursing her dog, which had begun its snarling again.

'It must have been taken from me in the dark as we went through the tunnel,' affirmed the Squire to the room in general and perhaps the station-master in particular. 'I am a magistrate and have some experience in these things. I sat completely off my guard, a prey for anybody, my hands stretched out before me, grappling with that dog, that seemed – why, goodness me! yes he *did*, now that I think of it – that seemed to be held about fifteen inches off my nose on purpose to attack me. That's when the thing must have been done. But now – which of them could it have been?'

He meant which of the passengers. As he looked hard at us in rotation, especially at the guard and station-master who had not been in the carriage, the lady gave a shriek and threw the dog into the middle of the room.

'I see it all,' she said faintly. 'He has a habit of snatching at things with his mouth. He must have snatched the case out of your pocket, sir, and dropped it from the window. You will find it in the tunnel.'

'Who has?' asked the lunatic, while the Squire stared in wonder.

'My poor little Wasp. Ah, villain! beast! it is he that has done all this mischief.'

'He might have taken the pocket-book,' I said, thinking it time to speak, 'but he could not have dropped it out, for I put the window up as we went into the tunnel.'

It seemed a nonplus, and her face fell again. 'There was the other window,' she said in a minute. 'He might have dropped it there. I heard his bark quite close to it.'

'*I* pulled up that window, madam,' said the lunatic. 'If the dog did take it out of the pocket it may be in the carriage now.'

The guard rushed out to search it. The Squire followed, but the station-master remained where he was and closed the door after them. A thought came over me that he was stopping to keep the two passengers in view.

No, the pocket-book could not be found in the carriage. As they came back, the Squire was asking the guard if he knew who the nobleman was who had got out at the last station with his servant. But the guard did not know.

'He said they knew him on the line.'

'Very likely, sir. I have not been on this line above a month or two.'

'Well, this is an unpleasant affair,' said the lunatic impatiently. 'And the question is, what's to be done? It appears pretty evident that your pocket-book was taken in the carriage, sir. Of the four passengers, I suppose the one who left us at the last station must be held exempt from suspicion, being a nobleman. Another got out here and has disappeared; the other two are present. I propose that we should both be searched.'

'I'm sure I am quite willing,' said the lady, and she got up at once.

I think the Squire was about to disclaim any wish so to act, but the lunatic was resolute, and the station-master agreed with him. There was no time to be lost, for the train was ready to start again, her time being up, and the lunatic was turned out. The lady went into another room with two women called by the station-master, and *she* was turned out. Neither of them had the pocket-book.

'Here's my card, sir,' said the lunatic, handing one to Mr Todhetley. 'You know my name, I dare say. If I can be of any future assistance to you in this matter, you may command me.'

'Bless my heart!' cried the Squire as he read the name on the card. 'How could you allow yourself to be searched, sir?'

'Because, in such a case as this, I think it only right and fair that everyone who has the misfortune to be mixed up in it *should* be searched,' replied the lunatic, as they went out together. 'It is a satisfaction to both parties. Unless you offered to search me, you could not have offered to search that woman, and I suspected her.'

'Suspected *her*!' cried the Squire, opening his eyes.

'If I didn't suspect, I doubted. Why on earth did she cause her dog to make all that row the moment we got into the tunnel? It must have been done then. I should not be startled out of my senses if I heard that that silent man by my side and hers was in league with her.'

The Squire stood in a kind of amazement, trying to recall what he could of the little man in spectacles and see if things would fit into one another.

'Don't you like her look?' he asked suddenly.

'No, I *don't!* said the lunatic, turning himself about. 'I have a prejudice against painted women: they put me in mind of Jezebel. Look at her hair. It's awful.'

He went out in a whirlwind and took his seat in the carriage not a moment before it puffed off.

'*Is* he a lunatic?' I whispered to the Squire.

'He a lunatic!' he roared. 'You must be a lunatic for asking it, Johnny. Why, that's . . . that's . . .'

Instead of saying any more, he showed me the card, and the name nearly took my breath away. He is a well-known London man, of science, talent and position, and of worldwide fame.

'Well, I thought him nothing better than an escaped maniac.'

'*Did* you?' said the Squire. 'Perhaps he returned the compliment on you, sir. But now . . . Johnny, who has got my pocket-book?'

As if it was any use asking me? As we turned back to the station-master's room, the lady came into it, evidently resenting the search, though she had seemed to acquiesce in it so readily.

'They were rude, those women. It is the first time I ever had the misfortune to travel with men who carry pocket-books to lose them, and I hope it will be the last,' she pursued in scornful passion meant for the Squire. 'One generally meets with *gentlemen* in a first-class carriage.'

The emphasis came out with a shriek, and it told on him. Now that she was proved innocent, he was as vexed as she for having listened to the advice of the scientific man – but I can't help calling him a lunatic still. The Squire's apologies might have disarmed a cross-grained hyena, and she came around with a smile.

'If anyone *has* got the pocket-book,' she said, as she stroked her dog's ears, 'it must be that silent man with the gold spectacles. There was no one else, sir, who could have reached you without getting up to do it. And I declare on my honour that when that commotion first arose through my poor little dog, I felt for a moment something like a man's arm stretched across me. It could only have been his. I hope you have the numbers of the notes.'

'But I have not,' said the Squire.

The room was being invaded by this time. Two stray passengers, a friend of the station-master's and the porter who took the tickets had crept in. All thought the lady's opinion must be correct and said the spectacled man had got clear off with the pocket-book. There was no one else to pitch upon. A nobleman travelling with his servant would not be likely to commit a robbery; the lunatic was really the man his card represented him to be, for the station-master's friend had seen and recognized him; and the lady was proved innocent by search. Wasn't the Squire in a passion!

'That close reading of his was all a blind,' he said in sudden conviction. 'He kept his face down that we should not know him in future. He never looked at one of us! He never said a word! I shall go and find him.'

Away went the Squire, as fast as he could hurry, but came back in a moment to know which was the way out and where it led to. There was quite a small crowd of us by this time. Some fields lay beyond the station at the back, and a boy affirmed that he had seen a little gentleman in spectacles with a black bag in his hand making over the first stile.

'Now look here, boy,' said the Squire. 'If you catch that same man, I'll give you five shillings.'

Tod could not have flown faster than the boy did. He took the stile at a leap, and the Squire tumbled over it after him. Some boys and men joined in the chase, and a cow, grazing in the field, trotted after us and brought up the rear.

Such a shout from the boy! It came from behind the opposite hedge of the long field. I was over the gate first; the Squire came next. On the edge of the dry ditch sat the passenger, his legs dangling, his neck imprisoned in the boy's arms. I knew him at once. His hat and gold spectacles had fallen off in the scuffle, the black bag was wide open and had a tall bunch of something green sticking up from it. Some tools lay on the ground.

'Oh, you wicked hypocrite!' spluttered the Squire, not in the least knowing what he said in his passion. 'Are you not ashamed to have played upon me such a vile trick? How dare you go about to commit robberies!'

'I have not robbed you, at any rate,' said the man, his voice trembling a little and his face pale, while the boy loosed the neck but pinioned one of the arms.

'Not robbed me!' cried the Squire. 'Good heavens! Who do you suppose you have robbed, if not me? Here, Johnny, lad, you are a witness. He says he has not robbed me.'

'I did not know it was yours,' said the man meekly. 'Loose me, boy. I'll not attempt to run away.'

'Halloa! here! what's to do?' roared a big fellow, swinging himself over the gate. 'Any tramp been trespassing? Anybody wanting to be took up? I'm the parish constable.'

If he had said he was the parish engine, ready to let loose buckets of water on the offender, he could not have been more welcome. The Squire's face was rosy with satisfaction.

'Have you your handcuffs with you, my man?'

'I've not got them, sir, but I fancy I'm big enough and strong enough to take *him* without 'em. Something to spare, too.'

'There's nothing like handcuffs for safety,' said the Squire rather damped, for he believed in them as one of the country's institutions. 'Oh, you villain! Perhaps you can tie him with cords?'

The thief floundered out of the ditch and stood upon his feet. He did not look an ungentlemanly thief now you came to see and hear him, and his face, though scared, might have been thought an honest one. He picked up his hat and glasses and held them in his hand while he spoke in tones of earnest remonstrance.

'Surely, sir, you would not have me taken up for this slight offence! I did not know I was doing wrong, and I doubt if the law would condemn me. I thought it was public property!'

'Public property!' cried the Squire, turning red at the words. 'Of all the impudent brazen-faced rascals that are cheating the gallows, you must be the worst. My bank notes, public property!'

'Your what, sir?'

'My bank notes, you villain. How dare you repeat your insolent questions?'

'But I don't know anything about your bank notes, sir,' said the man meekly. 'I do not know what you mean.'

They stood facing each other, a sight for a picture: the Squire with his hands under his coat, dancing a little in rage, his face crimson; the other quite still, holding his hat and gold spectacles and looking at him in wonder.

'You don't know what I mean! When you confessed with your last breath that you had robbed me of my pocket-book!'

'I confessed – I have not sought to conceal – that I have robbed the ground of this rare fern,' said the man, handling carefully the green stuff in the black bag. 'I have not robbed you or anyone of anything else.'

The tone, simple, quiet, self-contained, threw the Squire in amazement. He stood staring.

'Are you a fool?' he asked. 'What do you suppose I have to do with your rubbishing ferns?'

'Nay, I supposed you owned them – that is, owned the land. You led me to believe so, in saying I had robbed you.'

'What I've lost is a pocket-book with ten five-pound bank notes in it. I lost it in the train. It must have been taken as we came through the tunnel, and you sat next but one to me,' reiterated the Squire.

The man put on his hat and glasses. 'I am a geologist and botanist, sir. I came here after this plant today – having seen it yesterday, but then I had not my tools with me. I don't know anything about the pocket-book and bank notes.'

So that was another mistake, for the botanist turned out of his pockets a heap of letters directed to him and a big book he had been reading in the train, a treatise on botany, to prove who he was. And, as if to leave no loophole for doubt, one stepped up who knew him and assured the Squire there was not a more learned man in his line, no, nor one more respected in the three kingdoms. The Squire shook him by the hand in apologizing and told him we had some valuable ferns near Dyke Manor if he would come and see them.

Like Patience on a monument, when we got back there sat the lady, waiting to see the prisoner brought in. Her face would have made a picture, too, when she heard the upshot and saw the hot Squire and the gold spectacles walking side by side in friendly talk.

'I think still he must have got it,' she said sharply.

'No, madam,' answered the Squire. 'Whoever may have taken it, it was not he.'

'Then there's only one man, and that is he whom you have let go on in the train,' she returned decisively. 'I thought his fidgety movements were not put on for nothing. He had secured the pocket-book somewhere and then made a show of offering to be searched. Ah, ha!'

And the Squire veered around again at this suggestion and began to suspect he had been doubly cheated. First, out of his money; next, out of his suspicions. One only thing in the whole bother seemed clear, and that was that the notes and case had gone for good. As, in point of fact, they had.

We were on the Chain Pier at Brighton, Tod and I. It was about eight or nine months after. I had put my arms on the rails at the end, looking at a pleasure party sailing by. Tod, next to me, was bewailing his ill-fortune in not possessing a yacht and opportunities of cruising in it.

'I tell you, no, I don't want to be made seasick.'

The words came from someone behind us. It seemed almost as though they were spoken in reference to Tod's wish for a yacht. But it was not *that* that made me turn around sharply; it was the sound of the voice, for I thought I recognized it.

Yes. There she was. The lady who had been with us in the carriage that day. The dog was not with her now, but her hair was more amazing than ever. She did not see me. As I turned, she turned and began to walk slowly back, arm in arm with a gentleman. And to see him – that is, to see them together – made me open my eyes. For it was the lord who had travelled with us.

'Look, Tod!' I said, and told him in a word who they were.

'What the deuce do they know of each other?' cried Tod with a frown, for he felt angry every time the thing was referred to. Not for the loss of the money but for what he called the stupidity of us all; saying always had *he* been there he should have detected the thief at once.

I sauntered after them. Why I wanted to learn which of the lords he was, I can't tell, for lords are numerous enough, but I had had a curiosity upon the point ever since. They encountered some people and were standing to speak to them, three ladies and a fellow in a black glazed hat with a piece of green ribbon around it.

'I was trying to induce my wife to take a sail,' the lord was saying, 'but she won't. She is not a very good sailor unless the sea has its best behaviour on.'

'Will you go tomorrow, Mrs Mowbray?' asked the man in the glazed hat, who spoke and looked like a gentleman. 'I will promise you perfect calmness. I am weather-wise and can assure you this little wind will have gone down before night, leaving us without a breath of air.'

'I will go on condition that your assurance proves correct.'

'All right. You, of course, will come, Mowbray?'

The lord nodded. 'Very happy.'

'When do you leave Brighton, Mr Mowbray?' asked one of the ladies.

'I don't know exactly. Not for some days.'

'A muff as usual, Johnny,' whispered Tod. 'That man is no lord. He is a Mr Mowbray.'

'But, Tod, he *is* the lord. It is the one who travelled with us; there's no mistake about that. Lords can't put off their titles as parsons can. Do you suppose his servant would have called him "my lord" if he had not been one?'

'At least there is no mistake that these people are calling him Mr Mowbray now.'

That was true. It was equally true that they were calling her Mrs Mowbray. My ears had been as quick as Tod's, and I don't deny I was puzzled. They turned to come up the pier again with the people, and the lady saw me standing there with Tod. Saw me looking at her, too, and I think she did not relish it, for she took a step backwards as one startled and then stared me full in the face as if asking who I might be. I lifted my hat.

There was no response. In another moment she and her husband were walking quickly down the pier together, and the other party went on to the end quietly. A man in a tweed suit and brown hat drawn low over his eyes was standing with his arms folded looking after the two with a queer smile upon his face. Tod marked it and spoke.

'Do you happen to know that gentleman?'

'Yes, I do,' was the answer.

'Is he a peer?'

'On occasion.'

'On occasion!' repeated Tod. 'I have a reason for asking,' he added. 'Do not think me impertinent.'

'Been swindled out of anything?' asked the man coolly.

'My father was some months ago. He lost a pocket-book with fifty pounds in it in a railway carriage. Those people were both in it but not then acquainted with each other.'

'Oh, weren't they!' said the man.

'No, they were not,' I put in, 'for I was there. He was a lord then.'

'Ah,' said the man, 'and had a servant in livery no doubt, who came up my-lording him unnecessarily every other minute. He is a member of the swell-mob, one of the cleverest of the *gentleman* fraternity, and the one who acts as servant is another of them.'

'And the lady?' I asked.

'She is a third. They have been working in concert for two or three years now and will give us trouble yet before their career is stopped. But for being singularly clever, we should have had them long ago. And so they did not know each other in the train! I dare say not!'

The man spoke with quiet authority. He was a detective come down from London to Brighton that morning, whether for a private trip or on business he did not say. I related to him what had passed in the train.

'Ay,' said he after listening. 'They contrived to put the lamp out before starting. The lady took the pocket-book during the commotion she caused the dog to make, and the lord received it from her hand when he gave her back the dog. Cleverly done! He had it about him, young sir, when he got out at the next station. *She* waited to be searched and to throw the scent off. Very ingenious, but they'll be a little too much so some fine day.'

'Can't you take them up?' demanded Tod.

'No.'

'I will accuse them of it,' he haughtily said. 'If I meet them again on this pier –'

'Which you won't do today,' interrupted the man.

'I heard them say they were not going for some days.'

'Ah, but they have seen you now. And I think – I'm not quite sure – that he saw me. They'll be off by the next train.'

'Who are *they?*' asked Tod, pointing to the end of the pier.

'Unsuspecting people whose acquaintance they have casually made here. Yes, an hour or two will see Brighton quit of the pair.'

And it was so. A train was starting within an hour, and Tod and I galloped to the station. There they were, in a first-class carriage, not apparently knowing each other, I verily believe, for he sat at one door and she at the other, passengers dividing them.

'Lambs between two wolves,' remarked Tod. 'I have a great mind to warn the people of the sort of company they are in. Would it be actionable, Johnny?'

The train moved off as he was speaking. And may I never write another word if I did not catch sight of the manservant and his cockade in the next carriage behind them!

Harriet E. Prescott

MR FURBUSH

This is the earliest story in the book, first published in the April 1865 edition of Harper's New Monthly Magazine, *yet, apart from a few quaint old spellings, such as 'clew' rather than 'clue', the story, and certainly the way the crime is solved, seems remarkably modern. Harriet Elizabeth Prescott (1835–1921), usually known as Hallie to her friends – and who added Spofford to her name after her marriage in 1865 – had a writing career lasting over sixty years. She was one of those many talented New England writers, like Mary E. Wilkins, who is also in this volume, though early in her career, until supported by her husband, she found herself having to write anything and everything in order to be able to support her ailing parents. That makes the ingenuity of this story, one of the last she wrote before her marriage, all the more remarkable.*

*Prescott returned to the character of Detective Furbush in one other story, 'In the Maguerriwock' (*Harper's New Monthly Magazine, *August 1868) but did not otherwise continue the character. That story, together with an earlier detective story, 'In a Cellar', were resurrected by Alfred Bendixen in* The Amber Gods and Other Stories *(1989) but the original 'Mr Furbush' was not included in any of her collections and has been all but forgotten.*

Mr Furbush

IT IS NOT very long since the community was startled by the report of an extraordinary murder that occurred at one of our fashionable hotels, under peculiar circumstances and in broad daylight, and without affording, as it appeared, the slightest clew to motive or murderer. Public curiosity, finding that nothing was likely to satisfy it, gradually dropped the matter, and as gradually it died out of the newspapers.

The person who was thus abruptly ushered from this world into the unknown region of the next was a young girl, some twenty summers old and possessed of great personal charms. She was the heiress to a small fortune, a mere annuity, but had resided since her childhood with her guardian, the wealthy and generous Mr Denbigh, who had always surrounded her with every luxury and elegance. When Mr Denbigh married he and his wife took their ward with them on the foreign tour they made, and the three had but just returned to America, residing temporarily at a hotel until their uptown mansion should be suitably prepared, when the sudden and terrible death of Miss Agatha More threw such a gloom over all their plans that the preparations were for a time abandoned, and Mr Denbigh's energies were called upon to assist his wife in rallying from the low nervous fever into which she had been thrown and prostrated by this tragedy, when, after returning with her husband from a drive, they had discovered it in all its horror.

Mr Denbigh was himself greatly afflicted by the death of his ward and the fearful manner of it – she had been strangled in her own handkerchief – for besides the debt of affection he owed her as a child of a dear dead friend, long years of familiarity, her extreme loveliness and the winning gentleness of her sweet and timid ways had given her a deep and warm place in his heart. Of late she had been a little out of health, not recovering rapidly from the great exhaustion and weakness of severe seasickness, and he had been unremitting in his endeavours to promote her comfort and happiness. While in making ready their new abode both he and his wife had paid such heed to the tastes and needs of Agatha, meaning, as Mr Denbigh said, that it should be felt by her to be as much her own home as theirs, without any sense of obligation, that now the place without her seemed too much a desert ever to enter upon it again.

Mrs Denbigh, moreover, must have felt sorely, it would seem, the loss of the gentle daily companion of three years; but even more than on her own account she appeared to resent the deed for the sake of her husband, to whom she was so passionately devoted, and no sooner was she able to lift her head from its pillow once more than she interested herself with revengeful vigour in the proceedings that had been undertaken. Mr Denbigh, personally, cared little to discover the perpetrator of the atrocious crime – he felt that no human justice of cord or gibbet could restore Agatha – but his wife, burdened with their bereavement and with her own weight of indignation, would not rest with the mystery unravelled. In the deepest mourning, discarding almost every ornament, impressing so upon them more deeply the emergencies of the case and commanding their sympathies, she was closeted every morning with the detectives of the police, sparing her husband as much of the painful duty as possible, as she would have walked over burning plough shares at a word from him.

It was at first supposed that the deed had been done for plunder, as various valuable jewels, gifts of the Denbighs and heirlooms from Miss More's own mother, were discovered to be missing, but they afforded in themselves insufficient reason and were subsequently discovered in a package picked up by one of the police themselves at a crossing of a crowded thoroughfare where they had apparently been purposely dropped. Neither did Miss More's lovers afford any clew to the miscreant. She had had several suitors and attendants, none of whom had Mr Denbigh favoured; and though Mrs Denbigh had urged Agatha to regard young Elliot with kindness, Mr Denbigh frowned, Agatha remained indifferent, and young Elliot – having taunted Mr Denbigh with the assurance that since he countenanced none of

Miss More's lovers it could be but from sinister intentions on his part – had withdrawn, vowing vengeance and declaring that, since he could not have her, nobody else should. Still, that was hardly murder. And the poor fellow was found, besides, to be in such a heartbroken state as to disarm suspicion. The only other accusation that could take shape and breath might have been directed toward Agatha's maid, but as she was able to prove that she was down in the laundry and had remained there uninterruptedly from nine until one, while the occurrence had taken place between the hours of eleven and twelve in the morning, and as she had evidently nothing to gain and much to lose by it, that idea was also dismissed, though both young Elliot and the servant-maid remained under surveillance. Finally, in despair, the Denbighs abandoned the investigation and departed to spend the winter in Madeira, returning in the spring to their city abode, whose adornment had been left to the tender mercies of the upholsterers, since they had themselves so completely lost interest in it.

Here the general course of the matter rested. One officer alone, Detective Furbush – a man of genteel proclivities, fond of fancy parties and the *haut ton*, curious in fine women and aristocratic defaulters and peculators – who had not at first been detailed upon the case but had been interested in the reports of it, having become at last much in earnest about it pursued it still, incidentally, on his own account and in a kind of amateur way. It seemed to him a fatal fascination, a predestination of events that kept his steps nearly always about the purlieus of the Margrand House.

One day that Detective Furbush had happened, in a spare hour, to take his little daughter into a photograph gallery, he lounged about a window while the child was undergoing the awful operation. Along the opposite side of the street from this window ran one end of the Margrand House with its countless windows and projections. The Margrand House fronted on a square, one end of it running down this street and always receiving, on its stone facings and adornments, the whole sheet of the noon sun. A thought suddenly occurred to Mr Furbush. So as soon as the operator was at leisure he attacked him with the enquiry if there were any picture of that fine building, the Margrand House, to which the operator replied affirmatively, and showed him one taken from the square. 'However,' said the operator, 'though it doesn't take in so much and was only what this one window could do for itself, I call this a prettier picture,' and he produced something which, having been taken at such a short focal distance, resembled the photographs of the rich architecture of some Venetian façade. 'It was the morning of the Great Walden Celebration,' continued the operator.

'What one?' asked Mr Furbush.

'The Great Walden Celebration.'

'Ah yes,' responded Mr Furbush, not letting the rest of his thought reach the air, running as it did: That was the morning of the More murder.

'And we let one of the boys try his hand at the craft,' resumed the operator, 'there being nothing doing, and it was such a lively scene in the street below, narrow as it is. And, as was to be expected from him, the crowd and procession turned into dot and line, and the whole of that part of the building opposite came out as if it had sat for its picture.'

'Exactly,' said Mr Furbush, as, rubbing his finger over his lips, he looked at the sheet on which the central portion of that side of the hotel, with its quaint windows and lintels and ornamentation were most minutely given. It was in that very portion of the house that Miss Agatha More's room had been situated; nay, so well was it all impressed upon him that Mr Furbush could tell the very window of the room in which she had met her cruel fate. Never was there such a coincidence, to Mr Furbush's mind, before or since, never such an interposition of Providence. The day that an unknown hand had brought Agatha More to her doom, perhaps the very hour, the sun had made a revelation of that room's interior upon this sheet of sensitized paper; his Ithuriel's spear had touched this shapeless darkness and turned it into form and truth. The Walden Celebration had defiled through the street and into the square at a somewhat earlier hour than the supposed hour of the murder, since it was to see the procession from a more advantageous point of view that Mr and Mrs Denbigh had driven out, and while they were gone the terrible action was thought to have been committed. Still the window might have a secret of its own to tell even concerning that.

Straightway Mr Furbush made a prize of the operator, and procuring, through channels always open to him, the strongest glasses and most accurate instruments, had the one chosen window in the picture magnified and photographed, remagnified and rephotographed, until under their powerful, careful, prolonged and patient labour a speck came into sight that would perhaps well reward them. Mr Furbush strained his eyes over it; to him it was a spot of greater possibilities than the nebula in Orion. This little white unresolved cloud again and again they subjected to the same process, and once more, as if a ghost had made apparition, it opened itself into an outline – into a substance – and they saw the fingers of a hand, a white hand, doubled but pliant, strong and shapely; a left hand, on its third finger wearing rings, one of which seemed at first a mere blot of light but, gradually, as the rest, answering the spell of the camera, showed itself a central stone set with five points, each point consisting of smaller stones. The colour, of course, could not be told; the form was that of a star. Held in the tight, fierce fingers of that clenched hand, between the pointed thumb and waxy knuckles, and one edge visible along the tips deep dinted into the thumb's side, was grasped an end of a laced handkerchief. Now the handkerchief of Agatha More, the instrument of her destruction, was always carried folded in the shape of its running knot in Mr Furbush's great wallet: a large, laced, embroidered handkerchief. That this was its photograph he needed but a glance to rest assured. All the rest of the dark deed was hidden beyond the angle of light afforded by the window frame. And whosoever the murderer might be, Mr Furbush said to himself with the pleasantry of the headsman, it was evident that the owner of this picture had a hand in it. And here he paid the photographer for his labours and bade him adieu.

Mr Furbush was now, however, not much better off than he had been before. He had the hand that did the deed in his possession, to be sure, but to whose body was he to affix that hand and how was he to do it? And in what did it differ from any other hand? In nothing but that fetter which made it his prisoner, that five-pointed star, that blot of light upon the third finger above a wedding-ring. A wedding-ring, that would seem to prove the hand to be a woman's; the five-pointed glittering ring, that proved the woman to be no pauper. Worn above the wedding-ring it must be its guard and was probably as inseparable as that. To identify that hand, to certify that ring, became the recreation of Mr Furbush's days and nights, so much to the detriment of all his other business that he fell into sad disrepute thereby at the Bureau. Mr Furbush became all at once a gay man, plunged into the dissipations of fashionable life – he had been there before, on similar necessity, and knew how to carry himself. His costume grew singularly correct; he handled his lorgnette at the opera like a coxcomb of the first milk-and-water; he procured invitations to ball and party and watched every lady who, for the moment, daintily ungloved herself; he was as constant at church as the sexton; he made a part of the *beau monde*. It was all in vain. And though Mr Furbush carried the photograph in his breast pocket, ready at any moment to descend like the hand of the Inquisition upon its victim, he might as well have carried there a pardon to all concerned for all the good it did him.

But the world goes round.

One starlit night Mr Furbush, pursuing some scent of other affairs along the princely avenue with its rows of palaces, took in, as was his wont, with every wink a whole scene to its last details. He saw the beggar on these steps shrink into shadow, the housemaid in that area listening to the beguiling voice of the footman-three-doors-off no longer keeping his distance; he saw, there, the gay scene offered by the bright balcony casement with its rich curtains still unclosed; he saw, yet beyond, the light streaming from between open doors down the shining steps at whose foot the carriage waited while a gentleman at its door hurried, with a pleasant word, the stately woman who came down to enter it beside him. She came down slowly, Mr Furbush noted, moving like a person whom organic difficulty of the heart indisposes to quick exertion; she was one of those whom Mr Furbush called magnificent – great coils of blue-black hair, twisted with diamonds, wreathing her queenly head tiara-wise, her features having the firmness and the pallor of marble, her eyes rivalling the diamonds in their steady splendour. A heavy cloak of ermine wrapped her velvet attire, and she was buttoning a glove as she descended. She paused a moment under the carriage lamp, giving her husband the ungloved hand to help her in. The carriage light flashed upon it, and in that second of its lingering Mr Furbush saw, plainly as he saw the stars above him, on the third finger of that left hand, above the wedding-ring, the circlet with its five-pointed star whose duplicate he carried.

Mr Furbush was thunderstruck. Here was what he had sought for thrice a twelvemonth, and unexpectedly blundering upon it turned him into stone. When he recovered himself with an emphatic 'Humph!' the carriage had rolled away and the doors were closed.

Mr Furbush was not the man to lose opportunities. The business in hand might go to the dogs; tomorrow would answer as well for that as tonight. For this there was no time like the present. Fortified with an outside subordinate he demanded entrance into the mansion alone, and announcing his intention to await the arrival home of the master and mistress made himself agreeable to the footman and butler in the upper hall until hour after hour pealing forth at last struck midnight as if they tolled a knell. The footman was asleep in his chair, the butler heard the mellifluous murmur of the visitor's voice by starts with a singing sensation as if his fingers were in his ears and out again momentarily. The wheels grated on the curb below, the horses hammered the pavement, the doors were flung apart and the master and mistress of the house returned from the entertainments they had shared. She was a little paler, a little more magnificent, a little more imposing in her height and dignity than before; there was only one emotion, though, apparent through it all, that she valued her beauty and power only for its influence on the man beside her. Mr Furbush's keen eye saw the quick heave and restless agitation that the heart kept up beneath the velvets, simply in the moment when her husband touched her hand helping her across the threshold, and saw the whole story of her eye as it rested that instant on his. He would have had the entire case at once – if he had not had it before.

'Mr and Mrs Denbigh,' said he, approaching them then. 'May I beg to see you alone for a few moments on a matter of importance?'

And in conformity with his request he was conducted through other apartments into a library, a place more secluded than they, a rather sombre room, wainscoted all its lofty height in bookcases and with here and there a glimmering bust. Mr Denbigh himself turned up the gas and closed the door.

'Your business, sir?' said he then to Mr Furbush.

'My business, sir, is more particularly with Mrs Denbigh, although I desire your presence. I am a member of the police . . .'

Mrs Denbigh, who yet stood with her hand laid passively along the back of a chair, slowly grasped the back until the glove that she wore with a quick crack ripped down the length of the finger, and the five-pointed ring protruded its sparkling face like the vicious head of a serpent.

'I am a member of the police,' continued Mr Furbush, quietly. 'I have something in my possession which I desire Mrs Denbigh to look at and see if it belongs to her.' Perhaps the woman breathed again. Whether she did or not he proceeded to open his great leathern wallet on the library table beneath the chandelier.

Mrs Denbigh moved forward with her slow majesty, dragging her velvets heavily and the cloak dropping from her shoulder.

Queer subjects, women, thought Mr Furbush. Ah! You had more spring in you once. As handsome a thing as a leopard!

But in spite of that calm deliberate step Mr Furbush saw her heart fluttering there like a white dove in its nest. She did not speak but waited a moment beside him. 'Will you be so kind,' said he, 'as to remove your glove?'

She quietly did so. Perhaps wonderingly.

'Excuse me, madam,' then continued he, lifting her hand as he spoke, doubling its cold fingers over one end of a running knot that a soiled handkerchief made, a laced embroidered handkerchief he had produced, and, powerless in his grasp, he laid hand and all – a white hand, doubled, but pliant, strong and shapely, holding in its fingers, between the pointed thumb and waxy knuckles, the laced handkerchief's end, just an edge visible along the tips deep dinted into the thumb's side; and with the five-pointed ring burning its bale-fire above it – laid the hand and all on the table beside the photograph that he spread there.

'Is it yours?' said he.

A detective has perhaps no right to any pity, but for a moment Mr Furbush would gladly have never heard of the More murder as he saw in the long, slow rise and fall of the bosom this woman's heart swing like a pendulum, a noiseless pendulum that ceases to vibrate. Her eyes wavered a moment between him and the table then, as if caught and chained by something that compelled their gaze, glared at and protruded over the sight they saw beneath them. Her own hand – her own executioner. A long shudder shook her from head to foot. Iron nerve gave way, the white lips parted, she threw her head back and gasped; with one wild look towards her husband she turned from him as if she would have fled and fell dead upon the floor.

'Hunt's up,' said Mr Furbush to his subordinate, coming out an hour or two later, and the two found some congenial oyster-opener while the chief explained how he had gone to get his wife's spoons from the maid who had appropriated them and taken service elsewhere. Mr Furbush made a night of it, but never a soul longed for daylight as he did. He had a notion that he had scarcely less than murdered – himself – and good fellow as he must needs be abroad that night, indoors the next day he put his household in sackcloth and ashes.

You will not find Mr Furbush's name on the list of detectives now. He has sickened of the business. He says there is too much night-work. He has found a patron now – a wealthy one apparently. He has opened one of the largest and most elegant photographing establishments in the city – he was always fond of chemicals, he says. He has still, in an inner drawer, some singular but fast-fading likenesses of a hand, a clenched, murderous hand – among them not the one Mr Denbigh burned. He has a few secrets appertaining to his profession, which no one else has yet obtained. Meanwhile, it has never been exactly explained how the story of the ring found the light.

Perhaps it was in order that Mr Furbush might never be convicted of compounding a felony!

Mary Fortune

TRACES OF CRIME

Though the names of Mary E. Braddon and Mrs Henry Wood were well known, that of Mary Fortune was for many years completely unknown, yet she was not only one of the most prolific writers of crime fiction, certainly in the Victorian period, but also one of the first to write a regular series about the work of the police. It is only in recent decades that her life and works have been rediscovered by the writer Lucy Sussex and others. Sussex has compiled a volume of Fortune's autobiographical writings, The Fortunes of Mary Fortune *(1989), which is both revealing and makes us aware how much more there is to learn of this remarkable woman. We're not even sure of her dates of birth and death, though she probably lived from around 1833 to 1910. She was born Mary Wilson in Belfast, Northern Ireland, where her father was a civil engineer. Her mother may well have died in childbirth or soon after, as young Mary never knew her. She and her father emigrated to Canada, and it was there that Mary married Joseph Fortune in 1851. Believing his daughter settled, the father set off to seek his fortune in Australia. However, Mary and her husband must have separated because, though he lived until 1861 (dying at the age of only thirty-five), Mary and her three-year-old son Georgie had already set off in 1855 to find her father in Australia, somewhere in the goldfields of Victoria. She spent the rest of her life in Australia, for many years in the nomadic world of the gold prospector. Alas, young Georgie died in January 1858, probably as a result of the poor living conditions.*

Mary began to write poems and stories for local newspapers almost as soon as she arrived in Australia, but these all paid poorly. Her most important work appeared in the newly formed Australian Journal *from 1865 on. All of these writings were published either anonymously or under the alias Waif Wander, later shortened to WW. Fortune maintained an astonishing output in order to scrape a living. It has been estimated that she wrote close on five hundred stories, many of them crime or mystery and often featuring detectives of the Australian police. Only one volume of her work appeared during her lifetime,* The Detective's Album *(1871), selecting seven stories from her long-running series in the* Australian Journal, *and it was the first book of detective fiction to be published in Australia. An expanded version, edited by Lucy Sussex, was published in Canada in 2003, but is currently not widely available.*

Eventually, encroaching blindness and old age forced Fortune to stop writing in 1909, and she probably died soon afterwards. It was not until the 1950s that the identity behind Waif Wander was discovered and not until the 1980s that the scale of her writing became apparent. Though many of these stories are fairly crudely written, especially the early ones, they are an accurate and directly personal reflection of life in the goldfields of Australia in the 1860s and 1870s. The following is one of her earliest such stories, part of a series 'Memoirs of an Australian Police Officer', published in the Australian Journal *of 2 December 1865.*

Traces of Crime

THERE ARE MANY who recollect full well the rush at Chinaman's Flat. It was in the height of its prosperity that an assault upon a female was committed of a character so diabolical in itself as to have aroused the utmost anxiety in the public as well as in the police to punish the perpetrator thereof.

The case was placed in my hands, and as it presented difficulties so great as to appear to an ordinary observer almost insurmountable, the overcoming of which was likely to gain approbation in the proper quarter, I gladly accepted the task.

I had little to go upon at first. One dark night, in a tent in the very centre of a crowded thoroughfare, a female had been preparing to retire to rest, her husband being in the habit of remaining at the public house until a late hour, when a man with a crape mask – who must have gained an earlier entrance – seized her and, in the prosecution of a criminal offence, had injured and abused the unfortunate woman so much that her life was despaired of.

Though there was a light burning at the time, the woman was barely able to describe his general appearance. He appeared to her like a German, had no whiskers, fair hair, was low in stature and stoutly built.

With one important exception, that was all the information she was able to give me on the subject. The exception, however, was a good deal to a detective, and I hoped might prove an invaluable aid to me. During the struggle she had torn the arm of the flannel shirt he wore and was under a decided impression that upon the upper part of the criminal's arm there was a small anchor and heart tattooed.

Now, I was well aware that in this colony to find a man with a tattooed arm was an everyday affair, especially on the diggings, where, I dare say, there is scarcely a person who has not come in contact more than once or twice with half a dozen men tattooed in the style I speak of – the anchor or heart, or both, being a favourite figure with those 'gentlemen' who are in favour of branding.

However, the clue was worth something, and even without its aid, not more than a couple of weeks had elapsed when, with the assistance of the local police, I had traced a man bearing in appearance a general resemblance to the man who had committed the offence to a digging about seven miles from Chinaman's Flat.

It is unnecessary that I should relate every particular as to how my suspicions were directed to this man who did not live on Chinaman's Flat and to all appearances had not left the diggings where he was camped since he first commenced working there. I say 'to all appearances', for it was with a certain knowledge that he had been absent from his tent on the night of the outrage that I one evening trudged down the flat where his tent was pitched, with my swag on my back, and sat down on a log not far from where he had kindled a fire for culinary or other purposes.

These diggings I will call McAdam's. It was a large and flourishing goldfield, and on the flat where my man was camped there were several other tents grouped, so that it was nothing singular that I should look about for a couple of bushes between which I might swing my little bit of canvas for the night.

After I had fastened up the rope, and thrown my tent over it in regular digger fashion, I broke down some bushes to form my bed and, having spread thereon my blankets, went up to my man – whom I shall in future call 'Bill' – to request permission to boil my billy on his fire.

It was willingly granted, so I lighted my pipe and sat down to await the boiling of the water, determined, if I could so manage it, to get this suspected man to accept me as a mate before I lay down that night.

Bill was also engaged in smoking and had not, of course, the slightest suspicion that in the rough, ordinary-looking digger before him he was contemplating the 'make-up' of a Victorian detective, who had already made himself slightly talked of among his comrades by one or two clever captures.

'Where did you come from, mate?' enquired Bill, as he puffed away leisurely at a cutty.

'From Burnt Creek,' I replied, 'and a long enough road it is in such d—d hot weather as this.'

'Nothing doing at Burnt Creek?'

'Not a thing – the place is cooked.'

'Are you in for a try here, then?' he asked, rather eagerly I thought.

'Well, I think so. Is there any chance, do you think?'

'Have you got a miner's right?' was his sudden question.

'I have,' said I, taking it out of my pocket and handing the bit of parchment for his inspection.

'Are you a hatter?'* enquired Bill as he returned the document.

'I am,' was my reply.

'Well, if you have no objections then, I don't mind going mates with you. I've got a pretty fair prospect, and the ground's going to run rather deep for one man, I think.'

'All right.'

So here was the very thing I wanted, settled without the slightest trouble. My object in wishing to go mates with this fellow will, I dare say, readily be perceived. I did not wish to risk my character for 'cuteness by arresting my gentleman without being sure that he was branded in the way described by the woman, and besides, in the close supervision which I should be able to keep over him while working together daily, Heaven knows what might transpire as additional evidence against him – at least, so I reasoned with myself. And it was with a partially relieved mind that I made my frugal supper, and made to believe to 'turn in', fatigued, as I might be supposed to be, after my long tramp.

But I didn't turn in, not I. I had other objects in view, if one may be said to have an object in view on one of the darkest nights of a moonless week, for dark enough the night in question became, even

* An independent miner who worked alone

before I had finished my supper and made my apparent preparations for bed.

We were not camped far enough from the business part of the rush to be very quiet. There was plenty of noise – the nightly noise of a rich goldfield – came down our way, and even in some of the tents close to us card-playing and drinking and singing and laughing were going on, so it was quite easy for me to steal unnoticed to the back of Bill's little tent and, by the assistance of a small slit made in the calico by my knife, have a look what my worthy was doing inside, for I was anxious to become acquainted with his habits and, of course, determined to watch him as closely as ever I could.

Well, the first specimen I had of his customs was certainly a singular one and was, it may be well believed, an exception to his general line of conduct. Diggers, or any other class of men, do not generally spend their evenings in cutting their shoes up into small morsels, and that was exactly what Bill was busily engaged in doing when I clapped my eye to the hole. He had already disposed of a good portion of the article when I commenced to watch him: the entire 'upper' of a very muddy blucher boot lying upon his rough table in a small heap and in the smallest pieces that one would suppose any person could have patience to cut up a dry, hard old leather boot.

It was rather a puzzler to me this, and that Bill was doing such a thing simply to amuse himself was out of the question. Indeed, without observing that he had the door of the tent closely fastened upon a warm evening and that he started at the slightest sound, the instincts of an old detective would alone have convinced me that Bill had some great cause to make away with those old boots. So I continued watching.

He had hacked away at the sole with an old but sharp butcher's knife, but it almost defied his attempts to separate it into pieces, and at length he gave them up in despair and, gathering up the small portions on the table, he swept them with the mutilated sole into his hat and, opening his tent door, went out.

I guessed very truly that he would make for the fire, and as it happened to be at the other side of a log from where I was hiding I had a good opportunity of continuing my espial. He raked together the few embers that remained near the log and, flinging the pieces of leather thereon, retired once more into his tent, calculating, no doubt, that the hot ashes would soon scorch and twist them up so as to defy recognition, while the fire he would build upon them in the morning would settle the matter most satisfactorily.

All this would have happened just so, no doubt, if I had not succeeded in scraping nearly every bit from the place where Bill had thrown them, so silent and quickly that I was in the shelter of my slung tent with my prize and a burn or two on my fingers before he himself had time to divest himself of his garments and blow out the light.

He did so very soon, however, and it was long before I could get asleep. I thought it over and over in all ways and looked upon it in all lights that I could think of, and yet, always connecting this demolished boot with the case in the investigation of which I was engaged, I could not make it out at all.

Had we overlooked, with all our fancied acuteness, some clue which Bill feared we had possession of to which this piecemeal boot was the key? And, if so, why had he remained so long without destroying it? It was, as I said before, a regular puzzler to me, and my brain was positively weary when I at length dropped off to sleep.

Well, I worked for a week with Bill, and I can tell you it was work I didn't at all take to. The unaccustomed use of the pick and shovel played the very mischief with my hands, but, for fear of arousing the suspicions of my mate, I durst not complain, having only to endure in silence – or as our Scotch friends would put it, 'grin and bide it'. And the worst of it was that I was gaining nothing – nothing whatever – by my unusual industry.

I had hoped that accidentally I should have got a sight of the anchor and heart, but I was day after day disappointed, for my mate was not very regular in his ablutions, and I had reckoned without my host in expecting that the very ordinary habit of a digger, namely, that of having a 'regular wash' at least every Sunday, would be a good and certain one for exposing the brand.

But, no, Bill allowed the Sunday to come and go without once removing what I could observe was the flannel shirt in which he had worked all the week. And then I began to swear at my own obtuseness. The fellow must be aware that his shirt was torn by the woman; of course he suspects that she may have seen the tattooing and will take blessed good care not to expose it, mate or no mate, thought I. And then I called myself a donkey, and during the few following days, when I was trusting to the chapter of accidents, I was also deliberating on the 'to be or not to be' of the question of arresting him at once and chancing it.

Saturday afternoon came again, and then the early knock-off time, and that sort of quarter holiday among the miners, namely four o'clock, was hailed by me with the greatest relief, and it was with the full determination of never again setting foot in the cursed claim that I shouldered my pick and shovel and proceeded tent-wards.

On my way I met a policeman and received from him a concerted signal that I was wanted at the camp, and so, telling Bill that I was going to see an old mate about some money that he owed me, I started at once.

'We've got something else in your line, mate,' said my old chum Joe Bennet, as I entered the camp, 'and one which, I think, will be a regular poser for you. The body of a man has been found in Pipeclay Gully, and we can scarcely be justified by appearances in giving even a surmise as to how he came by his death.'

'How do you mean?' I enquired. 'Has he been dead so long?'

'About a fortnight, I dare say, but we have done absolutely nothing as yet. Knowing you were on the ground, we have not even touched the body. Will you come up at once?'

'Of course I will!' And after substituting the uniform of the force for the digger's costume in which I was apparelled in case of an encounter with my 'mate', we went straight to Pipeclay.

The body had been left in charge of one of the police and was still lying undisturbed in the position in which it had been discovered. Not a soul was about – in fact, the gully had been rushed and abandoned and bore not the slightest traces of man's handiwork, saving and except the miner's holes and their surrounding little eminences of pipeclay from which the gully was named. And it was a veritable gully, running between two low ranges of hills, which hills were covered with an undergrowth of wattle and cherry trees and scattered over with rocks and indications of quartz, which have, I dare say, been fully tried by this time.

Well, on the slope of one of the hills, where it amalgamated as it were with the level of the gully and where the sinking had evidently been shallow, lay the body of the dead man. He was dressed in ordinary miner's fashion and, saving for the fact of a gun being by his side, one might have supposed that he had only given up his digging to lie down and die beside the hole near which he lay.

The hole, however, was full of water – quite full; indeed, the water was sopping out on the ground around it – and that the hole was an old one was evident by the crumbling edges around it and the fragments of old branches that lay rotting in the water.

Close to this hole lay the body, the attitude strongly indicative of the last exertion during life having been that of crawling out of the water hole, in which, indeed, still remained part of the unfortunate man's leg. There was no hat on his head, and in spite of the considerable decay of the body even an ordinary observer could not fail to notice a large fracture in the side of the head.

I examined the gun. It was a double-barrelled fowling piece, and one barrel had been discharged, while very apparent on the stock of the gun were blood marks that even the late heavy rain had failed to erase. In the pockets of the dead man was nothing, save what any digger might carry – pipe and tobacco, a cheap knife and a shilling or two, this was all – and so, leaving the body to be removed by the police, I thoughtfully retraced my way to the camp.

Singularly enough, during my absence a woman had been there, giving information about her husband on account of whose absence she was becoming alarmed. And as the caution of the policeman on duty at the camp had prevented his giving her any idea of the fact of the dead body having been discovered that very day, I immediately went to the address which the woman had left in order to discover, if possible, not only if it was the missing man but also to gain any information that might be likely to put me upon the scent of the murderer – for that the man had been murdered I had not the slightest doubt.

Well, I succeeded in finding the woman, a young and decidedly good-looking English woman of the lower class, and gained from her the following information:

About a fortnight before, her husband, who had been indisposed and in consequence not working for a day or two, had taken his gun one morning in order to amuse himself for an hour or two as well as to have a look at the ranges near Pipeclay Gully and do a little prospecting at the same time. He had not returned, but as he had suggested a possibility of visiting his brother, who was digging about four miles off, she had not felt alarmed until, upon communicating with the said brother, she had become aware that her husband had never been there. From the description I knew at once that the remains of the poor fellow lying in Pipeclay Gully were certainly those of the missing man, and with what care and delicacy I might possess I broke the tidings to the shocked wife, and after allowing her grief to have vent in a passion of tears I tried to gain some clue to the likely perpetrator of the murder.

Had she any suspicions? I asked. Was there any feud between her husband and any individual she could name?

At first she replied 'no', and then a sudden recollection appeared to strike her, and she said that some weeks ago a man had, during the absence of her husband, made advances to her under the feigned supposition that she was an unmarried woman. In spite of her decidedly repellent manner, he had continued his attentions until she, afraid of his impetuosity, had been obliged to call the attention of her husband to the matter, and he, of course feeling indignant, had threatened to shoot the intruder if he ever ventured near the place again. The woman described this man to me, and it was with a violent whirl of emotional excitement – as one feels who is on the eve of a great discovery – that I hastened to the camp, which was close by.

It was barely half past five o'clock, and in a few minutes I was on my way, with two or three other associates, to the scene of what I had no doubt had been a horrible murder. What my object was there was soon apparent. I had before tried the depth of the muddy water and found it was scarcely four feet, and now we hastened to make use of the remaining light of a long summer's day in draining carefully the said hole.

I was repaid for the trouble, for in the muddy mid-deep sediment at the bottom we uncovered a deeply imbedded blucher boot – and I dare say you will readily guess how my heart leaped up at the sight.

To old diggers the task which followed was not a very great one. We had provided ourselves with a 'tub', etc., and 'washed' every bit of the mud at the bottom of the hole. The only 'find' we had, however, was a peculiar bit of wood, which, instead of rewarding us for our exertions by lying like gold at the bottom of the dish in which we 'turned off', insisted upon floating on the top of the very first tub when it became loosened from its surrounding of clay.

It was a queer piece of wood and eventually quite repaid us for any trouble we might have had in its capture. A segment of a circle it was, or rather a portion of a segment of a circle, being neither more nor less than a piece broken out of one of those old-fashioned black wooden buttons that are still to be seen on the monkey-jacket of many an Australian digger as well as elsewhere.

Well, I fancied that I knew the identical button from whence had been broken this bit of wood, and that I could go and straightway fit it into its place without the slightest trouble in the world – singular, was it not ? – and as I carefully placed the piece in my pocket I could not help thinking to myself: Well, this does indeed and most truly look like the working of Providence.

There are many occasions when an apparent chance has effected the unravelling of a mystery which, but for the turning over of that particular page of fatality, might have remained a mystery to the day of judgement in spite of the most strenuous and most able exertions. Mere human acumen would never have discovered the key to the secret's hieroglyphic nor placed side by side the hidden links of a chain long enough and strong enough to tear the murderer from his fancied security and hang him as high as Haman. Such would almost appear to have been the case in the instance to which I am alluding, only that in place of ascribing the elucidation and the unravelling to that mythical power Chance, the impulse of some 'inner man' writes the word Providence.

I did not feel exactly like moralizing, however, when, after resuming my digger's 'make-up', I walked towards the tent of the man I have called Bill. No. I felt more and deeper than any mere moralist could understand. The belief that a higher power had especially called out and chosen one of his own creatures to be the instrument of his retributive power has, in our world's history, been the means of mighty evil, and I hope that not for an instant did such an idea take possession of me. I was not conscious of feeling that I had been chosen as a scourge and an instrument of earthly punishment, but I did feel that I was likely to be the means of cutting short the thread of a most unready fellow mortal's life – and a solemn responsibility it is to bring home to one's self, I can assure you.

The last flush of sunlight was fading low in the west when I reached our camping ground and found Bill seated outside on a log, indulging in his usual pipe in the greying twilight. I had, of course, determined upon arresting him at once and had sent two policemen around to the back of our tents in case of an attempted escape upon his part. And now, quite prepared, I sat down beside him, and, after feeling that the handcuffs were in their usual place in my belt, I lit my pipe and commenced to smoke also. My heart verily went pit-a-pat as I did so, for, long as I had been engaged in this sort of thing, I had not as yet become callous either as to the feelings of a wretched criminal or the excitement attendant more or less upon every capture of the sort.

We smoked in silence for some minutes, and I was listening intently to hear the slightest intimation of the vicinity of my mates. At length Bill broke the silence. 'Did you get your money?' he enquired.

'No,' I replied, 'but I think I will get it soon.'

Silence again, and then withdrawing the pipe from my mouth and quietly knocking the ashes out of it on the log, I turned towards my mate and said, 'Bill, what made you murder that man in Pipeclay Gully?'

He did not reply, but I could see his face pale and whiten in the grey dim twilight and at last stand out distinctly in the darkening like that of the dead man we found lying in the lonely gully. It was so entirely unexpected that he was completely stunned. Not the slightest idea had he that the body had ever been found, and it was on quite nerveless wrists that I locked the handcuffs as my mates came up and took him in charge.

Rallying a little, he asked huskily, 'Who said I did it?'

'No person,' I replied, 'but I know you did it.'

Again he was silent and did not contradict me, and so he was taken to the lock-up.

I was right about the broken button and had often noticed it on an old jacket of Bill's. The piece fitted to a nicety, and the cut-up blucher! Verily there was some powerful influence at work in the discovery of this murder, and again I repeat that no mere human wisdom could have accomplished it.

Bill, it would appear, thought so, too, for expressing himself so to me he made a full confession, not only of the murder but also of the other offence, for the bringing home to him of which I had been so anxious. When he found that the body of the unfortunate man had been discovered upon the surface in the broad light of day after he had left him dead in the bottom of the hole, he became superstitiously convinced that God himself had permitted the dead man to leave his hiding place for the purpose of bringing the murderer to justice.

It is no unusual thing to find criminals of his class deeply impregnated with superstition, and Bill insisted to the last that the murdered man was quite dead when he had placed him in the hole and where, in his anxiety to prevent the body from appearing above the surface, he had lost his boot in the mud and was too fearful of discovery to remain to try and get it out.

Bill was convicted, sentenced to death and hanged, many other crimes of a similar nature to that which he had committed on Chinaman's Flat having been brought home to him by his own confession.

Anna Katharine Green

THE HOUSE OF CLOCKS

The woman usually acknowledged as the pioneer female writer of detective fiction – and dubbed 'the mother of the detective novel' – is the American Anna Katharine Green (1846–1935). Her most famous book was her first, The Leavenworth Case *(1878), which introduced the character of her police detective, the middle-aged and rather portly Ebenezer Gryce. Though a police detective rather than a private one, Gryce shared many of the characteristics of Sherlock Holmes (who was not even a glint in Conan Doyle's eye at this time) – for example, he displays a remarkable depth of knowledge on such obscure subjects as what paper produces which type of ash when burnt, a topic on which Holmes would later write a monograph. Gryce is assisted in his investigations by a lawyer, Everett Raymond, who narrates the cases. Green's father, James Wilson Green, was an attorney, and he raised the girl after her mother died when Anna was only two. James ensured his daughter received a good education, and she initially wished to be a poet but was advised by no less a figure than Ralph Waldo Emerson to pursue a different form of writing. In the end she wrote thirty-six detective novels and many short stories. There are twelve novels featuring Gryce and, in three of them, starting with* That Affair Next Door *(1897), he is further assisted by an elderly spinster, Amelia Butterworth, a clear forerunner of Agatha Christie's Miss Marple. In the years just before the First World War Green wrote a series of stories featuring Violet Strange, a young debutante who keeps secret her role as an undercover detective. These stories were collected as* The Golden Slipper and Other Problems *(1915), and the story reprinted here is one of the oddest.*

The House of Clocks

I

Miss Strange was not in a responsive mood. This her employer had observed on first entering, yet he showed no hesitation in laying on the table behind which she had ensconced herself in the attitude of one besieged an envelope thick with enclosed papers.

'There,' said he. 'Telephone me when you have read them.'

'I shall not read them.'

'No?' he smiled, and, repossessing himself of the envelope, he tore off one end, extracted the sheets with which it was filled and laid them down still unfolded in their former place on the table top.

The suggestiveness of the action caused the corners of Miss Strange's delicate lips to twitch wistfully before settling into an ironic smile.

Calmly the other watched her.

'I am on a vacation,' she loftily explained, as she finally met his studiously non-quizzical glance. 'Oh, I know that I am in my own home!' she petulantly acknowledged as his gaze took in the room, 'and that the automobile is at the door and that I'm dressed for shopping, but for all that I'm on a vacation – a mental one,' she emphasized, 'and business must wait. I haven't got over the last affair,' she protested, as he maintained a discreet silence, 'and the season is so gay just now – so many balls, so many – But that isn't the worst. Father is beginning to wake up, and if he ever suspects . . .' A significant gesture ended this appeal.

The personage knew her father – everyone did – and the wonder had always been that she dared run the risk of displeasing one so implacable. Though she was his favourite child, Peter Strange was known to be quite capable of cutting her off with a shilling once his close, prejudiced mind conceived it to be his duty. And that he would so interpret the situation, if he ever came to learn the secret of his daughter's fits of abstraction and the sly bank account she was slowly accumulating, the personage holding out this dangerous lure had no doubt at all. Yet he only smiled at her words and remarked in casual suggestion, 'It's out of town this time – way out. Your health certainly demands a change of air.'

'My health is good. Fortunately, or unfortunately, as one may choose to look at it, it furnishes me with no excuse for an outing,' she steadily retorted, turning her back on the table.

'Ah, excuse me!' the insidious voice apologized. 'Your paleness misled me. Surely a night or two's change might be beneficial.'

She gave him a quick side look and began to adjust her boa.

To this hint he paid no attention.

'The affair is quite out of the ordinary,' he pursued in the tone of one rehearsing a part. But there he stopped. For some reason, not altogether apparent to the masculine mind, the pin of flashing stones (real stones) which held her hat in place had to be taken out and thrust back again, not once but twice. It was to watch this performance he had paused. When he was ready to proceed, he took the musing tone of one marshalling facts for another's enlightenment, 'A woman of unknown instincts . . .'

'Pshaw!' The end of the pin would strike against the comb holding Violet's chestnut-coloured locks.

'Living in a house as mysterious as the secret it contains. But . . .' here he allowed his patience apparently to forsake him, 'I will bore you no longer. Go to your teas and balls. I will struggle with my dark affairs alone.'

His hand went to the packet of papers she affected so ostentatiously to despise. He could be as nonchalant as she. But he did not lift them, he let them lie. Yet the young heiress had not made a movement or even turned the slightest glance his way.

'A woman difficult to understand! A mysterious house – possibly a mysterious crime!' Thus Violet kept repeating in silent self-communion, as flushed with dancing she sat that evening in a highly scented conservatory, dividing her attention between the compliments of her partner and the splash of a fountain bubbling in the heart of this mass of tropical foliage. And when, some hours later, she sat down in her chintz-furnished bedroom for a few minutes' thought before retiring, it was to draw from a little oak box at her elbow the half-dozen or so folded sheets of closely written paper which had been left for her perusal by her persistent employer.

Glancing first at the signature and finding it to be one already favourably known at the bar, she read with avidity the statement of events thus vouched for, finding them curious enough in all conscience to keep her awake for another full hour.

We here subscribe it:

I am a lawyer with an office in the Times Square Building. My business is mainly local, but sometimes I am called out of town, as witness the following summons received by me on the fifth of last October:

Dear Sir, –

I wish to make my will. I am an invalid and cannot leave my room. Will you come to me? The enclosed reference will answer for my respectability. If it satisfies you and you decide to accommodate me, please hasten your visit. I have not many days to live. A carriage will meet you at Highland Station at any hour you designate. Telegraph reply.

A. Postlethwaite, Gloom Cottage, —— , NJ

The reference given was a Mr Weed of Eighty-sixth Street – a well-known man of unimpeachable reputation. Calling him up at his business office, I asked him what he could tell me about Mr Postlethwaite of Gloom Cottage, —— , NJ

The answer astonished me. 'There is no Mr Postlethwaite to be found at that address. He died years ago. There is a Mrs Postlethwaite – a confirmed paralytic. Do you mean her?'

I glanced at the letter still lying open at the side of the telephone. 'The signature reads A. Postlethwaite.'

'Then it's she. Her name is Arabella. She hates the name, being a woman of no sentiment. Uses her initials even on her cheques. What does she want of you?'

'To draw her will.'

'Oblige her. It'll be experience for you.' And he slammed home the receiver.

I decided to follow the suggestion so forcibly emphasized, and the next day saw me at Highland Station. A superannuated horse and a still more superannuated carriage awaited me – both too old to serve a busy man in these days of swift conveyance. Could this be a sample of the establishment I was about to enter? Then I remembered that the woman who had sent for me was a helpless invalid and probably had no use for any sort of turnout.

The driver was in keeping with the vehicle and as noncommittal as the plodding beast he drove. If I ventured upon a remark, he gave me a long and curious look; if I went so far as to attack him with a direct question, he responded with a hitch of the shoulder or a dubious smile which conveyed nothing. Was he deaf or just unpleasant? I soon learned that he was not deaf, for suddenly, after a jog-trot of a mile or so through a wooded road which we had entered from the main highway, he drew in his horse, and, without glancing my way, spoke his first word. 'This is where you get out. The house is back there in the bushes.'

As no house was visible and the bushes rose in an unbroken barrier along the road, I stared at him in some doubt of his sanity.

'But –' I began, a protest into which he at once broke, with the sharp direction:

'Take the path. It'll lead you straight to the front door.'

'I don't see any path.'

For this he had no answer, and, confident from his expression that it would be useless to expect anything further from him, I dropped a coin into his hand and jumped to the ground. He was off before I could turn myself about.

'Something is rotten in the state of Denmark,' I quoted in startled comment to myself and, not knowing what else to do, stared down at the turf at my feet.

A bit of flagging met my eye, protruding from a layer of thick moss. Farther on I espied another – the second, probably, of many. This, no doubt, was the path I had been bidden to follow, and without further thought on the subject I plunged into the bushes which, with difficulty, I made give way before me.

For a moment all further advance looked hopeless. A more tangled, uninviting approach to a so-called home I had never seen outside of the tropics, and the complete neglect thus displayed should have prepared me for the appearance of the house I unexpectedly came upon just as the way seemed on the point of closing up before me.

But nothing could well prepare one for a first view of Gloom Cottage. Its location in a hollow which had gradually filled itself up with trees and some kind of prickly brush, its deeply stained walls, once picturesque enough in their grouping but too deeply hidden now amid rotting boughs to produce any other effect than that of shrouded desolation, the sough of these same boughs as they rapped a devil's tattoo against each other and the absence of even the rising column of smoke which bespeaks domestic life wherever seen – all gave to one who remembered the cognomen Cottage and forgot the pre-cognomen of Gloom a sense of buried life as sepulchral as that which emanates from the mouth of some freshly opened tomb.

But these impressions, natural enough to my youth, were necessarily transient and soon gave way to others more business-like. Perceiving the curve of an arch rising above the undergrowth still blocking my approach, I pushed my way resolutely through and presently found myself stumbling upon the steps of an unexpectedly spacious domicile, built not of wood, as its name of Cottage had led me to expect, but of carefully cut stone which, while showing every mark of time, proclaimed itself one of those early, carefully erected Colonial residences which it takes more than a century to destroy or even to wear to the point of dilapidation.

Somewhat encouraged, though failing to detect any signs of active life in the heavily shuttered windows frowning upon me from either side, I ran up the steps and rang the bell, which pulled as hard as if no hand had touched it in years.

Then I waited.

But not to ring again, for, just as my hand was approaching the bell a second time, the door fell back and I beheld in the black gap before me the oldest man I had ever come upon in my whole life. He was so old I was astonished when his drawn lips opened and he asked if I was the lawyer from New York. I would as soon have expected a mummy to wag its tongue and utter English, he looked so thin and dried and removed from this life and all worldly concerns.

But when I had answered his question and he had turned to marshal me down the hall towards a door I could dimly see standing open in the twilight of an absolutely sunless interior I noticed that his step was not without some vigour, despite the feeble bend of his withered body and the incessant swaying of his head, which seemed to be continually saying No!

'I will prepare madam,' he admonished me after drawing a ponderous curtain two inches or less aside from one of the windows. 'She is very ill, but she will see you.'

The tone was senile, but it was the senility of an educated man, and as the cultivated accents wavered forth my mind changed in regard to the position he held in the house. Interested anew, I sought to give him another look, but he had already vanished through the doorway, and so noiselessly it was more like a shadow's flitting than a man's withdrawal.

The darkness in which I sat was absolute, but gradually, as I continued to look about me, the spaces lightened and certain details came out, which to my astonishment were of a character to show that the plain if substantial exterior of this house with its choked-up approaches and weedy gardens was no sample of what was to be found inside. Though the walls surrounding me were dismal because unlighted, they betrayed a splendour unusual in any country house. The frescoes and paintings were of an ancient order, dating from days when life and not death reigned in this isolated dwelling, but in them high art reigned supreme, an art so high and so finished that only great wealth combined with the most cultivated taste could have produced such effects.

I was still absorbed in the wonder of it all when the quiet voice of the old gentleman who had let me in reached me again from the doorway, and I heard, 'Madam is ready for you. May I trouble you to accompany me to her room.'

I rose with alacrity. I was anxious to see madam, if only to satisfy myself that she was as interesting as the house in which she was self-immured.

I found her a great deal more so. But, before I enter upon our interview, let me mention a fact which had attracted my attention in my passage to her room. During his absence my guide evidently had pulled aside other curtains than those of the room in which he had left me. The hall, no longer a tunnel of darkness, gave me a glimpse as we went by of various secluded corners, and it seemed as if everywhere I looked I saw – a clock. I counted four before I reached the staircase, all standing on the floor and all of ancient make, though differing much in appearance and value. A fifth one rose grim and tall at the stair foot, and under an impulse I have never understood I stopped when I reached it to note the time. But it had paused in its task and faced me with motionless hands and silent works – a fact which somehow startled me, perhaps because just then I encountered the old man's eye watching me with an expression as challenging as it was unintelligible.

I had expected to see a woman in bed. I saw instead, a woman sitting up. You felt her influence the moment you entered her presence. She was not young, she was not beautiful – never had been, I should judge – she had not even the usual marks about her of an ultra-strong personality; but that her will was law, had always been and would continue to be law so long as she lived, was patent to any eye at the first glance. She exacted obedience consciously and unconsciously, and she exacted it with charm. Some few people in the world possess this power. They frown, and the opposing will weakens; they smile, and all hearts succumb. I was hers from the moment I crossed the threshold until . . . But I will relate the happenings of that instant when it comes.

She was alone, or so I thought, when I made my first bow to her stern but not unpleasing presence. Seated in a great chair, with a silver tray before her containing such little matters as she stood in hourly need of, she confronted me with a piercing gaze startling to behold in eyes so colourless. Then she smiled, and in obedience to that smile I seated myself in a chair placed very near her own. Was she too paralysed to express herself clearly? I waited in some anxiety until she spoke, when this fear vanished. Her voice betrayed the character her features failed to express. It was firm, resonant and instinct with command. Not loud but penetrating and of a quality which made one listen with his heart as well as with his ears. What she said is immaterial. I was there for a certain purpose, and we entered immediately upon the business of that purpose. She talked, and I listened, mostly without comment. Only once did I interrupt her with a suggestion, and, as this led to definite results, I will proceed to relate the occurrence in full.

In the few hours remaining to me before leaving New York I had learned (no matter how) some additional particulars concerning herself and family, and when after some minor bequests she proceeded to name the parties to whom she desired to leave the bulk of her fortune, I ventured, with some astonishment at my own temerity, to remark, 'But you have a young relative! Is she not to be included in this partition of your property?'

A hush. Then a smile came to life on her stiff lips, such as is seldom seen, thank God, on the face of any woman, and I heard, 'The young relative of whom you speak is in the room. She has known for some time that I have no intention of leaving anything to her. There is, in fact, small chance of her ever needing it.'

The latter sentence was a muttered one, but that it was loud enough to be heard in all parts of the room I was soon assured, for a quick sigh, which was almost a gasp, followed from a corner I had hitherto ignored, and upon glancing that way I perceived, peering upon us from the shadows, the white face of a young girl in whose drawn features and wide, staring eyes I beheld such evidences of terror that in an instant, whatever predilection I had hitherto felt for my client, vanished in distrust if not positive aversion.

I was still under the sway of this new impression when Mrs Postlethwaite's voice rose again, this time addressing the young girl.

'You may go,' she said with such force in the command for all its honeyed modulation that I expected to see its object fly the room in frightened obedience.

But though the startled girl had lost none of the terror which had made her face like a mask, no power of movement remained to her. A picture of hopeless misery, she stood for one breathless moment with her eyes fixed in unmistakable appeal on mine, then she began to sway so helplessly that I leaped with bounding heart to catch her. As she fell into my arms I heard her sigh as before. No common anguish spoke in that sigh. I had stumbled unwittingly upon a tragedy to the meaning of which I held but a doubtful key.

'She seems very ill,' I observed with some emphasis, as I turned to lay my helpless burden on a nearby sofa.

'She's doomed.' The words were spoken with gloom and with an attempt at commiseration which no longer rang true in my ears. 'She is as sick a woman as I am myself,' continued Mrs Postlethwaite. 'That is why I made the remark I did, never imagining she would hear me at that distance. Do not put her down. My nurse will be here in a moment to relieve you of your burden.'

A tinkle accompanied these words. The resolute woman had stretched out a finger, of whose use she was not quite deprived, and touched a little bell standing on the tray before her an inch or two from her hand.

Pleased to obey her command I paused at the sofa's edge, and taking advantage of the momentary delay studied the youthful countenance pressed unconsciously to my breast.

It was one whose appeal lay less in its beauty, though that was of a touching quality, than in the story it told, a story, which for some unaccountable reason – I did not pause to determine what one – I felt it to be my immediate duty to know. But I asked no questions then – I did not even venture a comment – and yielded her up with seeming readiness when a strong but none-too-intelligent woman came running in with arms outstretched to carry her off. When the door had closed upon these two, the silence of my client drew my attention back to herself.

'I am waiting,' was her quiet observation, and without any further reference to what had just taken place under our eyes she went on with the business previously occupying us.

I was able to do my part without any too great display of my own disturbance. The clearness of my remarkable client's instructions, the definiteness with which her mind was made up as to the disposal of every dollar of her vast property, made it easy for me to master each detail and make careful note of every wish. But this did not prevent the ebb and flow within me of an undercurrent of thought full of question and uneasiness. What had been the real purport of the scene to which I had just been made a surprised witness? The few, but certainly unusual, facts which had been given me in regard to the extraordinary relations existing between these two closely connected women will explain the intensity of my interest. Those facts shall be yours.

Arabella Merwin, when young, was gifted with a peculiar fascination which, as we have seen, had not altogether vanished with age. Consequently she had many lovers, among them two brothers, Frank and Andrew Postlethwaite. The latter was the older, the handsomer and the most prosperous (his name is remembered yet in connection with South American schemes of large importance), but it was Frank she married.

That real love, ardent if unreasonable, lay at the bottom of her choice is evident enough to those who followed the career of the young couple. But it was a jealous love which brooked no rival, and, as Frank Postlethwaite was of an impulsive and erratic nature, scenes soon occurred between them which, while revealing the extraordinary force of the young wife's character, led to no serious break until after her son was born, and this notwithstanding the fact that Frank had long given up making a living and that they were openly dependent on their wealthy brother, now fast approaching the millionaire status.

This brother – the Peruvian King, as some called him – must have been an extraordinary man. Though cherishing his affection for the spirited Arabella to the point of remaining a bachelor for her sake, he betrayed none of the usual signs of disappointed love but, on the contrary, made every effort to advance her happiness, not only by assuring to herself and husband an adequate income but by doing all he could in other and less open ways to lessen any sense she might entertain of her mistake in preferring for her lifemate his self-centred and unstable brother. She should have adored him, but, though she evinced gratitude enough, there is nothing to prove that she ever gave Frank Postlethwaite the least cause to cherish any other sentiment towards his brother than that of honest love and unqualified respect. Perhaps he never did cherish any other. Perhaps the change which everyone saw in the young couple immediately after the birth of their only child was due to another cause. Gossip is silent on this point. All that it insists upon is that from this time evidences of a growing estrangement between them became so obvious that even the indulgent Andrew could not blind himself to it, showing his sense of trouble not by lessening their income, for that he doubled, but by spending more time in Peru and less in New York where the two were living.

However – and here we enter upon those details which I have ventured to characterize as uncommon – he was in this country and in the actual company of his brother when the accident occurred which terminated both their lives. It was the old story of a skidding motor, and Mrs Postlethwaite, having been sent for in great haste to the small inn into which the two injured men had been carried, arrived only in time to witness their last moments. Frank died first and Andrew some few minutes later – an important fact, as was afterwards shown when the latter's will came to be read.

This will was a peculiar one. By its provisions the bulk of the King's great property was left to his brother Frank, but with this especial stipulation that, in case his brother failed to survive him, the full legacy as bequeathed to him should be given unconditionally to his widow. Frank's demise, as I have already stated, preceded his brother's by several minutes, and consequently Arabella became the chief legatee, and that is how she obtained her millions. But – and here a startling feature comes in – when the will came to be administered the secret underlying the break between Frank and his wife was brought to light by a revelation of the fact that he had practised a great deception upon her at the time of his marriage. Instead of being a bachelor as was currently believed, he was in reality a widower and the father of a child. This fact, so long held secret, had become hers when her own child was born; and constituted as she was, she not only never forgave the father but conceived such a hatred for the innocent object of their quarrel that she refused to admit its claims or even to acknowledge its existence.

But later – after his death, in fact – she showed some sense of obligation towards one who under ordinary conditions would have shared her wealth. When the whole story became heard and she discovered that this secret had been kept from his brother as well as from herself and that consequently no provision had been made in any way for the child thus thrown directly upon her mercy, she did the generous thing and took the forsaken girl into her own home. But she never betrayed the least love for her, her whole heart being bound up in her boy who was, as all agree, a prodigy of talent.

But this boy, for all his promise and seeming strength of constitution, died when barely seven years old, and the desolate mother was left with nothing to fill her heart but the uncongenial daughter of her husband's first wife. The fact that this child, slighted as it had hitherto been, would, in the event of her uncle having passed away before her father, have been the undisputed heiress of a large portion of the wealth now at the disposal of her arrogant stepmother, led many to expect, now that the boy was no more, that Mrs Postlethwaite would proceed to acknowledge the little Helena as her heir and give her that place in the household to which her natural claims entitled her.

But no such result followed. The passion of grief into which the mother was thrown by the shipwreck of all her hopes left her hard and implacable, and when, as very soon happened, she fell a victim to the disease which tied her to her chair and made the wealth which had come to her by such a peculiar ordering of circumstances little else than a mockery even in her own eyes, it was upon this child she expended the full fund of her secret bitterness.

And the child? What of her? How did she bear her unhappy fate when she grew old enough to realize it? With a resignation which was the wonder of all who knew her. No murmurs escaped her lips nor was the devotion she invariably displayed to the exacting invalid, who ruled her as well as all the rest of her household with a rod of iron, ever disturbed by the least sign of reproach. Though the riches, which in those early days poured into the home in a measure far beyond the needs of its mistress, were expended in making the house beautiful rather than in making the one young life within it happy, she never was heard to utter so much as a wish to leave the walls within which fate had immured her. Content, or seemingly content, with the only home she knew, she never asked for change or demanded friends or amusements. Visitors ceased coming. Desolation followed neglect. The garden, once a glory, succumbed to a riot of weeds and undesirable brush until a towering wall seemed to be drawn about the house, cutting it off from the activities of the world as it cut it off from the approach of sunshine by day and the comfort of a starlit heaven by night. And yet the young girl continued to smile, though with a pitifulness of late, which some thought betokened secret terror and others the wasting of a body too sensitive for such unwholesome seclusion.

These were the facts, known if not consciously specialized, which gave to the latter part of my interview with Mrs Postlethwaite a poignancy of interest which had never attended any of my former experiences. The peculiar attitude of Miss Postlethwaite towards her indurate tormentor awakened in my agitated mind something much deeper than curiosity, but when I strove to speak her name with the intent of enquiring more particularly into her condition, such a look confronted me from the steady eye immovably fixed upon my own that my courage – or was it my natural precaution – bade me subdue the impulse and risk no attempt which might betray the depth of my interest in one so completely outside the scope of the present moment's business. Perhaps Mrs Postlethwaite appreciated my struggle; perhaps she was wholly blind to it. There was no reading the mind of this woman of sentimental name but inflexible nature, and, realizing the fact more fully with every word she uttered, I left her at last with no further betrayal of my feelings than might be evinced by the earnestness with which I promised to return for her signature at the earliest possible moment.

This she had herself requested, saying as I rose, 'I can still write my name if the paper is pushed carefully along under my hand. See to it that you come while the power remains to me.'

I had hoped that in my passage downstairs I might run upon someone who would give me news of Miss Postlethwaite, but the woman who approached to conduct me downstairs was not of an appearance to invite confidence, and I felt forced to leave the house with my doubts unsatisfied.

Two memories, equally distinct, followed me. One was a picture of Mrs Postlethwaite's fingers groping among her belongings on the little tray perched upon her lap and another of the intent and strangely bent figure of the old man who had acted as my usher listening to the ticking of one of the great clocks. So absorbed was he in this occupation that he not only failed to notice me when I went by but he did not even lift his head at my cheery greeting. Such mysteries were too much for me and led me to postpone my departure from town until I had sought out Mrs Postlethwaite's doctor and propounded to him one or two leading questions. First, would Mrs Postlethwaite's present condition be likely to hold good until Monday; and, secondly, was the young lady living with her as ill as her stepmother said.

He was a mild old man of the easy-going type, and the answers I got from him were far from satisfactory. Yet he showed some surprise when I mentioned the extent of Mrs Postlethwaite's anxiety about her stepdaughter and paused, in the dubious shaking of his head, to give me a short stare in which I read as much determination as perplexity.

'I will look into Miss Postlethwaite's case more particularly,' were his parting words. And with this one gleam of comfort I had to be content.

Monday's interview was a brief one and contained nothing worth repeating. Mrs Postlethwaite listened with stoical satisfaction to the reading of the will I had drawn up and upon its completion rang her bell for the two witnesses awaiting her summons in an adjoining room. They were not of her household but to all appearances honest villagers with but one noticeable characteristic, an overweening idea of Mrs Postlethwaite's importance. Perhaps the spell she had so liberally woven for others in other and happier days was felt by them at this hour. It would not be strange; I had almost fallen under it myself so great was the fascination of her manner even in this wreck of her bodily powers when, triumph assured, she faced us all in a state of complete satisfaction.

But before I was again quit of the place all my doubts returned and in fuller force than ever. I had lingered in my going as much as decency would permit, hoping to hear a step on the stair or see a face in some doorway which would contradict Mrs Postlethwaite's cold assurance that Miss Postlethwaite was no better. But no such step did I hear, and no face did I see save the old, old one of the ancient friend or relative whose bent frame seemed continually to haunt the halls. As before, he stood listening to the monotonous ticking of one of the clocks, muttering to himself and quite oblivious of my presence.

However, this time I decided not to pass him without a more persistent attempt to gain his notice. Pausing at his side I asked him, in the friendly tone I thought best calculated to attract his attention, how Miss Postlethwaite was today. He was so intent upon his task, whatever that was, that while he turned my way it was with a glance as blank as that of a stone image.

'Listen!' he admonished me. 'It still says No! No! I don't think it will ever say anything else.'

I stared at him in some consternation then at the clock itself, which was the tall one I had found run down at my first visit. There was nothing unusual in its quiet tick, so far as I could hear and, with a compassionate glance at the old man who had turned breathlessly again to listen, proceeded on my way without another word.

The old fellow was daft. A century old and daft.

I had worked my way out through the vines, which still encumbered the porch, and was taking my first steps down the walk when some impulse made me turn and glance up at one of the windows.

Did I bless the impulse? I thought I had every reason for doing so when, through a network of interlacing branches, I beheld the young girl with whom my mind was wholly occupied standing with her head thrust forward watching the descent of something small and white which she had just released from her hand.

A note! A note written by her and meant for me! With a grateful look in her direction (which was probably lost upon her as she had already drawn back out of sight), I sprang for it only to meet with disappointment. For it was no billet-doux I received from amid the clustering brush where it had fallen but a small square of white cloth showing a line of fantastic embroidery. Annoyed beyond measure, I was about to fling it down again when the thought that it had come from her hand deterred me, and I thrust it into my vest pocket. When I took it out again – which was soon after I had taken my seat in the car – I discovered what a mistake I should have made if I had followed my first impulse. For, upon examining the stitches more carefully, I perceived that what I had considered a mere decorative pattern was in fact a string of letters, and that these letters made words, and that these words were:

IDONOTWANTTODIEBUTISURELYWILLIF

Or, in plain writing: 'I do not want to die, but I surely will if –'

Finish the sentence for me. That is the problem I offer you. It is not a case for the police but one well worth your attention if you succeed in reaching the heart of this mystery and saving this young girl.

Only, let no delay occur. The doom, if doom it is, is imminent. Remember that the will is signed.

II

'She is too small. I did not ask you to send me a midget.' Thus spoke Mrs Postlethwaite to her doctor, as he introduced into her presence a little figure in nurse's cap and apron. 'You said I needed care, more care than I was receiving. I answered that my old nurse could give it, and you objected that she or someone else must look after Miss Postlethwaite. I did not see the necessity, but I never contradict a doctor. So I yielded to your wishes, but not without the proviso (you remember that I made a proviso) that whatever sort of young woman you chose to introduce into this room she should not be fresh from the training schools and that she should be strong, silent and capable.

And you bring me this mite of a woman – is she a woman? She looks more like a child, of pleasing countenance enough, but who can no more lift me –'

'Pardon me!' Little Miss Strange had advanced. 'I think, if you will allow me the privilege, madam, that I can shift you into a much more comfortable position.' And with a deftness and ease certainly not to be expected from one of her slight physique Violet raised the helpless invalid a trifle more upon her pillow.

The act, its manner and the smile accompanying it could not fail to please, and undoubtedly did, though no word rewarded her from lips not much given to speech save when the occasion was imperative. But Mrs Postlethwaite made no further objection to her presence, and, seeing this, the doctor's countenance relaxed and he left the room with a much lighter step than that with which he had entered it.

And thus it was that Violet Strange – an adept in more ways than one – became installed at the bedside of this mysterious woman whose days, if numbered, still held possibilities of action which those interested in young Helena Postlethwaite's fate would do well to recognize.

Miss Strange had been at her post for two days and had gathered up the following:

That Mrs Postlethwaite must be obeyed.

That her stepdaughter (who did not wish to die) would die if she knew it to be the wish of this domineering but apparently idolized woman.

That the old man of the clocks, while senile in some regards, was very alert and quite youthful in others. If a century old – which she began greatly to doubt – he had the language and manner of one in his prime when unaffected by the neighbourhood of the clocks, which seemed in some non-understandable way to exercise an occult influence over him. At table he was an entertaining host, but neither there nor elsewhere would he discuss the family or dilate in any way upon the peculiarities of a household of which he manifestly regarded himself as the least important member. Yet no one knew them better, and when Violet became quite assured of this, as well as of the futility of looking for explanation of any kind from either of her two patients, she resolved upon an effort to surprise one from him.

She went about it in this way. Noting his custom of making a complete round of the clocks each night after dinner, she took advantage of Mrs Postlethwaite's inclination to sleep at this hour to follow him from clock to clock in the hope of overhearing some portion of the monologue with which he bent his head to the swinging pendulum or put his ear to the hidden works. Soft-footed and discreet, she tripped along at his back and, at each pause he made, paused herself and turned her ear his way. The extreme darkness of the halls, which were more sombre by night than by day, favoured this attempt, and she was able, after a failure or two, to catch the 'No! no! no! no!' which fell from his lips in seeming repetition of what he heard the most of them say.

The satisfaction in his tone proved that the denial to which he listened chimed in with his hopes and gave ease to his mind. But he looked his oldest when, after pausing at another of the many timepieces, he echoed in answer to its special refrain 'Yes! yes! yes! yes!' and fled the spot with shaking body and a distracted air.

The same fear and the same shrinking were observable in him as he returned from listening to the least conspicuous one, standing in a short corridor, where Violet could not follow him. But when, after a hesitation which enabled her to slip behind the curtain hiding the drawing-room door, he approached and laid his ear against the great one standing, as if on guard, at the foot of the stairs, she saw by the renewed vigour he displayed that there was comfort for him in its message even before she caught the whisper with which he left it and proceeded to mount the stairs, 'It says No! It always says No! I will heed it as the voice of Heaven.'

But one conclusion could be the result of such an experiment to a mind like Violet's. This partly touched old man not only held the key to the secret of this house but was in a mood to divulge it if once he could be induced to hear command instead of dissuasion in the tick of this one large clock. But how could he be induced? Violet returned to Mrs Postlethwaite's bedside in a mood of extreme thoughtfulness.

Another day passed, and she had not yet seen Miss Postlethwaite. She was hoping each hour to be sent on some errand to that young lady's room, but no such opportunity was granted her. Once she ventured to ask the doctor, whose visits were now very frequent, what he thought of the young lady's condition. But, as this question was necessarily put in Mrs Postlethwaite's presence, the answer was naturally guarded and possibly not altogether frank.

'Our young lady is weaker,' he acknowledged. 'Much weaker,' he added with marked emphasis and his most professional air, 'or she would be here instead of in her own room. It grieves her not to be able to wait upon her generous benefactress.'

The word fell heavily. Had it been used as a test? Violet gave him a look, though she had much rather have turned her discriminating eye upon the face staring up at them from the pillow. Had the alarm expressed by others communicated itself at last to the physician? Was the charm which had held him subservient to the mother dissolving under the pitiable state of the child, and was he trying to aid the little detective-nurse in her effort to sound the mystery of her condition?

His look expressed benevolence, but he took care not to meet the gaze of the woman he had just lauded, possibly because that gaze was fixed upon him in a way to tax his moral courage.

The silence which ensued was broken by Mrs Postlethwaite. 'She will live – this poor Helena – how long?' she asked, with no break in her voice's wonted music.

The doctor hesitated, then with a candour hardly to be expected from him, answered, 'I do not understand Miss Postlethwaite's case. I should like, with your permission, to consult some New York physician.'

'Indeed!'

A single word, but as it left this woman's thin lips Violet recoiled, and, perhaps, the doctor did. Rage can speak in one word as well as in a dozen, and the rage which spoke in this one was of no common order, though it was quickly suppressed, as was all other show of feeling when she added, with a touch of her old charm, 'Of course you will do what you think best – as you know, I never interfere with a doctor's decisions – but,' and here her natural ascendancy of tone and manner returned in all its potency, 'it would kill me to know that a stranger was approaching Helena's bedside. It would kill her. She's too sensitive to survive such a shock.'

Violet recalled the words worked with so much care by this young girl on a minute piece of linen – I do not want to die – and watched the doctor's face for some sign of resolution. But embarrassment was all she saw there, and all she heard him say was the conventional reply, 'I am doing all I can for her. We will wait another day and note the effect of my latest prescription.'

Another day!

The deathly calm which overspread Mrs Postlethwaite's features as this word left the physician's lips warned Violet not to let another day go by without some action. But she made no remark and, indeed, betrayed but little interest in anything beyond her own patient's condition. That seemed to occupy her wholly. With consummate art she gave the appearance of being under Mrs Postlethwaite's complete thrall and watched with fascinated eyes every movement of the one unstricken finger which could do so much.

This little detective of ours could be an excellent actor when she chose.

III

To make the old man speak! To force this conscience-stricken but rebellious soul to reveal what the clock forbade! How could it be done?

This continued to be Violet's great problem. She pondered it so deeply during all the remainder of the day that a little pucker settled on her brow which someone (I will not mention who) would have been pained to see. Mrs Postlethwaite, if she noticed it at all, probably ascribed it to her anxieties as nurse, for never had Violet been more assiduous in her attentions. But Mrs Postlethwaite was no longer the woman she had been and possibly never noted it at all.

At five o'clock Violet suddenly left the room. Slipping down into the lower hall, she went the round of the clocks herself, listening to every one. There was no perceptible difference in their tick. Satisfied of this and that it was simply the old man's imagination which had supplied them each with separate speech, she paused before the huge one at the foot of the stairs – the one whose dictate he had promised himself to follow – and with an eye upon its broad, staring dial muttered wistfully, 'Oh! for an idea! For an idea!'

Did this cumbrous relic of old-time precision turn traitor at this ingenuous plea? The dial continued to stare, the works to sing, but Violet's face suddenly lost its perplexity. With a wary look about her and a listening ear turned towards the stair top she stretched out her hand and pulled open the door guarding the pendulum and peered in at the works, smiling slyly to herself as she pushed it back into place and retreated upstairs to the sick room.

When the doctor came that night she had a quiet word with him outside Mrs Postlethwaite's door. Was that why he was on hand when old Mr Dunbar stole from his room to make his nightly circuit of the halls below? Something quite beyond the ordinary was in the good physician's mind, for the look he cast at the old man was quite unlike any he had ever bestowed upon him before, and when he spoke it was to say with marked urgency, 'Our beautiful young lady will not live a week unless I get at the seat of her malady. Pray that I may be enabled to do so, Mr Dunbar.'

A blow to the aged man's heart which called forth a feeble, 'Yes, yes,' followed by a wild stare which imprinted itself upon the doctor's memory as the look of one hopelessly old, who hears for the first time a distinct call from the grave which has long been awaiting him!

A solitary lamp stood in the lower hall. As the old man picked his slow way down, its small hesitating flame flared up as in a sudden gust then sank down flickering and faint as if it, too, had heard a call which summoned it to extinction.

No other sign of life was visible anywhere. Sunk in twilight shadows, the corridors branched away on either side to no place in particular and serving to all appearance (as many must have thought in days gone by) as a mere hiding place for clocks.

To listen to their united hum the old man paused, looking at first a little distraught but settling at last into his usual self as he started forward upon his course. Did some whisper, hitherto unheard, warn him that it was the last time he would tread that weary round? Who can tell? He was trembling very much when, with his task nearly completed, he stepped out again into the main hall and crept rather than walked back to the one great clock to whose dictum he made it a practice to listen last.

Chattering the accustomed words, 'They say "Yes!" They are all saying "Yes!" now, but this one will say "No!"' he bent his stiff old back and laid his ear to the unresponsive wood. But the time for no had passed. It was Yes! yes! yes! yes! now, and, as his straining ears took in the word, he appeared to shrink where he stood, and, after a moment of anguished silence, broke forth into a low wail amid whose lamentations one could hear, 'The time has come! Even the clock she loves best bids me speak. Oh! Arabella, Arabella!'

In his despair he had not noticed that the pendulum hung motionless or that the hands stood at rest on the dial. If he had he might have waited long enough to have seen the careful opening of the great clock's tall door and the stepping forth of the little lady who had played so deftly upon his superstition.

He was wandering the corridors like a helpless child when a gentle hand fell on his arm and a soft voice whispered in his ear, 'You have a story to tell. Will you tell it to me? It may save Miss Postlethwaite's life.'

Did he understand? Would he respond if he did, or would the shock of her appeal restore him to a sense of the danger attending disloyalty? For a moment she doubted the wisdom of this startling measure, then she saw that he had passed the point of surprise and that, stranger as she was, she had but to lead the way for him to follow, tell his story and die.

There was no light in the drawing-room when they entered. But old Mr Dunbar did not seem to mind that. Indeed, he seemed to have lost all consciousness of present surroundings; he was even oblivious of her. This became quite evident when the lamp, in flaring up again in the hall, gave a momentary glimpse of his crouching, half-kneeling figure. In the pleading gesture of his trembling, outreaching arms Violet beheld an appeal, not to herself but to some phantom of his imagination, and when he spoke, as he presently did, it was with the freedom of one to whom speech is life's last boon and the ear of the listener quite forgotten in the passion of confession long suppressed.

'She has never loved me,' he began, 'but I have always loved her. For me no other woman has ever existed, though I was sixty-five years of age when I first saw her and had long given up the idea that there lived a woman who could sway me from my even life and fixed lines of duty. Sixty-five, and she a youthful bride! Was there ever such folly! Happily I realized it from the first and piled ashes on my hidden flame. Perhaps that is why I adore her to this day and only give her over to reprobation because Fate is stronger than my age – stronger even than my love.

'She is not a good woman, but I might have been a good man if I had never known the sin which drew a line of isolation about her and within which I, and only I, have stood with her in silent companionship. What was this sin, and in what did it have its beginning? I think its beginning was in the passion she had for her husband. It was not the everyday passion of her sex in this land of equable affections, but one of foreign fierceness, jealousy and insatiable demand. Yet he was a very ordinary man. I was once his tutor, and I know. She came to know it, too, when – but I am rushing on too fast, I have much to tell before I reach that point.

'From the first I was in their confidence. Not that either he or she put me there, but that I lived with them and was always around and could not help seeing and hearing what went on between them. Why he continued to want me in the house and at his table when I could no longer be of service to him I have never known. Possibly habit explains all. He was accustomed to my presence and so was she; so accustomed they hardly noticed it, as happened one night when, after a little attempt at conversation, he threw down the book he had caught up and, addressing her by name, said without a glance my way, and quite as if he were alone with her, "Arabella, there is something I ought to tell you. I have tried to find the courage to do so many times before now but have always failed. Tonight I must." And then he made his great disclosure – how, unknown to his friends and the world, he was a widower when he married her and the father of a living child.

'With some women this might have passed with a measure of regret and some possible contempt for his silence, but not so with her. She rose to her feet – I can see her yet – and for a moment stood facing him in the still, overpowering manner of one who feels the icy pang of hate enter where love has been. Never was a moment more charged – I could not breathe while it lasted – and when at last she spoke it was with an impetuosity of concentrated passion, hardly less dreadful than her silence had been.

'"You a father! A father already!" she cried, all her sweetness swallowed up in ungovernable wrath. "You whom I expected to make so happy with a child? I curse you and your brat. I . . ."

'He strove to placate her, to explain, but rage has no ears, and before I realized my own position the scene became openly tempestuous. That her child should be second to another woman's seemed to awaken demon instincts within her. When he ventured to hint that his little girl needed a mother's care, her irony bit like corroding acid. He became speechless before it and had not a protest to raise when she declared that the secret he had kept so long and so successfully he must continue to keep to his dying day, that the child he had failed to own in his first wife's lifetime should remain disowned in hers and if possible be forgotten. She should never give the girl a thought nor acknowledge her in any way.

'She was Fury embodied, but the fury was of that grand order which allures rather than repels. As I felt myself succumbing to its fascination and beheld how he was weakening under it even more perceptibly than myself, I started from my chair and sought to glide away before I should hear him utter a fatal acquiescence.

'But the movement I made unfortunately drew their attention to me, and after an instant of silent contemplation of my distracted countenance Frank said, as though he were the elder by the forty years which separated us, "You have listened to Mrs Postlethwaite's wishes. You will respect them, of course."

'That was all. He knew and she knew that I was to be trusted, but neither of them has ever known why.

'A month later her child came and was welcomed as though it were the first to bear his name. It was a boy, and their satisfaction was so great that I looked to see their old affection revive. But it had been cleft at the root, and nothing could restore it to life. They loved the child – I have never seen evidence of greater parental passion than they both displayed – but there their feelings stopped. Towards each other they were cold. They did not even unite in worship of their treasure. They gloated over him and planned for him, but always apart. He was a child in a thousand, and, as he developed, the mother especially nursed all her energies for the purpose of ensuring for him a future commensurate with his talents. Never a very conscientious woman, and alive to the advantages of wealth as demonstrated by the power wielded by her rich brother-in-law, she associated all the boy's prospects with money, great money, such money as Andrew had accumulated and now had at his disposal for his natural heirs.

'Hence came her great temptation, a temptation to which she yielded to the lasting trouble of us all. Of this I must now make confession though it kills me to do so and will soon kill her. The deeds of the past do not remain buried, however deep we dig their graves, but rise in an awful resurrection when we are old – old . . .'

Silence. Then a tremulous renewal of his painful speech.

Violet held her breath to listen. Possibly the doctor, hidden in the darkest corner of the room, did so also.

'I never knew how she became acquainted with the terms of her brother-in-law's will – he certainly never confided them to her, and as certainly the lawyer who drew up the document never did – but that she was well aware of its tenor is as positive a fact as that I am the most wretched man alive tonight. Otherwise, why the darksome deed into which she was betrayed when both the brothers lay dying among strangers of a dreadful accident?

'I was witness to that deed. I had accompanied her on her hurried ride and was at her side when she entered the inn where the two Postlethwaites lay. I was always at her side in great joy or in great trouble, though she professed no affection for me and gave me but scanty thanks.

'During our ride she had been silent, and I had not disturbed that silence. I had much to think of. Should we find him living, or should we find him dead? If dead, would it sever the relations between us two? Would I ever ride with her again?

'When I was not dwelling on this theme I was thinking of the parting look she gave her boy, a look which had some strange promise in it. What had that look meant, and why did my flesh creep and my mind hover between dread and a fearsome curiosity when I recalled it? Alas! There was reason for all these sensations, as I was soon to learn.

'We found the inn seething with terror and the facts worse than had been represented in the telegram. Her husband was dying. She had come just in time to witness the end. This they told her before she had taken off her veil. If they had waited – if I had been given a full glimpse of her face – but it was hidden, and I could only judge of the nature of her emotions by the stern way in which she held herself.

'"Take me to him," was the quiet command with which she met this disclosure. Then, before any of them could move, "And his brother, Mr Andrew Postlethwaite? Is he fatally injured too?"

'The reply was unequivocal. The doctors were uncertain which of the two would pass away first.

'You must remember that at this time I was ignorant of the rich man's will and consequently of how the fate of a poor child of whom I had heard only one mention hung in the balance at that awful moment. But in the breathlessness which seized Mrs Postlethwaite at this sentence of double death I realized from my knowledge of her that something more than grief was at prey upon her impenetrable heart, and I shuddered to the core of my being when she repeated in that voice which was so terrible because so expressionless, "Take me to them."

'They were lying in one room, her husband nearest the door, the other in a small alcove some ten feet away. Both were unconscious;

both were surrounded by groups of frightened attendants who fell back as she approached. A doctor stood at the bed head of her husband, but as her eye met his he stepped aside with a shake of the head and left the place empty for her.

'The action was significant. I saw that she understood what it meant and with constricted heart watched her as she bent over the dying man and gazed into his wide-open eyes, already sightless and staring. Calculation was in her look and calculation only; and calculation, or something equally unintelligible, sent her next glance in the direction of his brother. What was in her mind? I could understand her indifference to Frank, even at the crisis of his fate, but not the interest she showed in Andrew. It was an absorbing one, altering her whole expression. I no longer knew her for my dear young madam, and the jealousy I had never felt towards Frank rose to frantic resentment in my breast as I beheld what very likely might be a tardy recognition of the other's well-known passion, forced into disclosure by the exigencies of the moment.

'Alarmed by the strength of my feelings and fearing an equal disclosure on my own part I sought for a refuge from all eyes and found it in a little balcony opening out at my right. On to this balcony I stepped and found myself face to face with a starlit heaven. Had I only been content with my isolation and the splendour of the spectacle spread out before me! But no, I must look back upon that bed and the solitary woman standing beside it! I must watch the settling of her body into rigidity as a voice rose from beside the other Postlethwaite saying, "It is a matter of minutes now," and then – and then – the slow creeping of her hand to her husband's mouth, the outspreading of her palm across the livid lips, its steady clinging there, smothering the feeble gasps of one already moribund until the quivering form grew still and Frank Postlethwaite lay dead before my eyes!

'I saw and made no outcry, but she did, bringing the doctor back to her side with the startled exclamation, "Dead? I thought he had an hour's life left in him, and he has passed before his brother."

'I thought it hate, the murderous impulse of a woman who sees her enemy at her mercy and can no longer restrain the passion of her long-cherished antagonism. And, while something within me rebelled at the act, I could not betray her, though silence made a murderer of me, too. I could not. Her spell was upon me as in another instant it was upon everyone else in the room. No suspicion of one so self-repressed in her sadness disturbed the universal sympathy, and, encouraged by this blindness of the crowd, I vowed within myself never to reveal her secret. The man was dead, or as good as dead, when she touched him, and now that her hate was expended she would grow gentle and good.

'But I knew the worthlessness of this hope as well as my misconception of her motive when Frank's child by another wife returned to my memory, and Bella's sin stood exposed.

'But only to myself. I alone knew that the fortune now wholly hers, and in consequence her boy's, had been won by a crime. That if her hand had fallen in comfort on her husband's forehead instead of in pressure on his mouth he would have outlived his brother long enough to have become owner of his millions – in which case a rightful portion would have been insured to his daughter, now left a penniless waif. The thought made my hair rise as, the proceedings over, I faced her and made my first and last effort to rid my conscience of its new and intolerable burden.

'But the woman I had known and loved was no longer before me. The crown had touched her brows, and her charm, which had been mainly sexual up to this hour, had merged into an intellectual force with which few men's mentality could cope. Mine yielded at once to it. From the first instant I knew that a slavery of spirit, as well as of heart, was henceforth to be mine.

'She did not wait for me to speak; she had assumed the dictator's attitude at once.

'"I know of what you are thinking," said she, "and it is a subject you may dismiss at once from your mind. Mr Postlethwaite's child by his first wife is coming to live with us. I have expressed my wishes in this regard to my lawyer, and there is nothing left to be said. You, with your close mouth and dependable nature, are to remain here as before and occupy the same position towards my boy that you did towards his father. We shall move soon into a larger house, and the nature of our duties will be changed and their scope greatly increased. But I know that you can be trusted to enlarge with them and meet every requirement I shall see fit to make. Do not try to express your thanks. I see them in your face."

'Did she – or just the last feeble struggle my conscience was making to break the bonds in which she held me and win back my own respect? I shall never know, for she left me on completion of this speech not to resume the subject then or ever.

'But though I succumbed outwardly to her demands I had not passed the point where inner conflict ends and peace begins. Her recognition of Helena and her reception into the family calmed me for a while and gave me hope that all would yet be well. But I had never sounded the full bitterness of madam's morbid heart, well as I thought I knew it. The hatred she had felt from the first for her husband's child ripened into frenzied dislike when she found her a living image of the mother whose picture she had come across among Frank's personal effects. To win a tear from those meek eyes instead of a smile to the sensitive lips was her daily play. She seemed to exult in the joy of impressing upon the girl by how little she had missed a great fortune, and I have often thought, much as I tried to keep my mind free from all extravagant and unnecessary fancies, that half of the money she spent in beautifying this house and maintaining art industries and even great charitable institutions was spent with the base purpose of demonstrating to this child the power of immense wealth and in what ways she might expect to see her little brother expend the millions in which she had been denied all share.

'I was so sure of this that one night, while I was winding up the clocks with which Mrs Postlethwaite in her fondness for old timepieces has filled the house, I stopped to look at the little figure toiling so wearily upstairs to bed without a mother's kiss. There was an appeal in the small wistful face which smote my hard old heart, and possibly a tear welled up in my own eye when I turned back to my duty.

'Was that why I felt the hand of Providence upon me, when in my halt before the one clock to which any superstitious interest was attached

– the great one at the foot of the stairs – I saw that it had stopped and at the one minute of all minutes in our wretched lives, four minutes past two? The hour, the minute in which Frank Postlethwaite had gasped his last under the pressure of his wife's hand! I knew it – the exact minute, I mean – because Providence meant that I should know it. There had been a clock on the mantelpiece of the hotel room where he and his brother had died, and I had seen her glance steal towards it at the instant she withdrew her palm from her husband's lips. The stare of that dial and the position of its hands had lived still in my mind as I believed it did in hers.

'Four minutes past two! How came our old timepiece here to stop at that exact moment on a day when duty was making its last demand upon me to remember Frank's unhappy child? There was no one to answer, but as I looked and looked I felt the impulse of the moment strengthen into purpose to leave those hands undisturbed in their silent accusation. She might see and, moved by the coincidence, tremble at her treatment of Helena.

'But if this happened – if she saw and trembled – she gave no sign. The works were started up by some other hand, and the incident passed. But it left me with an idea. That clock soon had a way of stopping and always at that one instant of time. She was forced at length to notice it, and I remember an occasion when she stood stock still with her eyes on those hands and failed to find the banister with her hand, though she groped for it in her frantic need for support.

'But no command came from her to remove the worn-out piece, and soon its tricks and every lesser thing were forgotten in the crushing calamity which befell us in the sickness and death of little Richard.

'Oh, those days and nights! And oh, the face of the mother when the doctors told her that the case was hopeless! I asked myself then, and I have asked myself a hundred times since, which of all the emotions I saw pictured there bit the deepest and made the most lasting impression on her guilty heart? Was it remorse? If so, she showed no change in her attitude towards Helena unless it was by an added bitterness. The sweet looks and gentle ways of Frank's young daughter could not win against a hate sharpened by disappointment.

Useless for me to hope for it. Release from the remorse of years was not to come in that way. As I realized this I grew desperate and resorted again to the old trick of stopping the clock at the fatal hour. This time her guilty heart responded. She acknowledged the stab and let all her miseries appear. But how? In a way to wring my heart almost to madness and not benefit the child at all. She had her first stroke that night. I had made her a helpless invalid.

'That was eight years ago, and since then what? Stagnation. She lived with her memories and I with mine. Helena only had a right to hope, and hope perhaps she did until . . . Is that the great clock talking? Listen! They all talk, but I heed only the one. What does it say? Tell! tell! tell! Does it think I will be silent now when I come to my own guilt? That I will seek to hide my weakness when I could not hide her sin?'

'Explain!' It was Violet speaking, and her tone was stern in its command. 'Of what guilt do you speak? Not of guilt towards Helena; you pitied her too much . . .'

'But I pitied my dear madam more. It was that which affected me and drew me into crime against my will. Besides, I did not know – not at first – what was in the little bowl of curds and cream I carried to the girl each day. She had eaten them in her stepmother's room and under her stepmother's eye as long as she had strength to pass from room to room, and how was I to guess that it was not wholesome? Because she failed in health from day to day? Was not my dear madam failing in health also, and was there poison in her cup? Innocent at that time, why am I not innocent now? Because . . . Oh, I will tell it all, as though at the bar of God. I will tell all the secrets of that day.

'She was sitting with her hand trembling on the tray from which I had just lifted the bowl she had bid me carry to Helena. I had seen her so a hundred times before, but not with just that look in her eyes or just that air of desolation in her stony figure. Something made me speak, something made me ask if she were not quite so well as usual, and something made her reply with the dreadful truth that the doctor had given her just two months more to live. My fright and mad anguish stupefied me – for I was not prepared for this, no, not at all – and unconsciously I stared down at the bowl I held, unable to breathe or move or even to meet her look.

'As usual she misinterpreted my emotion.

'"Why do you stand like that?" I heard her say in a tone of great irritation. "And why do you stare into that bowl? Do you think I mean to leave that child to walk these halls after I am carried out of them for ever? Do you measure my hate by such a petty yardstick as that? I tell you that I would rot above ground rather than enter it before she did!"

'I had believed I knew this woman, but what soul ever knows another's? What soul ever knows itself?

'"Bella!" I cried, the first time I had ever presumed to address her so intimately. "Would you poison the girl?" And from sheer weakness my fingers lost their clutch, and the bowl fell to the floor, breaking into a dozen pieces.

'For a minute she stared down at these from over her tray, and then she remarked very low and very quietly, "Another bowl, Humphrey, and fresh curds from the kitchen. I will do the seasoning. The doses are too small to be skipped. You won't?" – I had shaken my head – "But you will! It will not be the first time you have gone down the hall with this mixture."

'"But that was before I knew . . ." I began.

'"And now that you do, you will go just the same." Then, as I stood hesitating, a thousand memories overwhelming me in an instant, she added in a voice to tear the heart, "Do not make me hate the only being left in this world who understands and loves me."

'She was a helpless invalid and I a broken man, but when that word "love" fell from her lips I felt the blood start burning in my veins and all the crust of habit and years of self-control loosen about my heart and make me young again. What if her thoughts were dark and her wishes murderous! She was born to rule and sway men to her will, even to their own undoing.

'"I wish I might kiss your hand," was what I murmured, gazing at her white fingers groping over her tray.

'"You may," she answered, and hell became Heaven to me for a brief instant. Then I lifted myself and went obediently about my task.

'But, puppet though I was, I was not utterly without sympathy. When I entered Helena's room and saw how her startled eyes fell shrinkingly on the bowl I set down before her my conscience leaped to life and I could not help saying, "Don't you like the curds, Helena? Your brother used to love them very much."

'"His were . . ."

'"What, Helena?"

'"What these are not," she murmured.

'I stared at her, terror-stricken. So she knew and yet did not seize the bowl and empty it out of the window! Instead, her hand moved slowly towards it and drew it into place before her.

'"Yet I must eat," she said, lifting her eyes to mine in a sort of patient despair, which yet was without accusation.

'But my hand had instinctively gone to hers and grasped it.

'"Why must you eat it?" I asked. "If – if you do not find it wholesome, why do you touch it?"

'"Because my stepmother expects me to," she cried, "and I have no other will than hers. When I was a little, little child my father made me promise that if I ever came to live with her I would obey her simplest wish. And I always have. I will not disappoint the trust he put in me."

'"Even if you die of it?"

'I do not know whether I whispered these words or only thought them. She answered as though I had spoken.

'"I am not afraid to die. I am more afraid to live. She may ask me some day to do something I feel to be wrong."

'When I fled down the hall that night I heard one of the small clocks speak to me. "Tell!" it cried, "Tell! tell! tell! tell!" I rushed away from it with beaded forehead and rising hair.

'Then another's note piped up. "No!" it droned. "No! no! no! no!" I stopped and took heart. Disgrace the woman I loved on the brink of the grave? I who asked no other boon from Heaven than to see her happy, gracious and good? Impossible. I would obey the great clock's voice; the others were mere chatterboxes.

'But it has at last changed its tune for some reason, quite changed its tune. Now it is "Yes! Yes!" instead of "No!" and in obeying it I save Helena. But what of Bella and, O God, what of myself?'

A sigh, a groan then a long and heavy silence into which there finally broke the pealing of the various clocks striking the hour. When all were still again and Violet had drawn aside the *portière* it was to see the old man on his knees, and between her and the thin streak of light entering from the hall the figure of the doctor hastening to Helena's bedside.

When with inducements needless to name they finally persuaded the young girl to leave her unholy habitation it was in the arms which had upheld her once before and to a life which promised to compensate her for her twenty years of loneliness and unsatisfied longing.

But a black shadow yet remained which she must cross before reaching the sunshine!

It lay at her stepmother's door.

In the plans made for Helena's release Mrs Postlethwaite's consent had not been obtained, nor was she supposed to be acquainted with the doctor's intentions towards the child whose death she was hourly awaiting.

It was, therefore, with an astonishment bordering on awe that on their way downstairs they saw the door of her room open and herself standing alone and upright on the threshold – she who had not been seen to take a step in years. In the wonder of this miracle of suddenly restored power the little procession stopped – the doctor with his hand upon the rail, the lover with his burden clasped yet more protectingly to his breast. That a little speech awaited them could be seen from the force and fury of the gaze which the indomitable woman bent upon the lax and half-unconscious figure she beheld thus sheltered and conveyed. Having but one arrow left in her exhausted quiver she launched it straight at the innocent breast which had never harboured against her a defiant thought.

'Ingrate!' was the word she hurled in a voice from which all its seductive music had gone for ever. 'Where are you going? Are they carrying you alive to your grave?'

A moan from Helena's pale lips, then silence. She had fainted at that barbed attack. But there was one there who dared to answer for her, and he spoke relentlessly. It was the man who loved her.

'No, madam, we are carrying her to safety. You must know what I mean by that. Let her go quietly, and you may die in peace. Otherwise –'

She interrupted him with a loud call, startling into life the echoes of that haunted hall, 'Humphrey! Come to me, Humphrey!'

But no Humphrey appeared.

Another call, louder and more peremptory than before, 'Humphrey! I say, Humphrey!'

But the answer was the same – silence and only silence. As the horror of this grew, the doctor spoke, 'Mr Humphrey Dunbar's ears are closed to all earthly summons. He died last night at the very hour he said he would – four minutes after two.'

'Four minutes after two!' It came from her lips in a whisper but with a revelation of her broken heart and life. 'Four minutes after two!' And, defiant to the last, her head rose, and for an instant, for a mere breath of time, they saw her as she had looked in her prime, regal in form, attitude and expression. Then the will which had sustained her through so much faltered and succumbed, and with a final reiteration of the words 'Four minutes after two!' she broke into a rattling laugh and fell back into the arms of her old nurse.

And, below, one clock struck the hour and then another. But not the big one at the foot of the stairs. That still stood silent with its hands pointing to the hour and minute of Frank Postlethwaite's hastened death.

Elizabeth Corbett

THE POLISH REFUGEE

Elizabeth Burgoyne Corbett (1846–1930), who usually wrote as Mrs George Corbett, was a prolific author for her day, predominantly of serials and stories for magazines and newspapers. Only a few of these made it into book form, so she soon faded into obscurity after her death in 1930. She produced a wide variety of work but is best remembered today (when she is remembered at all) for her detective stories and the novel New Amazonia: A Foretaste of the Future *(1889), a strongly feminist, pro-suffragette story set five centuries hence in a Utopian Ireland. Her detective works include* Secrets of a Private Enquiry Office *(1891), from which the following story is selected, continuing with* Behind the Veil *(1891), subtitled* Revelations by a Lady Detective, *and* When the Sea Gives Up Its Dead *(1894), which also features a female sleuth.*

The Polish Refugee

OF MEDIUM HEIGHT, slight build, clear, healthy complexion, beautiful dark eyes and black hair that curled in bewitching waves over the fine brow. The possessor of regular, intellectual features, small, delicately shaped hands and feet and a moustache so perfect in its size, its shape, its neatness and its glossy blackness that it was the admiration of the one sex and the envy of the other.

Such was Feodor Plotnitzky, a young gentleman who taught German, French and the violin to quite a host of pupils and who, to do him justice, was thoroughly able to do all he undertook. He claimed to be the scion of a noble house, compelled to seek safety in England, the El Dorado of political refugees from despotic persecution from time immemorial. His manners were perfect and quite justified a belief in the superiority of origin and bringing up of Count Feodor Plotnitzky, who, however, would modestly and sadly disclaim all desire of being addressed by the title which was his by right, saying that as England had proved such a haven of refuge to him and his, he felt honoured by being addressed by the simple English prefix 'Mr'.

This was all very well, but it seemed impossible for anyone to make up his mind to vulgarize him by a mode of address to which a street sweeper could lay claim. He was so bewilderingly handsome, accomplished and polished that some folk were actually inclined to temporize with his title in the opposite direction, and address him as 'Prince'.

'Oh! he is just heavenly!' sighed Miss Philippa Sudds, and, hardened observer of humanity as I was by this time, I could almost have found it in my heart to echo Miss Philippa's enthusiastic remark. I will at least say this much. I have never, before or since, seen so perfect a specimen of humanity, and, after once seeing him, I could no longer be surprised at the fact that the majority of his young lady pupils fell madly in love with him.

Perhaps the reader would like to know how I happened to be acquainted with this Polish marvel. I can soon explain how it came about. Jones informed me one day that a well-known baronet, whom we will call Sir Selby Grant, had been to the office during my absence and had invoked the aid of our firm in bringing certain family affairs to a satisfactory issue.

'This,' said our chief, 'is the gist of what the baronet said to me. "I have an only daughter, whom I love very dearly and to whom I am never inclined to deny anything in reason. She is now eighteen years old and has seen very little of society, having only just left school. She is considered a very handsome girl, and great expectations of her future have been held by our relatives and friends. As I have no other children, and the estates are not entailed, she will have a large fortune some day. I have looked forward with eagerness to the time when she would have completed her education and would be able to take the place of mistress of my establishment, for my life has had little domestic happiness to brighten it since I lost my dear wife six years ago.

"'Unfortunately, my anticipations have not all been realized. Miss Grant is quite as affectionate and quite as eager to promote my comfort as I hoped she would be, but I find her sad and preoccupied, and more than once I have surprised her in tears. I have had considerable difficulty in inducing her to give me her entire confidence but have at last discovered that she has not returned to me heart-whole. This, in itself, is matter for considerable regret in any case at her age. But what struck me as almost incredible is the fact that she does not believe her affection reciprocated, though the subject of it is nothing better than a teacher of languages.

"'I could almost have brought myself to be angry with my unhappy Mabel were I not so grieved at the genuine trouble the poor child is in and so full of admiration of the way in which she bravely strives to conquer her unfortunate passion. Again, failing this outlet for the vexation inseparable from so disappointing an affair, I might have emptied the vials of wrath upon this foreign professor, who has apparently been taking a base advantage of his opportunities to worm himself into the hearts of his pupils.

"'But here again I am foiled. Miss Grant protests that the fault, if fault there be, is entirely her own. She says that the professor, who by the way, is called Count Feodor Plotnitzky, has never, by word or deed, given either herself or any other young lady the slightest encouragement to believe that he entertains more than friendly – or, at the most, brotherly – affection for them. And yet they are one and all in love with him! I cannot understand it. Even Miss Minervina Prout, the lady principal of the school my daughter attended, speaks of this young man as if his equal had never been seen upon earth, though I will do her the justice to remark that she feels quite an innocent, motherly affection for him.

"'"He is," she said, 'the most capable teacher I have ever had in the school. The progress his pupils make under his tuition is perfectly miraculous when compared with the results of lessons by former tutors. His terms are rather high, but his abilities more than justify their exaction. His pupils, so far from evincing distaste of the coming lessons, as has generally been the case, look forward to their tasks with eagerness, and I have only to threaten to debar them from attending the violin or language lessons to make my young ladies do anything I require of them. So, you see, our Polish teacher has influence outside the actual sphere of his own duties.'

"'Influence! I should think so! Poor, innocent Miss Minervina never seemed to suspect that this wonderfully beneficent influence was owing to the fact that the pupils were each and all in love with the versatile Polish count, who was so unassuming that he actually preferred to be addressed as 'Mr'. I could discover nothing to the detriment of my gentleman, and I preferred not to horrify Miss Minervina by betraying my daughter's secret.

"'Nevertheless, I want to make an end of the affair either one way or the other, and I have come to you to help me. I am convinced that if the object of her affections is proved utterly unworthy my daughter will soon be cured of her infatuation, which owes its origin quite as much to the conviction that the man is as good and sensible as it is given anyone to be as it does to the fact that his exterior is of almost unrivalled beauty. I remember, as a youth, being desperately enamoured of a certain lady whom I accredited with all the virtues under the sun. My love evaporated with remarkable promptitude when I learned that my goddess was endowed with several objectionable vices in lieu of virtues. I believe my daughter to be of the same temperament as myself and that she would scorn to waste her affections on an unworthy object.

"'If, on the other hand, this count proves to be a true, manly fellow with no other drawback than his poverty I will gladly see him married to my girl. She will have money enough for both, and I do not wish to wreck her happiness in a foolish chase for more wealth. You must give me all the information you can gather about Count Plotnitzky. In order to afford the man nothing but fair play, your remuneration shall be the same whether he is proved to be an impostor and a cheat, or whether he turns out to be all that is desirable. What I wish to impress upon you is the necessity for making a most careful investigation of the man's private life and antecedents in order that no irreparable blunder may be made. My daughter's happiness is everything to me, or I would not submit anyone to the indignity of espionage.'"

Jones, having thoroughly grasped the duties expected of us and having come to terms with this rare English gentleman, took me into his confidence, and together we arranged our immediate plan of campaign. We decided that the best proceeding would be for me to go to lodge for a time at the same boarding-house which the professor patronized. Sir Selby, on the pretence of a desire to present Professor Plotnitzky with some token of his appreciation of the progress his daughter had made in languages and on the violin, had obtained his address from Miss Minervina. As the professor was out when he called he had not obtained the interview he sought and had since decided to postpone it awhile until a communication from us should determine his future course of action.

Fortunately for our project, Mrs Hales had a vacant room at my disposal. I represented myself as a literary gentleman who was studying up a special subject and wished to live in a quiet way apart from his too numerous circle of acquaintances until all arrangements for his new book were completed.

The next morning I made the acquaintance of my fellow boarders at breakfast. Upon the whole they were rather a nice lot, some dozen in all, but I felt little special interest in any of them except my young professor and his mother. Yes, although I had not heard of this lady before, it was none the less a fact that Mrs Hales numbered among her boarders a lady known as Mrs Plotnitzky.

'You know, sir, Mrs Plotnitzky, or "Madame" as we all call her, is really a countess. But she is, like her son, very modest and insists upon dropping the title. She says that now she has lost all her fortune and cannot afford to keep an establishment of her own, it is absurd to use a title. But anyone can see, the moment they look at her, that she is a thorough aristocrat. And so beautiful as she is, too! No wonder her son, who dotes on her, is so handsome, and so clever, and so . . .'

Here followed, if possible, a more enthusiastic panegyric of Professor Plotnitzky's amiabilities and virtues than I had even heard of before, and I was, at the end of this conversation, which took place after Madame had gone to her own room and after the other boarders had departed in pursuance of their various avocations, forced to the conclusion that Mrs Hales must also be included among the professor's worshippers.

And by the time I had been in the house twenty-four hours I was no longer surprised at the unbounded fascination which the irresistible Feodor exercised over all with whom he came in contact, for I could not withstand his influence myself. Not that I was particularly desirous of doing so, for I had sought his acquaintance armed with a vague distrust of my man, which in anyone else would have militated against the formation of a speedy liking. But ordinary prejudices were of no power here, and I positively delighted in such share as I could procure of this man's society.

There was only one thing, if possible, while I stayed with Mrs Hales that I preferred to a chat with Feodor, and that was the privilege of a little conversation with Madame, his mother. How perfectly beautiful and charming she was! What a world of resignation dwelt in the expressive eyes! And what inimitable dignity lurked in every detail of her appearance, from her silver-white hair down to the small daintily shod foot which protruded from beneath the handsome dresses in which her devoted son loved to clothe her. What . . . but there, I am turning just as enthusiastically rhapsodical as everyone else whoever comes across these people, and to this day I do not know which I was the most in love with – the mother or the son.

It was touching to see the perfect affection and concord in which the two lived, and but for one thing I should have gone away to assure my baronet that there was not the slightest rift within the lute in this case and that he need not hesitate to give the young professor any encouragement that would be likely to induce him to marry Miss Mabel Grant.

I was slightly puzzled to note that Madame's eyes, however cheerful they might look in his immediate presence, always followed the departing figure of her son with a wistful sadness and anxiety hard to account for under the circumstances. For it must be remembered that, though not more than five or six and twenty, his prospects were of the brightest and he was evidently gifted with perfect health. He had now the chance of more pupils than he could accept. He had, when possessed of more leisure than at present, given considerable attention to musical composition, and one of his cantatas was going to be produced very shortly by Mr August Manns at a Crystal Palace Saturday concert.

Certainly, he was banished from his native land, besides being shorn of his title and estates by despotic usurpers, but he had so many compensative blessings that I could not conceive of any ordinary reason for anxiety on Madame's part. When I explained the situation to Jones he was strongly of opinion that all was not so fair and above board with the professor as it might be and that something detrimental to the good opinion everybody held of him would yet turn up.

Of course, I began an enthusiastic disclaimer, and, equally of course, Jones cut me off with an impatient, 'For Heaven's sake, man, keep it short! I shall hate these people soon if I hear much more about their virtues and perfections. Anyhow, I shall have a fine laugh at you when the inevitable exposure takes place.'

It was no use arguing the matter with Jones, and as my private opinion did not weigh much in the affair I felt it quite as much a matter of love as of duty to ferret out all I could about the antecedents of the Plotnitzkys and prove that there was nothing of the impostor about them.

But my cautious enquiries produced no useful information. Mrs Hales confessed that she knew naught of her lodgers beyond what they had told her, which was nothing more nor less than that the two were dependent upon the son's exertions for a livelihood, that they were of aristocratic birth and that they had been deprived of their possessions by invaders.

When I tackled Madame, very carefully, I met with no more satisfactory solution of the mystery. I had read up the history of Poland very diligently and dwelt, when in conversation with the gentle old lady, at great length upon the enormities perpetrated by Russia, Austria and Prussia upon her native land and was especially eulogistic on the patriotism of such men as Kosciusko. But if I expected to rouse Madame's dormant national enthusiasm I was mistaken, for she completely lost that air of high-bred calmness and distinction which so well became her, being decidedly nervous and anxious to change the subject.

I eventually asked her, in as unconcerned a manner as possible, what part of Poland she came from, but she simply replied that she never cared to speak of her native place as to do so only served to awaken painful memories. Then, rising, she left the room, upon the plea that she did not feel well.

Now, though I had obtained no positive information, when I came to ponder upon the negative aspects of the case I found much to think about and make me feel apprehensive lest all my high opinions of this fascinating pair were going to be 'unshipped', to use a nautical phrase.

Evidently Madame had strong reasons for the silence which she maintained concerning the past of her son and herself. I wanted to be able to show the baronet that they really were the aristocrats they seemed to be, but it appeared as if I were going to be foiled by the unconscious subjects of our little experiment themselves.

Refugees abounded in and near London, and so many of them were eventually proved to be fugitives for criminal instead of political reasons that it was of imperative importance that those who had nothing disgraceful to conceal should be perfectly open regarding their past. Why then, I reflected, was Madame so secretive? It was while pondering this question that a certain doubt entered my head for the first time.

It was one of the many recommendations of this mother and son that they spoke English with a perfectly pure and native accent. Could it be that they were not Poles after all and that the land of the Lecszinskys and Sobieskis knew them not? The supposition was startling, for if proved to be impostors in one direction it was natural to suppose that all was not well with them in other ways.

I had been nearly a week masquerading as a literary gentleman without having made any actual or definite discoveries when our handsome young friend came home one day looking very ill indeed and complaining of frightful pains in his head. Every mother is alarmed when her only child is smitten with sudden illness, but I never saw anything to equal Madame's terror and prostration. We soon had a doctor on the spot who found the mother almost as helpless as the son, who, after lying down on his bed dressed as he had come home, seemed incapable of further effort or movement.

'He must be got into bed at once,' said the doctor. 'He has been overworked, and I should fancy he has had a great deal of worry with the result that he has broken down. It will be a case of brain fever, I expect. I will look in again in an hour, by which time you will have him as comfortable as possible.'

I was the only man in the house at the time, and Mrs Hales was unfeignedly thankful that I should be at hand to render assistance in undressing poor Feodor, who was by this time quite unconscious. But when I offered to commence this necessary duty at once, Madame became terribly excited and implored both Mrs Hales and myself to leave the room, saying that she could manage very well herself.

As this was clearly an utter impossibility, for the old lady was very fragile, I gently resisted her importunities and said that I would leave the room after seeing our patient safely in bed.

But Madame became so excited and distressed that we hardly knew what to do until Mrs Hales whispered, 'I am afraid the poor old lady will be laid up, too, if we do not humour her. Just go into the next room while I try to persuade her. I will come for you directly.'

In two minutes she followed me, not, however, to urge me to return, but because Madame had fiercely refused to allow her to remain and had then locked the door behind her to prevent intrusion on our part. We listened anxiously at the door, determined to break it open if necessary. It was just as we expected. We heard the old lady panting with exertion for a few moments, and then a smothered shriek told us that something was amiss.

In another second I had put my back to the wall and my foot to the door, forcing the latter from its hinges with very little trouble.

A singular spectacle met our gaze. Madame had fallen fainting to the floor while Feodor had sprung from the bed and was wildly pacing the room, uttering unintelligible sentences, probably in some language which we did not understand. I promptly raised Madame and carried her into the adjoining room, placing her upon the couch *pro tem*. Then I hurried back to Feodor's assistance. He had already collapsed again, and Mrs Hales was preventing him from sinking.

Together we placed him upon the bed, having previously turned the covers down ready to receive him. Then we rapidly proceeded to divest him of his upper clothing. No sooner, however, had we removed the vest than we made a startling discovery, which fully accounted for Madame's reluctance to permit us to remain in the room.

A dramatic situation is none the less dramatic because it is hailed in commonplace language, and Mrs Hales's horrified exclamation – 'Oh, my goodness gracious! It's a woman!' – was just as much of a surprise to me as if her discovery had been announced in classical phraseology.

A woman! Well, this was a complication I had never thought of!

But I judged it best to leave Mrs Hales in possession while I attended to Madame's wants and held myself prepared to render immediate help should it be necessary. However, my aid was not needed as the patient remained quiet for a while. Not so Madame.

On recovering from her swoon she looked into my face, and, reading there that her secret was betrayed, she gave way to an outburst of grief which made me feel very sorry for her, saying that her darling Feodor was now ruined.

I used my best endeavours to console her but had not made much progress in this direction when the doctor appeared. He was considerably surprised to find that his patient was a woman who had been masquerading in man's clothes, but he was discreet and promised to keep the secret until the mother could be induced to give her reasons for taking part in so strange a farce.

A few hours later our interesting patient was in the care of a competent nurse who had been summoned after all traces of Feodor's assumption of masculinity, even to the smart little false moustache, had been removed, and we had persuaded Madame of the advisability of being perfectly open and candid now that there was no longer any possibility of concealing Feodor's true sex.

This, in brief, is the lady's story. She and her daughter were not Poles, as I had begun to suspect. But Madame was really the widow of an English baronet, and her daughter, whose real name was Feodore, had been born and brought up under the happiest auspices. Unfortunately, the estates of Sir Godfrey Bryant were strictly entailed, and when he was killed in the hunting field it was found that for neither wife nor child had any provision been made. The new baronet was greedy, insolent and cruel and barely gave his aunt and cousin time to vacate the beloved home which they had never dreamed of losing.

For Lady Bryant to think of throwing herself upon the charity of erstwhile friends was as impossible as it was for her to attempt to earn her own livelihood at her age. But Feodore proved equal to the burdens laid upon her brave young shoulders. After a good deal of anxious thought she announced her plan of campaign to her mother, but it was some time before she could induce her to agree to it, though the reasons she urged were cogent enough.

'I shall never have the same chance of earning a livelihood by appearing as my natural self that I should have if I posed as an interesting male foreign refugee,' she had said, and the sequel proved that she was right.

A certain noble lord was taken into confidence, and his recommendations and testimonials soon procured employment for the young professor. Her own abilities and personal qualities did the rest.

All things considered, I saw no reason why the brave girl's secret should be made public, and, as the doctor and Mrs Hales were also of my opinion, Miss Bryant might have figured again as a Polish professor after her recovery but for one thing. I urged Lady Bryant to permit me to explain the real state of affairs to Sir Selby Grant, since his daughter was so much in love with Feodore that it would require a strong remedy to cure her – nothing short of the truth, in fact.

Lady Bryant was not so reluctant as might have been imagined, for she was actually acquainted with Sir Selby and knew him for a generous, kind-hearted gentleman who would respect the confidence placed in him.

But she scarcely anticipated the actual result of this confidence. I made it my business to see Sir Selby at once and explain the whole affair to him, and he, in his turn, told his daughter that she had bestowed her maiden affections upon a woman. So far from this producing any ill effect upon the girl, she said that there was now nothing which need prevent her from visiting her dear friend. Her father agreed with her, and even accompanied her to pay his respects to his old friend Lady Bryant.

Matters were kept very quiet for a time, but as soon as Miss Bryant was convalescent she and her mother were taken to Grant Lodge to pay a long visit to the baronet and his daughter.

The last time I heard of them Miss Bryant had become Lady Grant. Her mother was comfortably established in a dower house attached to the Grant estate, and she was perfectly idolized by her stepdaughter Mabel, who had consented to marry Lord Gutherton at no distant date.

As for myself, I received such a handsome special *douceur* for my pains that a few such well-paid cases would have enabled me to enter my name on the retiring list long ago.

Mary E. Wilkins

THE LONG ARM

Mary Eleanor Wilkins (1852–1930) – who became Mary Wilkins Freeman after her marriage in 1902 – was one of the best of the New England regional writers in the years up to and just after the end of the nineteenth century. She was best known for her short stories and particularly her ghost stories, some of which were collected in The Wind in the Rose-Bush *(1903). Her novel* Pembroke *(1894) contains echoes of much of Mary's own life, exploring a series of romantic entanglements and disappointments in a small town in Massachusetts. The subtext of sexual tension and repression reflects Mary's own strict religious upbringing and what some have suggested were her suppressed lesbian tendencies. Wilkins had a strong attachment for her childhood friend Mary Wales, with whom she lived for sixteen years before her marriage to Dr Charles Freeman. Though Wilkins initially revelled in her marriage, chiefly because it meant she was no longer thought of as an old spinster, it was not a happy relationship, and the couple later separated after Dr Freeman's decline into alcoholism.*

'The Long Arm' has become recognized as one of the nineteenth century's significant lesbian texts. It is one of the few detective stories that Mary Wilkins wrote, and it came about when her friend Joseph Edgar Chamberlin, then editor of Youth's Companion *magazine, wrote to her about the notorious case of Lizzie Borden, who was tried but acquitted of the murder of her father and stepmother in Fall River, Massachusetts, in August 1892. The crime was never solved. Chamberlin suggested to Mary that maybe they could try to solve the crime in fiction. How much Chamberlin contributed to the final story is not known, and it is probable that Wilkins wrote it entirely while incorporating suggestions by Chamberlin. The final story won a $2,000 story contest sponsored by* The Critic *in July 1895 and was syndicated in many*

US newspapers and published complete in Britain in Chapman's Magazine *in August 1895. While it doesn't solve the Lizzie Borden case it was the first, and remains the most important, story to be inspired by the murders.*

The Long Arm

I
The Tragedy

*From notes written by Miss Sarah Fairbanks
immediately after the report of the Grand Jury.*

AS I TAKE my pen to write this I have a feeling that I am in the witness box – for, or against myself, which? The place of the criminal in the dock I will not voluntarily take. I will affirm neither my innocence nor my guilt. I will present the facts of the case as impartially and as coolly as if I had nothing at stake. I will let all who read this judge me as they will.

This I am bound to do, since I am condemned to something infinitely worse than the life-cell or the gallows. I will try my own self in lieu of judge and jury; my guilt or my innocence I will prove to you all, if it be in mortal power. In my despair I am tempted to say I care not which it may be, so something be proved. Open condemnation could not overwhelm me like universal suspicion.

Now, first, as I have heard is the custom in the courts of law, I will present the case. I am Sarah Fairbanks, a country schoolteacher, twenty-nine years of age. My mother died when I was twenty-three. Since then, while I have been teaching at Digby, a cousin of my father's, Rufus Bennett, and his wife have lived with my father. During the long summer vacation they returned to their little farm in Vermont, and I kept house for my father.

For five years I have been engaged to be married to Henry Ellis, a young man whom I met in Digby. My father was very much opposed to the match and had told me repeatedly that if I insisted upon marrying him in his lifetime he would disinherit me. On this account Henry never visited me at my own home, while I could not bring myself to break off my engagement. Finally, I wished to avoid an open rupture with my father. He was quite an old man, and I was the only one he had left of a large family.

I believe that parents should honour their children as well as children their parents, but I had arrived at this conclusion: in nine-tenths of the cases wherein children marry against their parents' wishes, even when the parents have no just grounds for opposition, the marriages are unhappy.

I sometimes felt that I was unjust to Henry and resolved that, if ever I suspected that his fancy turned towards any other girl, I would not hinder it, especially as I was getting older and, I thought, losing my good looks.

A little while ago a young and pretty girl came to Digby to teach the school in the south district. She boarded in the same house with Henry. I heard that he was somewhat attentive to her, and I made up my mind I would not interfere. At the same time it seemed to me that my heart was breaking. I heard her people had money, too, and she was an only child. I had always felt that Henry ought to marry a wife with money because he had nothing himself and was not very strong.

School closed five weeks ago, and I came home for the summer vacation. The night before I left Henry came to see me and urged me to marry him. I refused again, but I never before had felt that my father was so hard and cruel as I did that night. Henry said that he should certainly see me during the vacation, and when I replied that he must not come he was angry and said . . . but such foolish things are not worth repeating. Henry has really a very sweet temper and would not hurt a fly.

The very night of my return home Rufus Bennett and my father had words about some maple sugar which Rufus made on his Vermont farm and sold to father, who made a good trade for it to some people in Boston. That was father's business. He had once kept a store but had given it up and sold a few articles that he could make a large profit on here and there at wholesale. He used to send to New Hampshire and Vermont for butter, eggs and cheese. Cousin Rufus thought father did not allow him enough profit on the maple sugar, and in the dispute father lost his temper and said that Rufus had given him underweight. At that, Rufus swore an oath and seized father by the throat. Rufus's wife screamed, 'Oh, don't! Don't! Oh, he'll kill him!'

I went up to Rufus and took hold of his arm.

'Rufus Bennett,' said I, 'you let go of my father!'

But Rufus's eyes glared like a madman's, and he would not let go. Then I went to the desk drawer where father had kept a pistol since some houses in the village were broken into. I got out the pistol, laid hold of Rufus again and held the muzzle against his forehead.

'You let go of my father,' said I, 'or I'll fire!'

Then Rufus let go, and father dropped like a log. He was purple in the face. Rufus's wife and I worked a long time over him to bring him to.

'Rufus Bennett,' said I, 'go to the well and get a pitcher of water.' He went, but when father had revived and got up Rufus gave him a look that showed he was not over his rage.

'I'll get even with you yet, Martin Fairbanks, old man as you are!' he shouted out and went into the outer room.

We got father to bed soon. He slept in the bedroom downstairs, out of the sitting-room. Rufus and his wife had the north chamber, and I had the south one. I left my door open that night and did not sleep. I listened; no one stirred in the night. Rufus and his wife were up very early in the morning, and before nine o'clock left for Vermont. They had a day's journey and would reach home about nine in the evening. Rufus's wife bade father goodbye, crying, while Rufus was getting their trunk downstairs; but Rufus did not go near father nor me. He ate no breakfast; his very back looked ugly when he went out of the yard.

That very day about seven in the evening, after tea, I had just washed the dishes and put them away and went out on the north doorstep where father was sitting and sat down on the lowest step. There was a cool breeze there; it had been a very hot day.

'I want to know if that Ellis fellow has been to see you any lately?' said father all at once.

'Not a great deal,' I answered.

'Did he come to see you the last night you were there,' said father.

'Yes, sir,' said I, 'he did come.'

'If you ever have another word to say to that fellow while I live I'll kick you out of the house like a dog, daughter of mine though you be,' said he. Then he swore a great oath and called God to witness. 'Speak to that fellow again, if you dare, while I live!' said he.

I did not say a word. I just looked up at him as I sat there. Father turned pale and shrank back and put his hand to his throat where Rufus had clutched him. There were some purple finger marks there.

'I suppose you would have been glad if he had killed me,' father cried out.

'I saved your life,' said I.

'What did you do with that pistol?' he asked.

'I put it back in the desk drawer.'

I got up and went around and sat on the west doorstep, which is the front one. As I sat there the bell rang for the Tuesday evening meeting, and Phoebe Dole and Maria Woods, two old maiden ladies, dressmakers, our next-door neighbours, went past on their way to the meeting. Phoebe stopped and asked if Rufus and his wife were gone. Maria went around the house. Very soon they went on, and several other people passed. When they had all gone it was as still as death.

I sat alone a long time until I could see by the shadows that the full moon had risen. Then I went to my room and went to bed.

I lay awake a long time crying. It seemed to me that all hope of marriage between Henry and me was over. I could not expect him to wait for me. I thought of that other girl. I could see her pretty face wherever I looked. But at last I cried myself to sleep.

At about five o'clock I awoke and got up. Father always wanted his breakfast at six o'clock, and I had to prepare it now.

When father and I were alone he always built the fire in the kitchen stove, but that morning I did not hear him stirring as usual, and I fancied that he must be so out of temper with me that he would not build the fire.

I went to my closet for a dark-blue calico dress which I wore to do housework in. It had hung there during all the school term.

As I took it off the hook my attention was caught by something strange about the dress I had worn the night before. This dress was made of thin summer silk; it was green in colour, sprinkled over with white rings. It had been my best dress for two summers, but now I was wearing it on hot afternoons at home for it was the coolest dress I had. The night before, too, I had thought of the possibility of Henry's driving over from Digby and passing the house. He had done this sometimes during the last summer vacation, and I wished to look my best if he did.

As I took down the calico dress I saw what seemed to be a stain on the green silk. I threw on the calico hastily and then took the green silk and carried it over to the window. It was covered with spots – horrible great splashes and streaks down the front. The right sleeve, too, was stained, and all the stains were wet.

'What have I got on my dress?' said I.

It looked like blood. Then I smelled of it, and it was sickening in my nostrils, but I was not sure what the smell of blood was like. I thought I must have got the stains by some accident the night before.

'If that is blood on my dress,' I said, 'I must do something to get it off at once or the dress will be ruined.'

It came to my mind that I had been told that bloodstains had been removed from cloth by an application of flour paste on the wrong side. I took my green silk and ran down the back stairs, which led – having a door at the foot – directly into the kitchen.

There was no fire in the kitchen stove, as I had thought. Everything was very solitary and still except for the ticking of the clock on the shelf. When I crossed the kitchen to the pantry, however, the cat mewed to be let in from the shed. She had a little door of her own by which she could enter or leave the shed at will, an aperture just large enough for her Maltese body to pass at ease beside the shed door. It had a little lid, too, hung upon a leathern hinge. On my way I let the cat in, then I went into the pantry and got a bowl of flour. This I mixed with water into a stiff paste, and applied to the under-surface of the stains on my dress. I then hung the dress up to dry in the dark end of a closet leading out of the kitchen which contained some old clothes of father's.

Then I made up the fire in the kitchen stove. I made coffee, baked biscuits and poached some eggs for breakfast.

Then I opened the door into the sitting-room and called, 'Father, breakfast is ready.' Suddenly I started. There was a red stain on the inside of the sitting-room door. My heart began to beat in my ears. 'Father!' I called out. 'Father!'

There was no answer.

'Father!' I called again as loud as I could scream. 'Why don't you speak? What is the matter?'

The door of his bedroom stood open. I had a feeling that I saw a red reflection in there. I gathered myself together and went across the sitting-room to father's bedroom door. His little looking-glass hung over his bureau opposite his bed, which was reflected in it.

That was the first thing I saw when I reached the door. I could see father in the looking-glass and the bed. Father was dead there; he had been murdered in the night.

II
The Knot of Ribbon

I think I must have fainted away, for presently I found myself on the floor, and for a minute I could not remember what had happened. Then I remembered, and an awful, unreasoning terror seized me. I must lock all the doors quick, I thought. Quick, or the murderer will come back.

I tried to get up, but I could not stand. I sank down again. I had to crawl out of the room on my hands and knees. I went first to the front door; it was locked with a key and a bolt. I went next to the north door, and that was locked with a key and a bolt. I went to the north shed door, and that was bolted. Then I went to the little-used east door in the shed, beside which the cat had her little passage-way, and that was fastened with an iron hook. It has no latch.

The whole house was fastened on the inside. The thought struck me like an icy hand: The murderer is in this house! I rose to my feet then. I unhooked that door and ran out of the house and out of the yard as for my life.

I took the road to the village. The first house, where Phoebe Dole and Maria Woods live, is across a wide field from ours. I did not intend to stop there, for they were only women and could do nothing; but seeing Phoebe looking out of the window, I ran into the yard.

She opened the window.

'What is it?' said she. 'What is the matter, Sarah Fairbanks?'

Maria Woods came and leaned over her shoulder. Her face looked almost as white as her hair, and her blue eyes were dilated. My face must have frightened her.

'Father – father is murdered in his bed!' I said.

There was a scream, and Maria Woods's face disappeared from over Phoebe Dole's shoulder – she had fainted. I do not know whether Phoebe looked paler – she is always very pale – but I saw in her black eyes a look which I shall never forget. I think she began to suspect me at that moment.

Phoebe glanced back at Maria, but she asked me another question.

'Has he had words with anybody?' said she.

'Only with Rufus,' I said, 'but Rufus is gone.'

Phoebe turned away from the window to attend to Maria, and I ran on to the village.

A hundred people can testify what I did next – can tell how I called for the doctor and the deputy sheriff; how I went back to my own home with the horror-stricken crowd; how they flocked in and looked at poor father; but only the doctor touched him, very carefully, to see if he were quite dead; how the coroner came, and all the rest.

The pistol was in the bed beside father, but it had not been fired; the charge was still in the barrel. It was bloodstained, and there was one bruise on father's head which might have been inflicted by the pistol used as a club. But the wound which caused his death was in his breast and made evidently by some cutting instrument, though the cut was not a clean one. The weapon must have been dull.

They searched the house lest the murderer should be hidden away.

I heard Rufus Bennett's name whispered by one and another. Everybody seemed to know that he and father had had words the night before. I could not understand how because I had told nobody except Phoebe Dole, who had had no time to spread the news, and I was sure that no one else had spoken of it.

They looked in the closet where my green silk dress hung and pushed it aside to be sure nobody was concealed behind it, but they did not notice anything wrong about it. It was dark in the closet, and besides, they did not look for anything like that until later.

All these people – the deputy sheriff, and afterwards the high sheriff and other out-of-town officers for whom they had telegraphed, and the neighbours – all hunted their own suspicion, and that was Rufus Bennett. All believed he had come back and killed my father. They fitted all the facts to that belief. They made him do the deed with a long, slender screw driver which he had recently borrowed from one of the neighbours and had not returned. They made his finger marks, which were still on my father's throat, fit the red prints of the sitting-room door. They made sure that he had returned and stolen into the house by the east-door shed while father and I sat on the doorsteps the evening before; that he had hidden himself away, perhaps in that very closet where my dress hung, and afterwards stolen out and killed my father and then escaped.

They were not shaken when I told them that every door was bolted and barred that morning. They themselves found all the windows fastened down, except a few which were open on account of the heat, and even these last were raised only the width of the sash, and fastened with sticks, so that they could be raised no higher. Father was very cautious about fastening the house, for he sometimes had considerable sums of money by him. The officers saw all these difficulties in the way, but they fitted them somehow to their theory, and two deputy sheriffs were at once sent to apprehend Rufus.

They had not begun to suspect me then, and not the slightest watch was kept on my movements. The neighbours were very kind and did everything to help me, relieving me altogether of all those last offices – in this case so much sadder than usual.

An inquest was held, and I told freely all I knew, except about the bloodstains on my dress. I hardly knew why I kept that back. I had no feeling then that I might have done the deed myself, and I could not bear to convict myself if I was innocent.

Two of the neighbours, Mrs Holmes and Mrs Adams, remained with me all that day. Towards evening, when there were very few in the house, they went into the parlour to put it in order for the funeral, and I sat down alone in the kitchen. As I sat there by the window I thought of my green silk dress, and wondered if the stains were out. I went to the closet and brought the dress out to the light. The spots and streaks had almost disappeared. I took the dress out into the shed and scraped off the flour paste, which was quite dry. I swept up the paste, burned it in the stove, took the dress upstairs to my own closet and bunged it in its old place. Neighbours remained with me all night.

At three o'clock in the afternoon of the next day, which was Thursday, I went over to Phoebe Dole's to see about a black dress to wear at the funeral. The neighbours had urged me to have my black silk dress altered a little and trimmed with crape.

I found only Maria Woods at home. When she saw me she gave a little scream and began to cry. She looked as if she had already been weeping for hours. Her blue eyes were bloodshot.

'Phoebe's gone over to . . . Mrs Whitney's to . . . try on her dress,' she sobbed.

'I want to get my black silk dress fixed a little,' said I.

'She'll be home pretty soon,' said Maria.

I laid my dress on the sofa and sat down. Nobody ever consults Maria about a dress. She sews well, but Phoebe does all the planning.

Maria Woods continued to sob like a child, holding her little soaked handkerchief over her face. Her shoulders heaved. As for me, I felt like a stone. I could not weep.

'Oh,' she gasped out finally. 'I knew . . . I knew! I told Phoebe . . . I knew just how it would be, I . . . knew!'

I roused myself at that.

'What do you mean?' said I.

'When Phoebe came home Tuesday night and said she heard your father and Rufus Bennett having words, I knew how it would be,' she choked out. 'I knew he had a dreadful temper.'

'Did Phoebe Dole know Tuesday night that father and Rufus Bennett had words?' said I.

'Yes,' said Maria Woods.

'How did she know?'

'She was going through your yard, the short cut to Mrs Ormsby's, to carry her brown alpaca dress home. She came right home and told me; and she overheard them.'

'Have you spoken of it to anybody but me?' said I.

Maria said she didn't know; she might have done so. Then she remembered hearing Phoebe herself speak of it to Harriet Sargent when she came in to try on her dress. It was easy to see how people knew about it.

I did not say any more, but I thought it was strange that Phoebe Dole had asked me if father had had words with anybody when she knew it all the time.

Phoebe came in before long. I tried on my dress, and she made her plan about the alterations and the trimming. I made no suggestions. I did not care how it was done, but if I had cared it would have made no difference. Phoebe always does things her own way. All the women in the village are in a manner under Phoebe Dole's thumb. The garments are visible proofs of her force of will.

While she was taking up my black silk on the shoulder seams, Phoebe Dole said, 'Let me see. You had a green silk made at Digby three summers ago, didn't you?'

'Yes,' I said.

'Well,' said she, 'why don't you have it dyed black? Those thin silks dye quite nice. It would make you a good dress.'

I scarcely replied, and then she offered to dye it for me herself. She had a recipe which she used with great success. I thought it was very kind of her but did not say whether I would accept her offer or not. I could not fix my mind upon anything but the awful trouble I was in.

'I'll come over and get it tomorrow morning,' said Phoebe.

I thanked her. I thought of the stains, and then my mind seemed to wander again to the one subject. All the time Maria Woods sat weeping. Finally Phoebe turned to her with impatience.

'If you can't keep calmer you'd better go upstairs, Maria,' said she. 'You'll make Sarah sick. Look at her! She doesn't give way – and think of the reason she's got.'

'I've got reason, too,' Maria broke out; then, with a piteous shriek, 'Oh, I've got reason.'

'Maria Woods, go out of the room!' said Phoebe. Her sharpness made me jump, half dazed as I was.

Maria got up without a word and went out of the room, bending almost double with convulsive sobs.

'She's been dreadfully worked up over your father's death,' said Phoebe calmly, going on with the fitting. 'She's terribly nervous. Sometimes I have to be real sharp with her for her own good.'

I nodded. Maria Woods has always been considered a sweet, weakly, dependent woman, and Phoebe Dole is undoubtedly very fond of her. She has seemed to shield her and take care of her nearly all her life. The two have lived together since they were young girls.

Phoebe is tall and very pale and thin, but she never had a day's illness. She is plain, yet there is a kind of severe goodness and faithfulness about her colourless face with the smooth bands of white hair over her ears.

I went home as soon as my dress was fitted. That evening Henry Ellis came over to see me. I do not need to go into details concerning that visit. It seems enough to say that he tendered the fullest sympathy and protection, and I accepted them. I cried a little for the first time, and he soothed and comforted me.

Henry had driven over from Digby and tied his horse in the yard. At ten o'clock he bade me good-night on the doorstep and was just turning his buggy around when Mrs Adams came running to the door.

'Is this yours?' said she, and she held out a knot of yellow ribbon.

'Why, that's the ribbon you have around your whip, Henry,' said I.

He looked at it.

'So it is,' he said. 'I must have dropped It.' He put it into his pocket and drove away.

'He didn't drop that ribbon tonight!' said Mrs Adams. 'I found it Wednesday morning out in the yard. I thought I remembered seeing him have a yellow ribbon on his whip.'

III
Suspicion Is Not Proof

When Mrs Adams told me she had picked up Henry's whip-ribbon Wednesday morning, I said nothing but thought that Henry must have driven over Tuesday evening after all and even come up into the yard, though the house was shut up and I in bed, to get a little nearer to me. I felt conscience-stricken because I could not help a thrill of happiness when my father lay dead in the house.

My father was buried as privately and as quietly as we could bring it about. But it was a terrible ordeal. Meantime, word came from Vermont that Rufus Bennett had been arrested on his farm. He was perfectly willing to come back with the officers and, indeed, had not the slightest trouble in proving that he was at his home in Vermont when the murder took place. He proved by several witnesses that he was out of the state long before my father and I sat on the steps together that evening and that he proceeded directly to his home as fast as the train and stage-coach could carry him.

The screw driver with which the deed was supposed to have been committed was found by the neighbour from whom it had been borrowed in his wife's bureau drawer. It had been returned, and she had used it to put a picture hook in her chamber. Bennett was discharged and returned to Vermont.

Then Mrs Adams told of the finding of the yellow ribbon from Henry Ellis's whip, and he was arrested, since he was held to have a motive for putting my father out of the world. Father's opposition to our marriage was well known, and Henry was suspected also of having had an eye to his money. It was found, indeed, that my father had more money than I had known myself.

Henry owned to having driven into the yard that night and to having missed the ribbon from his whip on his return, but one of the hostlers in the livery stables in Digby where he kept his horse and buggy came forward and testified to finding the yellow ribbon in the carriage room that Tuesday night before Henry returned from his drive. There were two yellow ribbons in evidence, therefore, and the one produced by the hostler seemed to fit Henry's whip-stock the more exactly.

Moreover, nearly the exact minute of the murder was claimed to be proved by the post-mortem examination, and by the testimony of the stable man as to the hour of Henry's return and the speed of his horse he was further cleared of suspicion – for, if the opinion of the medical experts was correct, Henry must have returned to the livery stable too soon to have committed the murder.

He was discharged, at any rate, though suspicion still clung to him. Many people believe now in his guilt; those who do not, believe in mine; and some believe we were accomplices.

After Henry's discharge, I was arrested. There was no one else left to accuse. There must be a motive for the murder; I was the only person left with a motive. Unlike the others, who were discharged after preliminary examination, I was held to the grand jury and taken to Dedham where I spent four weeks in jail awaiting the meeting of the grand jury.

Neither at the preliminary examination nor before the grand jury was I allowed to make the full and frank statement that I am making here. I was told simply to answer the questions that were put to me and to volunteer nothing, and I obeyed.

I know nothing about law. I wished to do the best I could, to act in the wisest manner, for Henry's sake and my own. I said nothing about the green silk dress. They searched the house for all manner of things at the time of my arrest, but the dress was not there; it was in Phoebe Dole's dye-kettle. She had come over after it one day when I was picking beans in the garden and had taken it out of the closet. She brought it back herself and told me this, after I had returned from Dedham, 'I thought I'd get it and surprise you,' said she. 'It's taken a beautiful black.'

She gave me a strange look – half as if she would see into my very soul in spite of me; half as if she were in terror of what she would see there – as she spoke. I do not know just what Phoebe Dole's look meant. There may have been a stain left on that dress after all, and she may have seen it.

I suppose if it had not been for that flour paste which I had learned to make, I should have hanged for the murder of my father. As it was, the grand jury found no bill against me because there was absolutely no evidence to convict me, and I came home a free woman. And if people were condemned for their motives, would there be enough hangmen in the world?

They found no weapon with which I could have done the deed. They found no bloodstains on my clothes. The one thing which told against me, aside from my ever-present motive, was the fact that on the morning after the murder the doors and windows were fastened. My volunteering this information had, of course, weakened its force as against myself.

Then, too, some held that I might have been mistaken in my terror and excitement, and there was a theory, advanced by a few, that the murderer had meditated making me also a victim and had locked the doors that he might not be frustrated in his designs but had lost heart at the last and had allowed me to escape and then fled himself. Some held that he had intended to force me to reveal the whereabouts of father's money, but his courage had failed him.

Father had quite a sum in a hiding-place which only he and I knew. But no search for money had been made, as far as anyone could see – not a bureau drawer had been disturbed, and father's gold watch was ticking peacefully under his pillow; even his wallet in his vest pocket had not been opened. There was a small roll of bank notes in it and some change; father never carried much money. I suppose if father's wallet and watch had been taken, I should not have been suspected at all.

I was discharged, as I have said, from lack of evidence and have returned to my home – free, indeed, but with this awful burden of suspicion on my shoulders. That brings me up to the present day. I returned yesterday evening. This evening Henry Ellis has been over to see me; he will not come again, for I have forbidden him to do so. This is what I said to him: 'I know you are innocent; you know I am innocent. To all the world beside we are under suspicion – I more than you, but we are both under suspicion. If we are known to be together, that suspicion is increased for both of us. I do not care for myself, but I do care for you. Separated from me the stigma attached to you will soon fade away, especially if you should marry elsewhere –'

Then Henry interrupted me. 'I will never marry elsewhere,' said he.

I could not help being glad that he said it, but I was firm. 'If you should see some good woman whom you could love, it will be better for you to marry elsewhere,' said I.

'I never will!' he said again. He put his arms around me, but I had strength to push him away.

'You never need, if I succeed in what I undertake before you meet the other,' said I. I began to think he had not cared for that pretty girl who boarded in the same house after all.

'What is that?' he said. 'What are you going to undertake?'

'To find my father's murderer,' said I.

Henry gave me a strange look, then, before I could stop him, he took me fast in his arms and kissed my forehead.

'As God is my witness, Sarah, I believe in your innocence,' he said, and from that minute I have felt sustained and fully confident of my power to do what I had undertaken.

My father's murderer I will find. Tomorrow I begin my search. I shall first make an exhaustive examination of the house, such as no officer in the case has yet made, in the hope of finding a clue. Every room I propose to divide into square yards by line and measure, and every one of these square yards I will study as if it were a problem in algebra.

I have a theory that it is impossible for any human being to enter any house and commit in it a deed of this kind and not leave behind traces which are the known quantities in an algebraic equation to those who can use them.

There is a chance that I shall not be quite unaided. Henry has promised not to come again until I bid him, but he is to send a detective here from Boston, one whom he knows. In fact, the man is a cousin of his, or else there would be small hope of our securing him even if I were to offer him a large price.

The man has been remarkably successful in several cases, but his health is not good; the work is a severe strain upon his nerves, and he is not driven to it from any lack of money. The physicians have forbidden him to undertake any new case for a year at least, but Henry is confident that we may rely upon him for this.

I will now lay aside this and go to bed. Tomorrow is Wednesday. My father will have been dead seven weeks. Tomorrow morning I will commence the work in which, if it be in human power, aided by a higher wisdom, I shall succeed.

IV
The Box of Clues

The pages which follow are from Miss Fairbanks's journal,
begun after the conclusion of the notes already given to the reader.

Wednesday night – I have resolved to record carefully each day the progress I make in my examination of the house. I began today at the bottom – that is, with the room least likely to contain any clue, the parlour. I took a chalk line and a yardstick and divided the floor into square yards, and every one of these squares I examined on my hands and knees. I found in this way literally nothing on the carpet but dust, lint, two common white pins and three inches of blue sewing-silk.

At last I got the dustpan and brush, and yard by yard swept the floor. I took the sweepings in a white pasteboard box out into the yard in the strong sunlight and examined them. There was nothing but dust and lint and five inches of brown woollen thread – evidently a ravelling of some dress material. The blue silk and the brown thread are the only possible clues which I found today, and they are hardly possible. Rufus's wife can probably account for them.

Nobody has come to the house all day. I went down to the store this afternoon to get some necessary provisions, and people stopped talking when I came in. The clerk took my money as if it were poison.

Thursday night – Today I have searched the sitting-room, out of which my father's bedroom opens. I found two bloody footprints on the carpet which no one had noticed before – perhaps because the carpet itself is red and white. I used a microscope which I had in my school work. The footprints, which are close to the bedroom door, pointing out into the sitting-room, are both from the right foot; one is brighter than the other, but both are faint. The foot was evidently either bare or clad only in a stocking – the prints are so widely spread. They are wider than my father's shoes. I tried one in the brightest print.

I found nothing else new in the sitting-room. The bloodstains on the doors, which have been already noted, are still there. They had not been washed away, first by order of the sheriff and next by mine. These stains are of two kinds: one looks as if made by a bloody garment brushing against it; the other, I should say, was made in the first place by the grasp of a bloody hand and then brushed over with a cloth. There are none of these marks upon the door leading to the bedroom – they are on the doors leading into the front entry and the china closet. The china closet is really a pantry, though I use it only for my best dishes and preserves.

Friday night – Today I searched the closet. One of the shelves, which is about as high as my shoulders, was bloodstained. It looked to me as if the murderer might have caught hold of it to steady himself. Did he turn faint after his dreadful deed? Some tumblers of jelly were ranged on that shelf, and they had not been disturbed. There was only that bloody clutch on the edge.

I found on this closet floor, under the shelves, as if it had been rolled there by a careless foot, a button, evidently from a man's clothing. It is an ordinary black enamelled metal trousers button; it had evidently been worn off and clumsily sewn on again, for a quantity of stout white thread is still clinging to it. This button must have belonged either to a single man or to one with an idle wife.

If one black button had been sewn on with white thread, another is likely to be. I may be wrong, but I regard this button as a clue.

The pantry was thoroughly swept – cleaned, indeed, by Rufus's wife the day before she left. Neither my father nor Rufus could have dropped it there, and they never had occasion to go to that closet. The murderer dropped the button.

I have a white pasteboard box which I have marked 'Clues.' In it I have put the button.

This afternoon Phoebe Dole came in. She is very kind. She had recut the dyed silk, and she fitted it to me. Her great shears clicking in my ears made me nervous. I did not feel like stopping to think about clothes. I hope I did not appear ungrateful, for she is the only soul besides Henry who has treated me as she did before this happened.

Phoebe asked me what I found to busy myself about, and I replied, 'I am searching for my father's murderer.' She asked me if I thought I should find a clue, and I replied, 'I think so.' I had found the button then, but I did not speak of it. She said Maria was not very well.

I saw her eyeing the stains on the doors, and I said I had not washed them off, for I thought they might yet serve a purpose in detecting the murderer. She looked closely at those on the entry door – the brightest ones – and said she did not see how they could help, for there were no plain finger marks there, and she should think they would make me nervous.

'I'm beyond being nervous,' I replied.

Saturday – Today I have found something which I cannot understand. I have been at work in the room where my father came to his dreadful end. Of course, some of the most startling evidences have been removed. The bed is clean and the carpet washed, but the worst horror of it all clings to that room. The spirit of murder seemed to haunt it. It seemed to me at first that I could not enter that room, but in it I made a strange discovery.

My father, while he carried little money about his person, was in the habit of keeping considerable sums in the house; there is no bank within ten miles. However, he was wary; he had a hiding place which he had revealed to no one but myself. He had a small stand in his room near the end of his bed. Under this stand, or rather under the top of it, he had tacked a large leather wallet. In this he kept all his spare money. I remember how his eyes twinkled when he showed it to me.

'The average mind thinks things have either got to be in or on,' said my father. 'They don't consider there's ways of getting around gravitation and calculation.'

In searching my father's room I called to mind that saying of his and his peculiar system of concealment, and then I made my discovery. I have argued that in a search of this kind I ought not only to search for hidden traces of the criminal but for everything which had been for any reason concealed. Something which my father himself had hidden, something from his past history, may furnish a motive for someone else.

The money in the wallet under the table, some five hundred dollars, had been removed and deposited in the bank. Nothing more was to be found there. I examined the bottom of the bureau and the undersides of the chair seats. There are two chairs in the room besides the cushioned rocker – green-painted wooden chairs with flag seats. I found nothing under the seats.

Then I turned each of the green chairs completely over, and examined the bottoms of the legs. My heart leaped when I found a bit of leather tacked over one. I got the tack-hammer and drew the tacks. The chair-leg had been hollowed out, and for an inch the hole was packed tight with cotton. I began picking out the cotton, and soon I felt something hard. It proved to be an old-fashioned gold band, quite wide and heavy, like a wedding-ring.

I took it over to the window and found this inscription on the inside: 'Let love abide for ever'. There were two dates: one in August forty years ago, and the other in August of the present year.

I think the ring had never been worn. While the first part of the inscription is perfectly clear, it looks old, and the last is evidently freshly cut.

This could not have been my mother's ring. She had only her wedding-ring, and that was buried with her. I think my father must have treasured this ring for years. But why? What does it mean? This can hardly be a clue, this can hardly lead to the discovery of a motive, but I will put it in the box with the rest.

Sunday night – Today, of course, I did not pursue my search. I did not go to church. I could not face old friends that could not face me. Sometimes I think that everybody in my native village believes in my guilt. What must I have been in my general appearance and demeanour all my life? I have studied myself in the glass and tried to discover the possibilities of evil that they must see in my face.

This afternoon about three o'clock, the hour when people here have just finished their Sunday dinner, there was a knock on the north door. I answered it, and a strange young man stood there with a large book under his arm. He was thin and cleanly shaved, with a clerical air.

'I have a work here to which I would like to call your attention,' he began, and I stared at him in astonishment, for why should a book agent be peddling his wares upon the Sabbath?

His mouth twitched a little.

'It's a Biblical Cyclopædia,' said he.

'I don't think I care to take it,' said I.

'You are Miss Sarah Fairbanks, I believe?'

'That is my name,' I replied stiffly.

'Mr Henry Ellis of Digby sent me here,' he said next. 'My name is Dix – Francis Dix.'

Then I knew it was Henry's first cousin from Boston, the detective who had come to help me. I felt the tears coming to my eyes. 'You are very kind to come,' I managed to say.

'I am selfish, not kind,' he returned, 'but you had better let me come in, or any chance of success in my book agency is lost if the neighbours see me trying to sell it on a Sunday. And, Miss Fairbanks, this is a *bona fide* agency. I shall canvass the town.'

He came in. I showed him all that I have written, and he read it carefully. When he had finished he sat still for a long time with his face screwed up in a peculiar meditative fashion.

'We'll ferret this out in three days at the most,' said he finally with a sudden clearing of his face and a flash of his eyes at me.

'I had planned for three years perhaps,' said I.

'I tell you, we'll do it in three days,' he repeated. 'Where can I get board while I canvass for this remarkable and interesting book under my arm? I can't stay here, of course, and there is no hotel. Do you think the two dressmakers next door, Phoebe Dole and the other one, would take me in?'

I said they had never taken boarders.

'Well, I'll go over and enquire,' said Mr Dix, and he had gone, with his book under his arm, almost before I knew it.

Never have I seen anyone act with the strange noiseless soft speed that this man does. Can he prove me innocent in three days? He must have succeeded in getting board at Phoebe Dole's, for I saw him go past to meeting with her this evening. I feel sure he will be over very early tomorrow morning.

V
The Evidence Points to One

Monday night – The detective came as I expected. I was up as soon as it was light, and he came across the dewy fields with his cyclopædia under his arm. He had stolen out from Phoebe Dole's back door.

He had me bring my father's pistol, then he bade me come with him out into the back yard.

'Now, fire it,' he said, thrusting the pistol into my hands. As I have said before, the charge was still in the barrel.

'I shall arouse the neighbourhood,' I said.

'Fire it,' he ordered.

I tried. I pulled the trigger as hard as I could.

'I can't do it,' I said.

'And you are a reasonably strong woman, too, aren't you?'

I said I had been considered so. Oh, how much I heard about the strength of my poor woman's arms and their ability to strike that murderous weapon home!

Mr Dix took the pistol himself, and drew a little at the trigger.

'I could do it,' he said, 'but I won't. It would arouse the neighbourhood.'

'This is more evidence against me,' I said despairingly. 'The murderer had tried to fire the pistol and failed.'

'It is more evidence against the murderer,' said Mr Dix.

We went into the house where he examined my box of clues long and carefully. Looking at the ring, he asked whether there was a jeweller in this village, and I said there was not. I told him that my father oftener went on business to Acton, ten miles away, than elsewhere.

He examined very carefully the button which I had found in the closet and then asked to see my father's wardrobe. That was soon done. Beside the suit in which father was laid away there was one other complete one in the closet in his room. Besides that, there were in this closet two overcoats, an old black frock-coat, a pair of pepper-and-salt trousers and two black vests. Mr Dix examined all the buttons; not one was missing.

There was still another old suit in the closet off the kitchen. This was examined, and no button found wanting.

'What did your father do for work the day before he died?' he then asked.

I reflected and said that he had unpacked some stores which had come down from Vermont and done some work out in the garden.

'What did he wear?'

'I think he wore the pepper-and-salt trousers and the black vest. He wore no coat while at work.'

Mr Dix went quietly back to father's room and his closet, I following. He took out the grey trousers and the black vest and examined them closely.

'What did he wear to protect these?' he asked.

'Why, he wore overalls!' I said at once. As I spoke I remembered seeing father go around the path to the yard with those blue overalls drawn up high under his arms.

'Where are they?'

'Weren't they in the kitchen closet?'

'No.'

We looked again, however, in the kitchen closet. We searched the shed thoroughly. The cat came in through her little door as we stood there and brushed around our feet. Mr Dix stooped and stroked her. Then he went quickly to the door, beside which her little entrance was arranged, unhooked it and stepped out. I was following him, but he motioned me back.

'None of my boarding-mistress's windows command us,' he said, 'but she might come to the back door.'

I watched him. He passed slowly around the little winding footpath which skirted the rear of our house and extended faintly through the grassy fields to the rear of Phoebe Dole's. He stopped, searched a clump of sweetbrier, went on to an old well and stopped there. The well had been dry many a year and was choked up with stones and rubbish. Some boards are laid over it, and a big stone or two to keep them in place.

Mr Dix, glancing across at Phoebe Dole's back door, went down on his knees, rolled the stones away then removed the boards and peered down the well. He stretched far over the brink and reached down. He made many efforts, then he got up and came to me and asked me to get for him an umbrella with a crooked handle or something that he could hook into clothing.

I brought my own umbrella, the silver handle of which formed an exact hook. He went back to the well, kneeled again, thrust in the umbrella and drew up, easily enough, what he had been fishing for. Then he came bringing it to me.

'Don't faint,' he said and took hold of my arm. I gasped when I saw what he had – my father's blue overalls all stained and splotched with blood!

I looked at them then at him.

'Don't faint,' he said again. 'We're on the right track. This is where the button came from – see, see!' He pointed to one of the straps of the overalls, and the button was gone. Some white thread clung to it.

Another black metal button was sewed on roughly with the same white thread that I found on the button in my box of clues.

'What does it mean?' I gasped out. My brain reeled.

'You shall know soon,' he said. He looked at his watch. Then he laid down the ghastly bundle he carried. 'It has puzzled you to know how the murderer went in and out and yet kept the doors locked, has it not?' he said.

'Yes.'

'Well, I am going out now. Hook that door after me.'

He went out, still carrying my umbrella. I hooked the door. Presently I saw the lid of the cat's door lifted, and his hand and arm thrust through. He curved his arm up towards the hook, but it came short by half a foot. Then he withdrew his arm, and thrust in my silver-handled umbrella. He reached the door hook easily enough with that.

Then he hooked it again. That was not so easy. He had to work a long time. Finally he accomplished it, unhooked the door again and came in.

'That was how!' I said.

'No, it was not,' he returned. 'No human being, fresh from such a deed, could have used such patience as that to fasten the door after him. Please hang your arm down by your side.'

I obeyed. He looked at my arm, then at his own.

'Have you a tape measure?' he asked.

I brought one out of my work-basket. He measured his arm, then mine and then the distance from the cat door to the hook.

'I have two tasks for you today and tomorrow,' he said. 'I shall come here very little. Find all your father's old letters and read them. Find a man or woman in this town whose arm is six inches longer than yours. Now I must go home, or my boarding-mistress will get curious.'

He went through the house to the front door, looked all ways to be sure no eyes were upon him, made three strides down the yard and was pacing soberly up the street with his cyclopædia under his arm.

I made myself a cup of coffee, then I went about obeying his instructions. I read old letters all the forenoon. I found packages in trunks in the garret; there were quantities in father's desk. I have selected several to submit to Mr Dix. One of them treats of an old episode in father's youth which must have years since ceased to interest him. It was concealed after his favourite fashion – tacked under the bottom of his desk. It was written forty years ago by Maria Woods, two years before my father's marriage – and it was a refusal of an offer of his hand. It was written in the stilted fashion of that day; it might have been copied from a 'Complete Letter-writer'.

My father must have loved Maria Woods as dearly as I love Henry to keep that letter so carefully all these years. I thought he cared for my mother. He seemed as fond of her as other men of their wives, though I did used to wonder if Henry and I would ever get to be quite so much accustomed to each other.

Maria Woods must have been as beautiful as an angel when she was a girl. Mother was not pretty; she was stout, too, and awkward, and I suppose people would have called her rather slow and dull. But she was a good woman and tried to do her duty.

Tuesday night – This evening was my first opportunity to obey the second of Mr Dix's orders. It seemed to me the best way to compare the average length of arms was to go to the prayer meeting. I could not go about the town with my tape measure and demand of people that they should hold out their arms. Nobody knows how I dreaded to go to the meeting, but I went, and I looked not at my neighbours' cold altered faces but at their arms.

I discovered what Mr Dix wished me to, but the discovery can avail nothing, and it is one he could have made himself. Phoebe Dole's arm is fully seven inches longer than mine. I never noticed it before, but she has an almost abnormally long arm. But why should Phoebe Dole have unhooked that door?

She made a prayer – a beautiful prayer. It comforted even me a little. She spoke of the tenderness of God in all the troubles of life and how it never failed us.

When we were all going out I heard several persons speak of Mr Dix and his Biblical Cyclopædia. They decided that he was a theological student, book-canvassing to defray the expenses of his education.

Maria Woods was not at the meeting. Several asked Phoebe how she was, and she replied, 'Not very well.'

It is very late. I thought Mr Dix might be over tonight, but he has not been here.

Wednesday – I can scarcely believe what I am about to write. Our investigations seem to point all to one person, and that person . . . It is incredible! I will not believe it.

Mr Dix came as before, at dawn. He reported, and I reported. I showed Maria Woods's letter. He said he had driven to Acton and found that the jeweller there had engraved the last date in the ring about six weeks ago.

'I don't want to seem rough, but your father was going to get married again,' said Mr Dix.

'I never knew him to go near any woman since mother died,' I protested.

'Nevertheless, he had made arrangements to be married,' persisted Mr Dix.

'Who was the woman?'

He pointed at the letter in my hand.

'Maria Woods!'

He nodded.

I stood looking at him, dazed. Such a possibility had never entered my head.

He produced an envelope from his pocket and took out a little card with blue and brown threads neatly wound upon it.

'Let me see those threads you found,' he said.

I got the box, and we compared them. He had a number of pieces of blue sewing-silk and brown woollen ravellings, and they matched mine exactly.

'Where did you find them?' I asked.

'In my boarding-mistress's piece-bag.'

I stared at him. 'What does it mean?' I gasped out.

'What do you think?'

'It is impossible!'

VI
The Revelation

Wednesday, continued – When Mr Dix thus suggested to me the absurd possibility that Phoebe Dole had committed the murder, he and I were sitting in the kitchen. He was near the table; he laid a sheet of paper upon it and began to write. The paper is before me.

'First,' said Mr Dix, and he wrote rapidly as he talked, 'whose arm is of such length that it might unlock a certain door of this house from the outside? Phoebe Dole's.

'Second, who had in her piece-bag bits of the same threads and ravellings found upon your parlour floor where she had not by your knowledge entered? Phoebe Dole.

'Third, who interested herself most strangely in your bloodstained green silk dress, even to dyeing it? Phoebe Dole.

'Fourth, who was caught in a lie while trying to force the guilt of the murder upon an innocent man? Phoebe Dole.'

Mr Dix looked at me. I had gathered myself together.

'That proves nothing,' I said. 'There is no motive in her case.'

'There is a motive.'

'What is it?'

'Maria Woods shall tell you this afternoon.'

He then wrote.

'Fifth, who was seen to throw a bundle down the old well in the rear of Martin Fairbanks's house at one o'clock in the morning? Phoebe Dole.'

'Was she . . . seen?' I gasped.

Mr Dix nodded. Then he wrote.

'Sixth, who had a strong motive, which had been in existence many years ago? Phoebe Dole.'

Mr Dix laid down his pen and looked at me again.

'Well, what have you to say?' he asked.

'It is impossible!'

'Why?'

'She is a woman.'

'A man could have fired that pistol, as she tried to do.'

'It would have taken a man's strength to kill with the kind of weapon that was used,' I said.

'No, it would not. No great strength is required for such a blow.'

'But she is a woman!'

'Crime has no sex.'

'But she is a good woman, a church member. I heard her pray yesterday afternoon. It is not in character.'

'It is not for you nor for me nor for any mortal intelligence to know what is or is not in character,' said Mr Dix.

He arose and went away. I could only stare at him in a half-dazed manner.

Maria Woods came this afternoon, taking advantage of Phoebe's absence on a dressmaking errand. Maria has aged ten years in the last few weeks. Her hair is white, her cheeks are fallen in, her pretty colour is gone.

'May I have the ring he gave me forty years ago?' she faltered. I gave it to her; she kissed it and sobbed like a child.

'Phoebe took it away from me before,' she said; 'but she shan't this time.'

Maria related with piteous sobs the story of her long subordination to Phoebe Dole. This sweet child-like woman had always been completely under the sway of the other's stronger nature. The subordination went back beyond my father's original proposal to her; she had, before he made love to her as a girl, promised Phoebe she would not marry; and it was Phoebe who, by representing to her that she was bound by this solemn promise, had led her to write a letter to my father declining his offer and sending back the ring.

'And, after all, we were going to get married if he had not died,' she said. 'He was going to give me this ring again, and he had had the other date put in. I should have been so happy!'

She stopped and stared at me with horror-stricken enquiry.

'What was Phoebe Dole doing in your back yard at one o'clock that night?' she cried.

'What do you mean?' I returned.

'I saw Phoebe come out of your back shed door at one o'clock that very night. She had a bundle in her arms. She went along the path about as far as the old well, then she stooped down and seemed to be working at something. When she got up she didn't have the bundle. I was watching at our back door. I thought I heard her go out a little while before and went downstairs and found that door unlocked. I went in quick and up to my chamber and into my bed when she started home across the fields. Pretty soon I heard her come in, then I heard the pump going. She slept downstairs; she went on to her bedroom. What was she doing in your back yard that night?'

'You must ask her,' said I. I felt my blood running cold.

'I've been afraid to,' moaned Maria Woods. 'She's been dreadful strange lately. I wish that book agent was going to stay at our house.'

Maria Woods went home in about an hour. I got a ribbon for her, and she has my poor father's ring concealed in her withered bosom. Again I cannot believe this.

Thursday – It is all over. Phoebe Dole has confessed! I do not know now in exactly what way Mr Dix brought it about, how he accused her of her crime. After breakfast I saw them coming across the fields. Phoebe came first, advancing with rapid strides like a man, Mr Dix followed and my father's poor old sweetheart tottered behind with her handkerchief at her eyes. Just as I noticed them, the front door bell rang. I found several people there, headed by the high sheriff. They crowded into the sitting-room just as Phoebe Dole came rushing in with Mr Dix and Maria Woods.

'I did it!' Phoebe cried out to me. 'I am found out, and I have made up my mind to confess. She was going to marry your father – I found it out. I stopped it once before. This time I knew I couldn't unless I killed him. She's lived with me in that house for over forty years. There are other ties as strong as the marriage one that are just as sacred. What right had he to take her away from me and break up my home?

'I overheard your father and Rufus Bennett having words. I thought folks would think he did it. I reasoned it all out. I had watched your cat go in that little door, I knew the shed door hooked, I knew how long my arm was. I thought I could undo it. I stole over here a little after midnight. I went all around the house to be sure nobody was awake. Out in the front yard I happened to think my shears were tied on my belt with a ribbon, and I untied them. I thought I put the ribbon in my pocket – it was a piece of yellow ribbon – but I suppose I didn't because they found it afterwards and thought it came off your young man's whip. I went around to the shed door, unhooked it and went in. The moon was light enough. I got out your father's overalls from the kitchen closet; I knew where they were. I went through the sitting-room to the parlour.

'In there I slipped off my dress and skirts and put on the overalls. I put a handkerchief over my face, leaving only my eyes exposed. I crept out then into the sitting-room. There I pulled off my shoes and went into the bedroom.

'Your father was fast asleep. It was such a hot night, the clothes were thrown back, and his chest was bare. The first thing I saw was that pistol on the stand beside his bed. I suppose he had had some fear of Rufus Bennett coming back after all. Suddenly I thought I'd better shoot him. It would be surer and quicker, and if you were aroused I knew that I could get away and everybody would suppose that he had shot himself.

'I took up the pistol and held it close to his head. I had never fired a pistol, but I knew how it was done. I pulled, but it would not go off. Your father stirred a little – I was mad with horror – I struck at his head with the pistol. He opened his eyes and cried out, then I dropped the pistol and took these' – Phoebe Dole pointed to the great shining shears hanging at her waist – 'for I am strong in my wrists. I only struck twice, over his heart.

'Then I went back into the sitting-room. I thought I heard a noise in the kitchen – I was full of terror then – and slipped into the sitting-room closet. I felt as if I were fainting and clutched the shelf to keep from falling.

'I felt that I must go upstairs to see if you were asleep, to be sure you had not waked up when your father cried out. I thought if you had I should have to do the same by you. I crept upstairs to your chamber. You seemed sound asleep, but, as I watched, you stirred a little, but instead of striking at you I slipped into your closet. I heard nothing more from you. I felt myself wet with blood. I caught something hanging in your closet, and wiped myself over with it. I knew by the feeling it was your green silk. You kept quiet, and I saw you were asleep, so I crept out of the closet and down the stairs, got my clothes and shoes and, out in the shed, took off the overalls and dressed myself. I rolled up the overalls and took a board away from the old well and threw them in as I went home. I thought if they were found it would be no clue to me. The handkerchief, which was not much stained, I put to soak that night and washed it out next morning before Maria was up. I washed my hands and arms carefully that night and also my shears.

'I expected Rufus Bennett would be accused of the murder and, maybe, hanged. I was prepared for that, but I did not like to think I had thrown suspicion upon you by staining your dress. I had nothing against you. I made up my mind I'd get hold of that dress – before anybody suspected you – and dye it black. I came in and got it, as you know. I was astonished not to see any more stains on it. I only found two or three little streaks that scarcely anybody would have noticed. I didn't know what to think. I suspected, of course, that you had found the stains and got them off, thinking they might bring suspicion upon you.

'I did not see how you could possibly suspect me in any case. I was glad when your young man was cleared. I had nothing against him. That is all I have to say.'

I think I must have fainted away then. I cannot describe the dreadful calmness with which that woman told this – that woman with the good face whom I had last heard praying like a saint in meeting. I believe in demoniacal possession after this.

When I came to, the neighbours were around me, putting camphor on my head and saying soothing things to me, and the old friendly faces had returned. But I wish I could forget!

They have taken Phoebe Dole away – I only know that. I cannot bear to talk any more about it when I think there must be a trial, and I must go!

Henry has been over this evening. I suppose we shall be happy after all when I have had a little time to get over this. He says I have nothing more to worry about. Mr Dix has gone home. I hope Henry and I may be able to repay his kindness some day.

A month later. I have just heard that Phoebe Dole has died in prison. This is my last entry. May God help all other innocent women in hard straits as He has helped me!

A HAND-TO-HAND STRUGGLE
from 'The Redhill Sisterhood' by C.L. Pirkis

C.L. Pirkis

THE REDHILL SISTERHOOD

The real lasting legacy of Catherine Louisa Pirkis (1839–1910) was not her writing but her work with animals. Along with her husband, Frederick, who had been an officer in the Royal Navy, she was active in the anti-vivisection movement and in 1891 the two set up the National Canine Defence League, which still exists today under the name Dogs Trust. Catherine and Frederick married in 1872, and he retired from the Navy in 1873 so that the two of them could work closely together on various humanitarian and animal projects. When Catherine died, at the end of September 1910, Frederick survived her by barely a week and the two were buried together at Kensal Green Cemetery in London.

Catherine was the daughter of Lewis Lyne the Comptroller-General of the Inland Revenue, and she had a comfortable upbringing. She turned to writing after her marriage and produced fourteen books, most of which look back to a bucolic past. But her first and last are of special interest. Her first, Disappeared from Her Home *(1877), published as by Mrs Fred E. Pirkis, was a mystery novel about the sudden disappearance of a young girl from a country home and the revelations that the search for her uncover. Her last, and also her best known, was* The Experiences of Loveday Brooke, Lady Detective *(1894), a collection of stories – including 'The Redhill Sisterhood', reprinted here – which had run in* The Ludgate *magazine the previous year. This was the first such series to feature a female detective to arise in the wake of the popularity of the Sherlock Homes stories, but Pirkis made Loveday Brooke very much her own woman and one not easily to be deceived.*

The Redhill Sisterhood

'THEY WANT YOU at Redhill, now,' said Mr Dyer, taking a packet of papers from one of his pigeon-holes. 'The idea seems to be gaining ground in manly quarters that in cases of mere suspicion, women detectives are more satisfactory than men, for they are less likely to attract attention. And this Redhill affair, so far as I can make out, is one of suspicion only.'

It was a dreary November morning. Every gas jet in the Lynch Court office was alight, and a yellow curtain of outside fog draped its narrow windows.

'Nevertheless, I suppose one can't afford to leave it uninvestigated at this season of the year with country-house robberies beginning in so many quarters,' said Miss Brooke.

'No, and the circumstances in this case certainly seem to point in the direction of the country-house burglar. Two days ago a somewhat curious application was made privately by a man giving the name of John Murray to Inspector Gunning of the Reigate police – Redhill, I must tell you, is in the Reigate police district. Murray stated that he had been a greengrocer somewhere in South London, had sold his business there and had, with the proceeds of the sale, bought two small houses in Redhill, intending to let the one and live in the other. These houses are situated in a blind alley known as Paved Court, a narrow turning leading off the London and Brighton coach road. Paved Court has been known to the sanitary authorities for the past ten years as a regular fever nest, and as the houses which Murray bought – numbers 7 and 8 – stand at the very end of the blind alley, with no chance of thorough ventilation, I dare say the man got them for next to nothing. He told the inspector that he had had great difficulty in procuring a tenant for the house he wished to let, number 8, and that consequently when, about three weeks back, a lady dressed as a nun made him an offer for it, he immediately closed with her. The lady gave her name simply as "Sister Monica", and stated that she was a member of an undenominational sisterhood that had recently been founded by a wealthy lady, who wished her name kept a secret. Sister Monica gave no references but instead paid a quarter's rent in advance, saying that she wished to take possession of the house immediately and open it as a home for crippled orphans.'

'Gave no references . . . home for cripples,' murmured Loveday, scribbling hard and fast in her notebook.

'Murray made no objection to this,' continued Mr Dyer, 'and, accordingly, the next day Sister Monica, accompanied by three other sisters and some sickly children, took possession of the house, which they furnished with the barest possible necessities from cheap shops in the neighbourhood. For a time, Murray said, he thought he had secured most desirable tenants, but during the last ten days suspicions as to their real character have entered his mind, and these suspicions he thought it his duty to communicate to the police. Among their possessions, it seems, these sisters number an old donkey and a tiny cart, and this they start daily on a sort of begging tour through the adjoining villages, bringing back every evening a perfect hoard of broken victuals and bundles of old garments. Now comes the extraordinary fact on which Murray bases his suspicions. He says, and Gunning verifies his statement, that, in whatever direction those sisters turn the wheels of their donkey cart, burglaries or attempts at burglaries are sure to follow. A week ago they went along towards Horley where, at an outlying house, they received much kindness from a wealthy gentleman. That very night an attempt was made to break into that gentleman's house – an attempt, however, that was happily frustrated by the barking of the house dog. And so on in other instances that I need not go into. Murray suggests that it might be as well to have the daily movements of these sisters closely watched and that extra vigilance should be exercised by the police in the districts that have had the honour of a morning call from them. Gunning coincides with this idea and so has sent to me to secure your services.'

Loveday closed her notebook. 'I suppose Gunning will meet me somewhere and tell me where I'm to take up my quarters?' she said.

'Yes, he will get into your carriage at Merstham – the station before Redhill – if you will put your hand out of the window with the morning paper in it. By the way, he takes it for granted that you will save the eleven-five train from Victoria. Murray, it seems, has been good enough to place his little house at the disposal of the police, but Gunning does not think espionage could be so well carried on there as from other quarters. The presence of a stranger in an alley of that sort is bound to attract attention, so he has hired a room for you in a draper's shop that immediately faces the head of the court. There is a private door to this shop of which you will have the key and can let yourself in and out as you please. You are supposed to be a nursery governess on the look-out for a situation, and Gunning will keep you supplied with letters to give colour to the idea. He suggests that you need only occupy the room during the day; at night you will find far more comfortable quarters at Laker's Hotel just outside the town.'

This was about the sum total of the instructions that Mr Dyer had to give.

The eleven-five train from Victoria that carried Loveday to her work among the Surrey Hills did not get clear of the London fog until well away on the other side of Purley. When the train halted at Merstham, in response to her signal a tall, soldier-like individual made for her carriage and, jumping in, took the seat facing her. He introduced himself to her as Inspector Gunning, recalled to her memory a former occasion on which they had met and then, naturally enough, turned the talk upon the present suspicious circumstances they were bent upon investigating.

'It won't do for you and me to be seen together,' he said. 'Of course, I am known for miles around, and anyone seen in my company will be at once set down as my coadjutor and spied upon accordingly. I walked from Redhill to Merstham on purpose to avoid recognition on the platform at Redhill and halfway here, to my great annoyance, found that I was being followed by a man in a workman's dress and carrying a basket of tools. I doubled, however, and gave him the slip, taking a short cut down a lane which, if he had been living in the place, he would have known as well as I did. By Jove!' – this was added with a sudden start – 'There is the fellow, I declare. He has weathered me after all and has no doubt taken good stock of us both with the train going at this snail's pace. It was unfortunate that your face should have been turned towards that window, Miss Brooke.'

'My veil is something of a disguise, and I will put on another cloak before he has a chance of seeing me again,' said Loveday.

All she had seen in the brief glimpse that the train had allowed was a tall, powerfully built man walking along a siding of the line. His cap was drawn low over his eyes, and in his hand he carried a workman's basket.

Gunning seemed much annoyed at the circumstance. 'Instead of landing at Redhill,' he said, 'we'll go on to Three Bridges and wait there for a Brighton train to bring us back. That will enable you to get to your room somewhere between the lights. I don't want to have you spotted before you've so much as started your work.'

Then they went back to their discussion of the Redhill sisterhood.

'They call themselves "undenominational", whatever that means,' said Gunning. 'They say they are connected with no religious sect whatever; they attend sometimes one place of worship, sometimes another, sometimes none at all. They refuse to give up the name of the founder of their order, and really no one has any right to demand it of them, for, as no doubt you see, up to the present moment the case is one of mere suspicion, and it may be a pure coincidence that attempts at burglary have followed their footsteps in this neighbourhood. By the way, I have heard of a man's face being enough to hang him, but until I saw Sister Monica's I never saw a woman's face that could perform the same kind office for her. Of all the lowest criminal types of faces I have ever seen I think hers is about the lowest and most repulsive.'

After the sisters, they passed in review the chief families resident in the neighbourhood.

'This,' said Gunning, unfolding a paper, 'is a map I have specially drawn up for you – it takes in the district for ten miles around Redhill, and every country house of any importance is marked in red ink. Here, in addition, is an index to those houses with special notes of my own to every one.'

Loveday studied the map for a minute or so then turned her attention to the index.

'Those four houses you've marked, I see, are those that have been already attempted. I don't think I'll run them through, but I'll mark them "doubtful"; you see, the gang – for, of course, it is a gang – might follow our reasoning on the matter and look upon those houses as our weak point. Here's one I'll run through, "house empty during winter months" – that means plate and jewellery sent to the bankers. Oh! and this one may as well be crossed off, "father and four sons all athletes and sportsmen" – that means firearms always handy. I don't think burglars will be likely to trouble them. Ah! now we come to something! Here's a house to be marked "tempting" in a burglar's list. "Wootton Hall, lately changed hands and rebuilt with complicated passages and corridors. Splendid family plate in daily use and left entirely to the care of the butler." I wonder, does the master of that house trust to his "complicated passages" to preserve his plate for him? A dismissed dishonest servant would supply a dozen maps of the place for half a sovereign. What do these initials "EL" against the next house in the list, North Cape, stand for?'

'Electric lighted. I think you might almost cross that house off also. I consider electric lighting one of the greatest safeguards against burglars that a man can give his house.'

'Yes, if he doesn't rely exclusively upon it. It might be a nasty trap under certain circumstances. I see this gentleman also has magnificent presentation and other plate.'

'Yes. Mr Jameson is a wealthy man and very popular in the neighbourhood. His cups and epergnes are worth looking at.'

'Is it the only house in the district that is lighted with electricity?'

'Yes, and, begging your pardon, Miss Brooke, I only wish it were not so. If electric lighting were generally in vogue it would save the police a lot of trouble on these dark winter nights.'

'The burglars would find some way of meeting such a condition of things, depend upon it. They have reached a very high development in these days. They no longer stalk about as they did fifty years ago with blunderbuss and bludgeon. They plot, plan, contrive and bring imagination and artistic resource to their aid. By the way, it often occurs to me that the popular detective stories – for which there seems to be a large demand at the present day – must be, at times, uncommonly useful to the criminal classes.'

At Three Bridges they had to wait so long for a return train that it was nearly dark when Loveday got back to Redhill. Mr Gunning did not accompany her thither, having alighted at a previous station. Loveday had arranged for her portmanteau to be sent direct to Laker's Hotel where she had engaged a room by telegram from Victoria Station. So, unburthened by luggage, she slipped quietly out of the Redhill Station and made her way straight for the draper's shop in the London Road. She had no difficulty in finding it, thanks to the minute directions given her by the inspector.

Street lamps were being lighted in the sleepy little town as she went along, and as she turned into the London Road shopkeepers were lighting up their windows on both sides of the way. A few yards down this road a dark patch between the lighted shops showed her where Paved Court led off from the thoroughfare. A side door of one of the shops that stood at the corner of the court seemed to offer a post of observation whence she could see without being seen, and here Loveday, shrinking into the shadows, ensconced herself in order to take stock of the little alley and its inhabitants. She found it much as it had been described to her – a collection of four-roomed houses of which more than half were unlet. Numbers 7 and 8 at the head of the court presented a slightly less neglected appearance than the other tenements. Number 7 stood in total darkness, but in the upper window of number 8 there showed what seemed to be a night-light burning, so Loveday conjectured that this possibly was the room set apart as a dormitory for the little cripples.

While she stood thus surveying the home of the suspected sisterhood, the sisters themselves – two, at least, of them – came into view with their donkey cart and their cripples on the main road. It was an odd little cortège. One sister, habited in a nun's dress of dark-blue serge, led the donkey by the bridle; another sister, similarly attired, walked alongside the low cart in which were seated two sickly looking children. They were evidently returning from one of their long country circuits, and, unless they had lost their way and been belated, it certainly seemed a late hour for the sickly little cripples to be abroad.

As they passed under the gas lamp at the corner of the court Loveday caught a glimpse of the faces of the sisters. It was easy, with Inspector Gunning's description before her mind, to identify the older and taller woman as Sister Monica, and a more coarse-featured and generally repellent face Loveday admitted to herself she had never before seen. In striking contrast to this forbidding countenance was that of the younger sister. Loveday could only catch a brief passing view of it, but that one brief view was enough to impress it on her memory as of unusual sadness and beauty. As the donkey stopped at the corner of the court Loveday heard this sad-looking young woman addressed as 'Sister Anna' by one of the cripples, who asked plaintively when they were going to have something to eat.

'Now, at once,' said Sister Anna, lifting the little one, as it seemed to Loveday, tenderly out of the cart and carrying him on her shoulder down the court to the door of number 8, which opened to them at their approach. The other sister did the same with the other child, then both sisters returned, unloaded the cart of sundry bundles and baskets and, this done, led off the old donkey and trap down the road, possibly to a neighbouring costermonger's stables.

A man coming along on a bicycle exchanged a word of greeting with the sisters as they passed then swung himself off his machine at the corner of the court and walked it along the paved way to the door of number 7. This he opened with a key and then, pushing the machine before him, entered the house.

Loveday took it for granted that this man must be the John Murray of whom she had heard. She had closely scrutinized him as he had passed her and had seen that he was a dark, well-featured man of about fifty years of age.

She congratulated herself on her good fortune in having seen so much in such a brief space of time, and coming forth from her sheltered corner turned her steps in the direction of the draper's shop on the other side of the road.

It was easy to find it. 'Golightly' was the singular name that figured above the shop front in which were displayed a variety of goods calculated to meet the wants of servants and the poorer classes generally. A tall, powerfully built man appeared to be looking in at this window. Loveday's foot was on the doorstep of the draper's private entrance, her hand on the door knocker, when this individual, suddenly turning, convinced her of his identity with the journeyman workman who had so disturbed Mr Gunning's equanimity. It was true he wore a bowler instead of a journeyman's cap, and he no longer carried a basket of tools, but there was no possibility for anyone with so good an eye for an outline as Loveday possessed not to recognize the carriage of the head and shoulders as that of the man she had seen walking along the railway siding. He gave her no time to make minute observation of his appearance but turned quickly away and disappeared down a by-street.

Loveday's work seemed to bristle with difficulties now. Here was she, as it were, unearthed in her own ambush, for there could be but little doubt that during the whole time she had stood watching those sisters that man, from a safe vantage point, had been watching her.

She found Mrs Golightly a civil and obliging person. She showed Loveday to her room above the shop, brought her the letters which Inspector Gunning had been careful to have posted to her during the day. Then she supplied her with pen and ink and, in response to Loveday's request, with some strong coffee that she said, with a little attempt at a joke, would 'keep a dormouse awake all through the winter without winking'.

While the obliging landlady busied herself about the room, Loveday had a few questions to ask about the sisterhood who lived down the court opposite. On this head, however, Mrs Golightly could tell her no more than she already knew, beyond the fact that they started every morning on their rounds at eleven o'clock punctually and that before that hour they were never to be seen outside their door.

Loveday's watch that night was to be a fruitless one. Though she sat with her lamp turned out and safely screened from observation until close upon midnight, with eyes fixed upon numbers 7 and 8 Paved Court, not so much as a door opening or shutting at either house rewarded her vigil. The lights flitted from the lower to the upper floors in both houses and then disappeared somewhere between nine and ten in the evening, and, after that, not a sign of life did either tenement show.

And all through the long hours of that watch, backwards and forwards there seemed to flit before her mind's eye, as if in some sort it were fixed upon its retina, the sweet, sad face of Sister Anna.

Why it was this face should so haunt her, she found it hard to say.

'It has a mournful past and a mournful future written upon it as a hopeless whole,' she said to herself. 'It is the face of an Andromeda! "Here am I," it seems to say, "tied to my stake, helpless and hopeless."'

The church clocks were sounding the midnight hour as Loveday made her way through the dark streets to her hotel outside the town. As she passed under the railway arch that ended in the open country road the echo of not-very-distant footsteps caught her ear. When she stopped they stopped, when she went on they went on, and she knew that once more she was being followed and watched, though the darkness of the arch prevented her seeing even the shadow of the man who was thus dogging her steps.

The next morning broke keen and frosty. Loveday studied her map and her country-house index over a seven o'clock breakfast and then set off for a brisk walk along the country road. No doubt in London the streets were walled in and roofed with yellow fog; here, however, bright sunshine played in and out of the bare tree boughs and leafless hedges on to a thousand frost spangles, turning the prosaic macadamized road into a gangway fit for Queen Titania herself and her fairy train.

Loveday turned her back on the town and set herself to follow the road as it wound away over the hill in the direction of a village called Northfield. Early as she was, she was not to have that road to herself. A team of strong horses trudged by on their way to their work in the fuller's-earth pits. A young fellow on a bicycle flashed past at a tremendous pace, considering the upward slant of the road. He looked hard at her as he passed then slackened pace, dismounted and awaited her coming on the brow of the hill.

'Good-morning, Miss Brooke,' he said, lifting his cap as she came alongside of him. 'May I have five minutes' talk with you?'

The young man who thus accosted her had not the appearance of a gentleman. He was a handsome, bright-faced young fellow of about two-and-twenty and was dressed in ordinary cyclists' dress; his cap was pushed back from his brow over thick, curly, fair hair, and Loveday, as she looked at him, could not repress the thought of how well he would look at the head of a troop of cavalry, giving the order to charge the enemy.

He led his machine to the side of the footpath.

'You have the advantage of me,' said Loveday. 'I haven't the remotest notion who you are.'

'No,' he said, 'although I know you, you cannot possibly know me. I am a north-countryman, and I was present, about a month ago, at the trial of old Mr Craven of Troyte's Hill – in fact, I acted as reporter for one of the local papers. I watched your face so closely as you gave your evidence that I should know it anywhere among a thousand.'

'And your name is . . . ?'

'George White, of Grenfell. My father is part-proprietor of one of the Newcastle papers. I am a bit of a literary man myself and sometimes figure as a reporter, sometimes as leader writer to that paper.' Here he gave a glance towards his side pocket, from which protruded a small volume of Tennyson's poems.

The facts he had stated did not seem to invite comment, and Loveday ejaculated merely, 'Indeed!'

The young man went back to the subject that was evidently filling his thoughts. 'I have special reasons for being glad to have met you this morning, Miss Brooke,' he went on, making his footsteps keep pace with hers. 'I am in great trouble, and I believe you are the only person in the whole world who can help me out of that trouble.'

'I am rather doubtful as to my power of helping anyone out of trouble,' said Loveday. 'So far as my experience goes, our troubles are as much a part of ourselves as our skins are of our bodies.'

'Ah, but not such trouble as mine,' said White eagerly. He broke off for a moment, then, with a sudden rush of words, told her what that trouble was. For the past year he had been engaged to be married to a young girl, who, until quite recently, had been fulfilling the duties of a nursery governess in a large house in the neighbourhood of Redhill.

'Will you kindly give me the name of that house?' interrupted Loveday.

'Certainly. Wootton Hall the place is called, and Annie Lee is my sweetheart's name. I don't care who knows it!' He threw his head back as he said this, as if he would be delighted to announce the fact to the whole world. 'Annie's mother,' he went on, 'died when she was a baby, and we both thought her father was dead also when suddenly, about a fortnight ago, it came to her knowledge that instead of being dead he was serving his time at Portland for some offence committed years ago.'

'Do you know how this came to Annie's knowledge?'

'Not the least in the world. I only know that I suddenly got a letter from her announcing the fact and, at the same time, breaking off her engagement with me. I tore the letter into a thousand pieces and wrote back saying I would not allow the engagement to be broken off but would marry her tomorrow if she would have me. To this letter she did not reply. There came instead a few lines from Mrs Copeland, the lady at Wootton Hall, saying that Annie had thrown up her engagement and joined some sisterhood and that she, Mrs Copeland, had pledged her word to Annie to reveal to no one the name and whereabouts of that sisterhood.'

'And I suppose you imagine I am able to do what Mrs Copeland is pledged not to do?'

'That's just it, Miss Brooke,' cried the young man enthusiastically. 'You do such wonderful things; everyone knows you do. It seems as if, when anything is wanted to be found out, you just walk into a place, look round you and, in a moment, everything becomes clear as noonday.'

'I can't quite lay claim to such wonderful powers as that. As it happens, however, in the present instance no particular skill is needed to find out what you wish to know, for I fancy I have already come upon the traces of Miss Annie Lee.'

'Miss Brooke!'

'Of course, I cannot say for certain, but it is a matter you can easily settle for yourself – settle, too, in a way that will confer a great obligation on me.'

'I shall be only too delighted to be of any . . . the slightest service to you,' cried White, enthusiastically as before.

'Thank you. I will explain. I came down here specially to watch the movements of a certain sisterhood who have somehow aroused the suspicions of the police. Well, I find that instead of being able to do this, I am myself so closely watched – possibly by confederates of these sisters – that unless I can do my work by deputy I may as well go back to town at once.'

'Ah! I see. You want me to be that deputy.'

'Precisely. I want you to go to the room in Redhill that I have hired, take your place at the window – screened, of course, from observation – at which I ought to be seated, watch as closely as possible the movements of these sisters and report them to me at the hotel where I shall remain shut in from morning until night. It is the only way in which I can throw my persistent spies off the scent. Now, in doing this for me you will be also doing yourself a good turn, for I have little doubt but what under the blue serge hood of one of the sisters you will discover the pretty face of Miss Annie Lee.'

As they had talked they had walked and now stood on the top of the hill at the head of the one little street that constituted the whole of the village of Northfield.

On their left hand stood the village schools and the master's house; nearly facing these, on the opposite side of the road beneath a clump of elms, stood the village pound. Beyond this pound, on either side of the way, were two rows of small cottages with tiny squares of garden in front, and in the midst of these small cottages a swinging sign beneath a lamp announced a 'Postal and Telegraph Office'.

'Now that we have come into the land of habitations again,' said Loveday, 'it will be best for us to part. It will not do for you and me to be seen together, or my spies will be transferring their attentions from me to you, and I shall have to find another deputy. You had better start on your bicycle for Redhill at once, and I will walk back at leisurely speed. Come to me at my hotel without fail at one o'clock and report proceedings. I do not say anything definite about remuneration, but I assure you, if you carry out my instructions to the letter your services will be amply rewarded by me and by my employers.'

There were yet a few more details to arrange. White had been, he said, only a day and night in the neighbourhood, and special directions as to the locality had to be given to him. Loveday advised him not to attract attention by going to the draper's private door but to enter the shop as if he were a customer and then explain matters to Mrs Golightly, who, no doubt, would be in her place behind the counter. Tell her he was the brother of the Miss Smith who had hired her room and ask permission to go through the shop to that room, as he had been commissioned by his sister to read and answer any letters that might have arrived there for her.

'Show her the key of the side door – here it is,' said Loveday, 'it will be your credentials – and tell her you did not like to make use of it without acquainting her with the fact.'

The young man took the key, endeavoured to put it in his waistcoat pocket, found the space there occupied and so transferred it to the keeping of a side pocket in his tunic.

All this time Loveday stood watching him.

'You have a capital machine there,' she said, as the young man mounted his bicycle once more, 'and I hope you will turn it to account in following the movements of these sisters about the neighbourhood. I feel confident you will have something definite to tell me when you bring me your first report at one o'clock.'

White once more broke into a profusion of thanks and then, lifting his cap to the lady, started his machine at a fairly good pace.

Loveday watched him out of sight down the slope of the hill

then, instead of following him as she had said she would 'at a leisurely pace', she turned her steps in the opposite direction along the village street.

It was an altogether ideal country village. Neatly dressed chubby-faced children, now on their way to the schools, dropped quaint little curtsies or tugged at curly locks as Loveday passed; every cottage looked the picture of cleanliness and trimness, and, though so late in the year, the gardens were full of late-flowering chrysanthemums and early-flowering Christmas roses.

At the end of the village Loveday came suddenly into view of a large, handsome, red-brick mansion. It presented a wide frontage to the road from which it lay back amid extensive pleasure grounds. On the right hand, and a little in the rear of the house, stood what seemed to be large and commodious stables, and immediately adjoining these stables was a low-built, red-brick shed that had evidently been recently erected.

That low-built, red-brick shed excited Loveday's curiosity.

'Is this house called North Cape?' she asked of a man who chanced at that moment to be passing with a pickaxe and shovel.

The man answered in the affirmative, and Loveday then asked another question. Could he tell her what was that small shed so close to the house. It looked like a glorified cow house; now what could be its use?

The man's face lighted up as if it were a subject on which he liked to be questioned. He explained that that small shed was the engine-house where the electricity that lighted North Cape was made and stored. Then he dwelt with pride upon the fact, as if he held a personal interest in it, that North Cape was the only house, far or near, that was thus lighted.

'I suppose the wires are carried underground to the house,' said Loveday, looking in vain for signs of them anywhere.

The man was delighted to go into details on the matter. He had helped to lay those wires, he said. They were two in number, one for supply and one for return, and were laid three feet below ground in boxes filled with pitch. These wires were switched on to jars in the engine-house where the electricity was stored and, after passing underground, entered the family mansion under its flooring at its western end.

Loveday listened attentively to these details and then took a minute and leisurely survey of the house and its surroundings. This done, she retraced her steps through the village, pausing, however, at the 'Postal and Telegraph Office' to dispatch a telegram to Inspector Gunning.

It was one to send the inspector to his cipher-book. It ran as follows:

'Rely solely on chemist and coal-merchant throughout the day. – LB'

After this she quickened her pace, and in something over three-quarters of an hour was back again at her hotel.

There she found more of life stirring than when she had quitted it in the early morning. There was to be a meeting of the Surrey Stags about a couple of miles off, and a good many hunting men were hanging about the entrance to the house, discussing the chances of sport after last night's frost. Loveday made her way through the throng in leisurely fashion, and not a man who did not have keen scrutiny from her sharp eyes. No, there was no cause for suspicion there. They were evidently one and all just what they seemed to be: loud-voiced, hard-riding men, bent on a day's sport. But – and here Loveday's eyes travelled beyond the hotel courtyard to the other side of the road – who was that man with a bill-hook hacking at the hedge there, a thin-featured, round-shouldered old fellow with a bent-about hat? It might be as well not to take it too rashly for granted that her spies had withdrawn and had left her free to do her work in her own fashion.

She went upstairs to her room. It was situated on the first floor in the front of the house and consequently commanded a good view of the high road. She stood well back from the window and, at an angle whence she could see and not be seen, took a long, steady survey of the hedger. And the longer she looked the more convinced she was that the man's real work was something other than the bill-hook seemed to imply. He worked, so to speak, with his head over his shoulder, and when Loveday supplemented her eyesight with a strong field-glass she could see more than one stealthy glance shot from beneath his bent-about hat in the direction of her window.

There could be little doubt about it: her movements were to be as closely watched today as they had been yesterday. Now it was of first importance that she should communicate with Inspector Gunning in the course of the afternoon. The question to solve was how it was to be done?

To all appearance Loveday answered the question in extraordinary fashion. She pulled up her blind, she drew back her curtain and seated herself in full view at a small table in the window recess. Then she took a pocket inkstand from her pocket, a packet of correspondence cards from her letter-case and, with rapid pen, set to work on them.

About an hour and a half afterwards White, coming in according to his promise to report proceedings, found her still seated at the window – not, however, with writing materials before her but with needle and thread in her hand with which she was mending her gloves.

'I return to town by the first train tomorrow morning,' she said as he entered, 'and I find these wretched things want no end of stitches. Now for your report.'

White appeared to be in an elated frame of mind. 'I've seen her!' he cried. 'My Annie, they've got her, those confounded sisters. But they shan't keep her – no, not if I have to pull the house down about their ears to get her out.'

'Well, now you know where she is you can take your time about getting her out,' said Loveday. 'I hope, however, you haven't broken faith with me and betrayed yourself by trying to speak with her, because, if so, I shall have to look out for another deputy.'

'Honour, Miss Brooke!' answered White indignantly. 'I stuck to my duty, though it cost me something to see her hanging over those kids and tucking them into the cart and never say a word to her, never so much as wave my hand.'

'Did she go out with the donkey cart today?'

'No, she only tucked the kids into the cart with a blanket and then went back to the house. Two old sisters, ugly as sin, went out with them. I watched them from the window, jolt, jolt, jolt, around the corner, out of sight, and then I whipped down the stairs and on to my machine and was after them in a trice and managed to keep them well in sight for over an hour and a half.'

'And their destination today was?'

'Wootton Hall.'

'Ah, just as I expected.'

'Just as you expected?' echoed White.

'I forgot. You do not know the nature of the suspicions that are attached to this sisterhood and the reasons I have for thinking that Wootton Hall, at this season of the year, might have an especial attraction for them.'

White continued staring at her. 'Miss Brooke,' he said presently in an altered tone, 'whatever suspicions may attach to the sisterhood, I'll stake my life on it, my Annie has had no share in any wickedness of any sort.'

'Oh, quite so. It is most likely that your Annie has, in some way, been inveigled into joining these sisters – has been taken possession of by them, in fact, just as they have taken possession of the little cripples.'

'That's it!' he cried excitedly. 'That was the idea that occurred to me when you spoke to me on the hill about them, otherwise you may be sure –'

'Did they get relief of any sort at the hall?' interrupted Loveday.

'Yes. One of the two ugly old women stopped outside the lodge gates with the donkey cart, and the other beauty went up to the house alone. She stayed there, I should think, about a quarter of an hour, and when she came back was followed by a servant carrying a bundle and a basket.'

'Ah! I've no doubt they brought away with them something else besides old garments and broken victuals.'

White stood in front of her, fixing a hard, steady gaze upon her.

'Miss Brooke,' he said presently in a voice that matched the look on his face, 'what do you suppose was the real object of these women in going to Wootton Hall this morning?'

'Mr White, if I wished to help a gang of thieves break into Wootton

Hall tonight, don't you think I should be greatly interested in procuring from them the information that the master of the house was away from home; that two of the menservants who slept in the house had recently been dismissed and their places had not yet been filled; also that the dogs were never unchained at night and that their kennels were at the side of the house at which the butler's pantry is not situated? These are particulars I have gathered in this house without stirring from my chair, and I am satisfied that they are likely to be true. At the same time, if I were a professed burglar I should not be content with information that was likely to be true but would be careful to procure such that was certain to be true and so would set accomplices to work at the fountain head. Now do you understand?'

White folded his arms and looked down on her.

'What are you going to do?' he asked in short, brusque tones.

Loveday looked him full in the face. 'Communicate with the police immediately,' she answered. 'And I should feel greatly obliged if you will at once take a note from me to Inspector Gunning at Reigate.'

'And what becomes of Annie?'

'I don't think you need have any anxiety on that head. I've no doubt that when the circumstances of her admission to the sisterhood are investigated it will be proved that she has been as much deceived and imposed upon as the man John Murray who so foolishly let his house to these women. Remember, Annie has Mrs Copeland's good word to support her integrity.'

White stood silent for a while.

'What sort of a note do you wish me to take to the inspector?' he presently asked.

'You shall read it as I write it, if you like,' answered Loveday. She took a correspondence card from her letter case, and, with an indelible pencil, wrote as follows: 'Wootton Hall is threatened tonight – concentrate attention there. LB'

White read the words as she wrote them with a curious expression passing over his handsome features.

'Yes,' he said, curtly as before. 'I'll deliver that, I give you my word, but I'll bring back no answer to you. I'll do no more spying for you – it's a trade that doesn't suit me. There's a straightforward way of doing straightforward work, and I'll take that way – no other – to get my Annie out of that den.'

He took the note, which she sealed and handed to him, and strode out of the room.

Loveday, from the window, watched him mount his bicycle. Was it her fancy, or did there pass a swift, furtive glance of recognition between him and the hedger on the other side of the way as he rode out of the courtyard?

Loveday seemed determined to make that hedger's work easy for him. The short winter's day was closing in now, and her room must consequently have been growing dim to outside observation. She lighted the gas chandelier which hung from the ceiling and, still with blinds and curtains undrawn, took her old place at the window, spread writing materials before her and commenced a long and elaborate report to her chief at Lynch Court.

About half an hour afterwards, as she threw a casual glance across the road, she saw that the hedger had disappeared but that two ill-looking tramps sat munching bread and cheese under the hedge to which his bill-hook had done so little service. Evidently the intention was, one way or another, not to lose sight of her so long as she remained in Redhill.

Meantime, White had delivered Loveday's note to the inspector at Reigate and had disappeared on his bicycle once more.

Gunning read it without a change of expression. Then he crossed the room to the fireplace and held the card as close to the bars as he could without scorching it.

'I had a telegram from her this morning,' he explained to his confidential man, 'telling me to rely upon chemicals and coals throughout the day, and that, of course, meant that she would write to me in invisible ink. No doubt this message about Wootton Hall means nothing . . .'

He broke off abruptly, exclaiming, 'Eh! what's this!' as, having withdrawn the card from the fire, Loveday's real message stood out in bold, clear characters between the lines of the false one.

Thus it ran:

North Cape will be attacked tonight – a desperate gang – be prepared for a struggle. Above all, guard the electrical engine-house. On no account attempt to communicate with me; I am so closely watched that any endeavour to do so may frustrate your chance of trapping the scoundrels. LB

That night when the moon went down behind Reigate Hill an exciting scene was enacted at North Cape. The *Surrey Gazette*, in its issue the following day, gave the subjoined account of it under the heading 'Desperate encounter with burglars'.

Last night North Cape, the residence of Mr Jameson, was the scene of an affray between the police and a desperate gang of burglars. North Cape is lighted throughout with electricity, and the burglars, four in number, divided in half – two being told to enter and rob the house, and two to remain at the engine-shed where the electricity is stored, so that, at a given signal, should need arise, the wires might be unswitched, the inmates of the house thrown into sudden darkness and confusion and the escape of the marauders thereby facilitated. Mr Jameson, however, had received timely warning from the police of the intended attack, and he, with his two sons, all well armed, sat in darkness in the inner hall awaiting the coming of the thieves. The police were stationed some in the stables, some in outbuildings nearer to the house and others in more distant parts of the grounds. The burglars effected their entrance by means of a ladder placed to a window of the servants' staircase, which leads straight down to the butler's pantry and to the safe where the silver is kept. The fellows, however, had no sooner got into the house than the police, issuing from their hiding-place outside, mounted the ladder after them and thus cut off their retreat. Mr Jameson and his two sons at the same moment attacked them in front, and thus overwhelmed by numbers the scoundrels were easily secured. It was at the engine-house outside that the sharpest struggle took place. The thieves had forced open the door of this engine-shed with their jemmies immediately on their arrival under the very eyes of the police who lay in ambush in the stables, and when one of the men, captured in the house, contrived to sound an alarm on his whistle, these outside watchers made a rush for the electrical jars in order to unswitch the wires. Upon this the police closed upon them, and a hand-to-hand struggle followed, and if it had not been for the timely assistance of Mr Jameson and his sons, who had fortunately conjectured that their presence here might be useful, it is more than likely that one of the burglars, a powerfully built man, would have escaped.

The names of the captured men are John Murray, Arthur and George Lee (father and son) and a man with so many aliases that it is difficult to know which is his real name. The whole thing had been most cunningly and carefully planned. The elder Lee, lately released from penal servitude for a similar offence, appears to have been prime mover in the affair. This man had, it seems, a son and a daughter who, through the kindness of friends, had been fairly well placed in life: the son at an electrical engineers' in London; the daughter as nursery governess at Wootton Hall. Directly this man was released from Portland he seems to have found out his children and done his best to ruin them both. He was constantly at Wootton Hall endeavouring to induce his daughter to act as an accomplice to a robbery of the house. This so worried the girl that she threw up her situation and joined a sisterhood that had recently been established in the neighbourhood. Upon this, Lee's thoughts turned in another direction. He induced his son, who had saved a little money, to throw up his work in London and join him in his disreputable career. The boy is a handsome young fellow but appears to have in him the makings of a first-class criminal. In his work as an electrical engineer he had made the acquaintance of the man John Murray, who, it is said, has been rapidly going downhill of late. Murray was the owner of the house rented by the sisterhood that Miss Lee had joined, and the idea evidently struck the brains of these three scoundrels that this sisterhood, whose antecedents were a little mysterious, might be utilized to draw off the attention of the police from themselves and from the especial house in the neighbourhood that they had planned to attack. With this end in view, Murray made an application to the police to have the sisters watched, and, still further to give colour to the suspicions he had endeavoured to set afloat concerning them, he and his confederates made feeble attempts at burglary upon the houses at which the sisters had called begging for scraps. It is a matter for congratulation that the plot, from beginning to end, has been thus successfully unearthed, and it is felt on all sides that great credit is due to Inspector Gunning and his skilled coadjutors for the vigilance and promptitude they have displayed throughout the affair.

Loveday read aloud this report with her feet on the fender of the Lynch Court office.

'Accurate, as far as it goes,' she said, as she laid down the paper.

'But we want to know a little more,' said Mr Dyer. 'In the first place, I would like to know what it was that diverted your suspicions from the unfortunate sisters?'

'The way in which they handled the children,' answered Loveday promptly. 'I have seen female criminals of all kinds handling children, and I have noticed that although they may occasionally – even this is rare – treat them with a certain rough sort of kindness, of tenderness they are utterly incapable. Now Sister Monica, I must admit, is not pleasant to look at; at the same time, there was something absolutely beautiful in the way in which she lifted the little cripple out of the cart, put his tiny thin hand around her neck and carried him into the house. By the way, I would like to ask some rapid physiognomist how he would account for Sister Monica's repulsiveness of feature as contrasted with young Lee's undoubted good looks – heredity, in this case, throws no light on the matter.'

'Another question,' said Mr Dyer, not paying much heed to Loveday's digression. 'How was it you transferred your suspicions to John Murray?'

'I did not do so immediately, although at the very first it had struck me as odd that he should be so anxious to do the work of the police for them. The chief thing I noticed concerning Murray, on the first and only occasion on which I saw him, was that he had had an accident with his bicycle, for in the right-hand corner of his lamp-glass there was a tiny star, and the lamp itself had a dent on the same side, had also lost its hook and was fastened to the machine by a bit of electric fuse. The next morning as I was walking up the hill towards Northfield I was accosted by a young man mounted on that self-same bicycle – not a doubt of it: star in glass, dent, fuse, all three.'

'Ah, that sounded an important keynote and led you to connect Murray and the younger Lee immediately.'

'It did, and, of course, also at once gave the lie to his statement that he was a stranger in the place and confirmed my opinion that there was nothing of the north-countryman in his accent. Other details in his manner and appearance gave rise to other suspicions. For instance, he called himself a press reporter by profession, and his hands were coarse and grimy as only a mechanic's could be. He said he was a bit of a literary man, but the Tennyson that showed so obtrusively from his pocket was new and in parts uncut and totally unlike the well-thumbed volume of the literary student. Finally, when he tried and failed to put my latch-key into his waistcoat pocket, I saw the reason lay in the fact that the pocket was already occupied by a soft coil of electric fuse, the end of which protruded. Now, an electric fuse is what an electrical engineer might almost unconsciously carry about with him, it is so essential a part of his working tools, but it is a thing that a literary man or a press reporter could have no possible use for.'

'Exactly, exactly. And it was no doubt that bit of electric fuse that turned your thoughts to the one house in the neighbourhood lighted by electricity and suggested to your mind the possibility of electrical engineers turning their talents to account in that direction. Now, will you tell me, what, at that stage of your day's work, induced you to wire to Gunning that you would bring your invisible-ink bottle into use?'

'That was simply a matter or precaution. It did not compel me to the use of invisible ink, if I saw other safe methods of communication. I felt myself being hemmed in on all sides with spies, and I could not tell what emergency might arise. I don't think I have ever had a more difficult game to play. As I walked and talked with the young fellow up the hill it became clear to me that if I wished to do my work I must lull the suspicions of the gang and seem to walk into their trap. I saw by the persistent way in which Wootton Hall was forced on my notice that it was wished to fix my suspicions there. I accordingly, to all appearance, did so and allowed the fellows to think they were making a fool of me.'

'Ha! ha! Capital that – the biter bit, with a vengeance! Splendid idea to make that young rascal himself deliver the letter that was to land him and his pals in jail. And he all the time laughing in his sleeve and thinking what a fool he was making of you! Ha, ha, ha!' And Mr Dyer made the office ring again with his merriment.

'The only person one is at all sorry for in this affair is poor little Sister Anna,' said Loveday pityingly. 'And yet, perhaps, all things considered, after her sorry experience of life she may not be so badly placed in a sisterhood where practical Christianity, not religious hysterics, is the one and only rule of the order.'

HE FLUNG HIMSELF UPON THE PANELS . . .
from 'The Villa of Simpkins' by Arabella Kenealy

Arabella Kenealy

THE VILLA OF SIMPKINS

Like Catherine Pirkis, Arabella Kenealy (1859–1938) was an ardent anti-vivisectionist and wrote a prize-winning essay on the subject, The Failure of Vivisection and the Future of Medical Research *(1909). She was by training a medical doctor and practised in London and Watford between 1888 and 1894, specializing in the care of women and children, before a severe attack of diphtheria forced her to retire and turn to writing. Not surprisingly, her first book was* Dr Janet of Harley Street *(1893), which, like her other novels, such as* Woman and the Shadow *(1898), championed the role of the independent 'new' woman. Yet Kenealy was also conscious of problems inherent in a totally liberated woman, which she finally confronted in* Feminism and Sex-Extinction *(1920) where she highlighted the importance of the distinction between the sexes.*

Kenealy was the daughter of Dr Edward Vaughan Kenealy, who had been the counsel for the defence in the notorious Tichborne case of 1874 regarding whether the claimant to the Tichborne baronetcy was genuine. Kenealy's conduct during this rather erratic trial was such that he was subsequently disbarred. This must have affected the whole Kenealy family, especially Arabella, who was only fifteen at the time, but it is probably also true that her father's irascibility and temperament rubbed off on Arabella as she, too, could be argumentative and difficult. This character trait also appears in the narrator of the following story. Kenealy had an interest in the occult, and in 1896 she wrote a series for The Ludgate *magazine, 'Some Experiences of Lord Syfret'. The stories themselves are genuine mysteries and not supernatural, but behind them is the suggestion that strange forces might be at work directing human actions. In the following story, for instance, Syfret has a premonition of disaster, but that is the only hint of the* outré.

The Villa of Simpkins

THERE IS AN atmosphere about houses. They who live and joy and grieve in them invest them with a kind of aura. So some houses come to wear a face of gloom, of gaiety, of tragedy or terror. This circumstance, to me so manifest, escapes the notice of most persons.

One can see that tiles are broken on the roof; another that the window curtains are in need of washing; another that the masonry demands repointing or the woodwork repainting; while a fourth condemns the sanitary arrangements. But the more intrinsic fact, the fact of desolation or disaster, that to my mind is most obvious, they miss, and even when perceived they refer to some detail of dilapidation or poverty. That my instinct is infallible, I do not claim – on the contrary, it has more than once deceived me – but in cases where it has been rooted and tenacious, even though proofs have not substantiated it, I am satisfied my conviction of mystery or calamity had had its origins in fact; that the sense I have of violence and murder in the midst of a smiling family is an echo, a shadow, a stain on the fabric of life left by some former catastrophe. Sometimes I have been able to justify it by raking up the ashes of the past. Sometimes – and this is singular – the tragedy has happened long after I have sensed it. Of this, what follows is an example.

Sauntering one day down a road in a suburban town, whither I had gone in search of adventure, I came upon a house a-building. It was a villa residence much after the style of other villa residences in the neighbourhood, a sixteen- or eighteen-roomed house divided from its fellows by an acre of geometrically laid-out garden wherein it stood with the pretentious and Pharisaical air of being some Englishman's castle. The structure was completed and men were painting the woodwork, gravelling the walks and putting in the other finishing touches which would, for a year or two, make its ostentatious freshness a reproach to its less lately smartened neighbours. There was nothing to stir one's interest. It was only another of the housings of opulent vulgarity with which the place abounded – housings that smacked of the shop and suggested sleek, overfed occupants in whom wine and good living had produced a kind of mental adiposity to act as buffer between their natures and the higher issues of life, as the flesh of physical plethora obliterated the lines divine of their persons.

I passed on unconcerned. At the further entrance to the drive a man was standing, overlooking the hinging of a gate. I took him to be the owner or builder. The man's face struck me. I stopped short. He glanced up, scowling as though he would have dispatched me about my business. Now I was interested. I had seldom seen a face of so much malignity. It struck me that I would not care to occupy a house planned by a fellow so evil. A shock of rough red hair and beard overgrew his face. His nose, slightly awry, was long and flattened at the nostrils with both cruelty and sensuality. His lips were thick and protrusive. The hand and wrist extended, directing the men, were shaggy with a coarse red thatch. One eye had a sinister droop. No, I should not care to tenant a house of his building.

'Do you want anything?' he demanded roughly after a minute. He was well dressed and apparently a person of some standing.

I returned his savage glance with a cool stare. 'I want nothing,' I said curtly.

He had more than a mind to enquire why then (with qualifications) I filled up the path. But he thought better of it. There is no law to prohibit a man from staring, and my manner proclaimed my determination to stare just so long as it pleased me.

'Hang you, you'll scrape the paint!' he shouted as one of the workmen stumbled and jammed the gate he was lifting against the post. The man grumbled something to the effect that the job was too much for two. 'Then go and be hanged to you,' the builder rasped. 'Get your wage in the office and march!'

The man mumbled sullenly again, 'I'm sick o' being swore at from mornin' to night.'

'Easy, mate,' his comrade counselled. 'Now then, stretch yer limbs, and in she goes.'

With an effort they hoisted the gate and lowered it, dropping the bolts into the sockets with a rush.

'Hang you!' the builder shouted again. 'It wasn't your fault you didn't snap the hinges.'

The labourers, panting, mopped their faces.

'You have a limited glossary, my friend,' I interposed, addressing the red-haired bully. 'Take the advice of an older man and curb your tongue. That "hang" of yours is not calculated to bring the best work out of men.'

He swung his evil eye upon me like a lamp. Only the self-control of habit prevented him from striking me. All at once his manner changed. He scanned me closely, then he raised his hat.

'Pardon, my lord,' he said, obsequiously. 'I did not recognize you. Your lordship does not know me, perhaps. My name is Simpkins. I have the honour to be your new agent at Rossmore.'

'The deuce you have!' I answered. 'From your credentials I should have supposed you a different man.' I resolved on the spot that never again, no matter how excellent his testimonials, would I engage a man without an interview.

'Your lordship misjudges me,' he submitted plausibly. 'I confess to being in bad humour. If you had much to do with this class you would find there is but one way of dealing with it.'

'It will not do at Rossmore,' I said, sharply. 'My people are not used to the treatment of dogs.'

'In dealing with your lordship's concerns I shall follow your lordship's wishes,' he responded, adding, with a spasm of independence, 'Here, I am attending to my own affairs.'

I liked him the better for his independence. I laughed and nodded him good-morning.

'Your temper is not pretty,' I said, as I walked off. 'Indeed, I was thinking I should not care to occupy a house built by a person so profane as yourself.'

He made two steps after me. His face paled in its circle of red hair. 'Do you mean *anything*?' he submitted hoarsely. There was an uneasy glitter in his eyes.

'Pooh!' I said. 'I shall not cancel our agreement for a few "hangs".'

His eyes still probed my face. My words had plainly relieved him. Yet I had a curious sense of something underlying all that appeared.

'When your six months are up, my friend,' I soliloquized, 'I shall exchange you for a steward of more prepossessing looks.'

* * *

A month later I strolled down the same road. I stopped short at the gates of Simpkins's house, the gates which had had so sulphurous a baptism. On one was painted the name 'Edenhome'. It struck my sense of humour. Was it of Simpkins's giving? Lurked there beneath that red thatch of his a corner for sentiment? I decided otherwise. Simpkins and sentiment were not compatible. The name was merely a lure for letting purposes.

I ran my eye over the house's face. Was it the place? Surely not. This was no house of only some months standing. I walked up the road and came back to it. This was the place, assuredly. I stood staring at it. What in the name of amazement had come to it? Where was the freshness that was to put its neighbours to the blush? The place had an air of ruin, of a house unrepaired for half a century. It was as though a blight had fallen on it. The paint of the gates had dulled into a dirty drab; the hinge-end was discoloured by a rust stain which, like a bloodstain, had trickled from the iron sockets. Someone had made it his business to scratch out the initial letter, so that the name stood on one gate 'denhome'. The abridgement seemed to scowl.

I opened the gate and went in. The same blight that had fallen on the house had fallen on the garden. The greater number of the shrubs had shrivelled and died. The walks were set with brown ghosts. The grass of the lawn had fallen in patches, giving an uncanny piebald look. As I approached I perceived that blinds had been put to the windows – fresh gay-looking blinds of a pink pattern. They only served to accentuate the gloom. Apparently, the house was about to be occupied. I wondered how anybody could have been induced to take it. Coming closer, I found I had been betrayed into a singular error, for the paint was fresh and unpeeled, the structure in excellent condition. There was nothing to explain the impression I had had of ruin.

I started, for of a sudden at an upper window, from among a daintiness of pink blind, a sinister face showed out. It was gone as soon as seen. But I knew the evil eye; I knew the Iscariot hair and beard; I knew the malign glance. Irritation succeeded. What business had Simpkins here? His duty was with my affairs a hundred miles away. I strode up the steps. The door stood ajar. I entered. Inside the house was as sombre as outside. Gloom and ill-omen possessed it like black-browed tenants. I mounted the stairs, my footsteps echoing hollowly and fleeing before me, noisy and afraid, like sound running amuck in the empty upper spaces. Suddenly they seemed to turn and come hustling back upon me – leaping, stumbling down the stairs as if in panic. A rumbling echo roared like distant thunder. For a moment I thought the house was about my ears – its premature decay had culminated in the falling of the roof. Then there was silence, the echoes slipping into quietude.

I went straight on, making for the room in which I had seen him. My temper was up. I determined to give Mr Simpkins a piece of my mind. At the top of the stairs I halted. Not a sound stirred. The landing was broad and well lighted. Into it, four doors opened. The construction was different from that which I had expected. There was a broad blank passage wall where I had supposed the door of the front room – the principal bedroom – would be. It was a construction as singular as it was unsightly. It had been so obvious to place the door of that centre room in the centre of this wall.

Suddenly, I felt faint. The passage was pervaded by a curious heavy odour, arising, I imagined, from the paint. My head throbbed.

I made for one of the rooms facing me. The air here was fresh. I threw up a window and leaned out. When I was quite myself I looked about the room. I was astonished to find it small. Holding my handkerchief to my nostrils I went down the passage and opened the other door, the only other door in the front wall. Another little room! And no Simpkins. Where could the fellow be? And where was the door of that room in which I had seen him? A room which must take up at least half the house front. I went all over the house. Not a sign of him – yet he could not have escaped without me seeing him. And why should he? My head throbbed heavily from the curious fumes. It did not smell like paint, nor was its effect like paint – probably an escape of gas.

I threw up another window. Doing so, I looked out. I was in the second small front room. To the left of me was the big bay window at which I had seen Simpkins. I went to the end of the corridor. From the window of the other room the bay showed to my right. I felt maddened. Where was the entrance to that room – where, doubtless, Simpkins still remained? Pacing the passage I heard a sound as though something dropped. I knocked angrily upon the wall.

'Simpkins,' I shouted, 'what is the meaning of this fool's play? Where and why are you hiding?'

My words came back to me like gibes out of the hollows of the house. I shouted again, only to be answered in the same strain. I went downstairs and out into the garden. I ran my eye over the house front. It was as though I were being mocked. For not only were the windows I had opened still thrown up but the three sashes of the bay, which before had been closed, were now raised. Out there in the daylight I could not help suspecting myself of some stupidity. There must be a door leading from one of the smaller side rooms to that centre room, a door I had missed. Yet I had carefully looked for such a door. Bah! My senses must have been fogged by that vapour. My head even now throbbed with it. A room without entrance was an absurdity.

I went back to the house. The door was shut fast. I rattled it. I threw my weight against it. It was fast locked. Yet I had left it ajar. Was I being fooled, or was I fooling myself? Had I indeed seen Simpkins? Was anything as it had seemed that morning? I strode to the nearest telegraph office and wired him at Rossmore. In an hour a reply came: 'Am here at your lordship's service – Simpkins.'

I took a course of Turkish baths and drank no wine for a week. If there be one thing I despise it is a man who cannot keep his head clear.

* * *

The villa of Simpkins faded from my mind, as did likewise, to some extent, my first impression of its builder. To say I ever liked him would mis-state the truth. But I could not help recognizing his exceptional business gifts and the zeal wherewith he prosecuted my affairs. I began to reconsider my intention of parting with him.

One morning, in my office, I received the following letter from Hopkins, a girl dismissed a year before from my employ for bungling some business whereon she had been set:

Honoured Lord – Pardon my addressing you, for I know you think low of me since the Smithson case; but any girl would have been frightened when Smithson took the carving-knife to her. But even Smithson's, honoured lord, was not as bad a place as this. Yet mistress and master is bride and bridegroom, and a nicer couple couldn't be. 'What is it?' you'd ask. It's the house, honoured lord. Yet it's a nice house and the kitchen and pantries are everything you could want for. But there's something about it. What that is, time, if I ever have the nerve to stop long enough, will show. It's called 'Denhome' on the gate . . . [*here I pricked up my ears*] . . . but young mistress calls it 'Edenhome', which we lay to soft-heartedness. Honoured lord, the Lovells are not gentry; which, when I found out, I never thought I could stop. But Mrs Lovell's an angel, and there's no stint, them having come into a fortune. I don't rightly know the facts, but as they taught us at the institute not to leave out anything, I mention that the Lovells got their money curious. Someone else had it, an uncle of theirs – Mr Sinkin his name is.

I paused in my reading of the letter, saying out loud: 'My dear young woman, you are disregarding one of my most stringent rules – that of getting names correctly.' I returned to the letter.

Well, he'd had the money – two thousand a year it is – for nearly ten years when it was proved it wasn't his but Lovell's. He'd kept back a will or something, they say; but it couldn't be proved. So he had to turn out. He must be a kind man, because he's built them this house and won't take any rent for it. He says it eases his conscience. And, of course, he can't help there being something horrible about the house. It's a nice view and polished floors but the strangest noises and feel about it. Mr Sinkin comes sometimes. He isn't a nice-looking gentleman, being cross-eyes and carroty, but he's wonderful kind and keeps telling master to look after his health, being delicate; and as Sinkin would get the money if master was to die, I call it kind. He's that careful of them nobody would expect – considering. The first time he came he was quite taken up because they didn't sleep in the best bedroom. 'It's a south aspic,' he said, quite angry, 'and a big atmosphery room. It was built special for you.' He quite stamped up and down the carpet, and mistress put her pretty white hand on his shoulder – though she's afraid of him – and she says, 'Uncle, we keep it for visitors. We keep it for you when you come. You've been so good to us.' He stared and looked quite queer. He was terribly vexed they didn't use the room he made for them. 'O, you keep it for me, do you?' he says. Then he burst out laughing. He laughs rather hoarse, and young mistress, she got nearer to master and put her hand to her throat. I was setting the table for dinner, and I wasn't hurrying. Mr Sinkin isn't good looking, but he's nice spoken, and though I only hung his greatcoat up for him he gave me five shillings and says, 'You look after my nephew and niece. I'm fond of 'em.'

It came up again at dinner. I had just handed him his pudding – mistress made it with her own hands – when he says again, shaking his fist playful at her, 'And don't let me hear any more of your not sleeping in the front bedroom – the room I built special, so sunny and healthy for poor Ned. Ned's lungs want a south aspic.' Master laughs and says, 'Why, uncle, all the front rooms are south.' Sinkin looked vexed. And I thought myself it was all they could do to please him and not argue. He says, frowning, 'It's the atmosperiness you want, Ned,' and he turned to mistress and says something about cubic feet and ends, 'So I look to you to see Ned sleeps there. His mother died consumptive.'

Mistress turned pale and caught the master's hand. 'O, Ned dear,' she says. 'I've no cough,' he answers. 'It's only uncle's over-kindness.' 'Ought he to go abroad?' she says to Sinkin, almost sobbing. 'He's best where he is,' he says short. 'The drains abroad are shocking.' 'Uncle,' she says, shivering, 'there's noises in the room – the strangest noises. Could it be rats?'

He looked hard at her and says slowly, 'Rats, in a new house – and a well-built house like this? Nonsense.' After a minute, 'There aren't noises every night?' he asks. 'No,' she says, 'only sometimes – horrid, rumbling noises, and I think the gas escapes. That's why I thought it must be rats. They say rats eat the pipes.'

I don't wonder he looked cross. It wasn't like mistress to argue so. Master broke out laughing. 'Uncle will think we're very ungrateful, Milly,' he says. 'And you can't be so silly as to think rats eat gas pipes.'

'Will you sleep there tonight, uncle?' she says. 'I should feel comfortable if somebody had slept there.'

He finished picking out a walnut. Then, 'There's nothing I'd like better,' he says. But after all, he fell asleep in the library. I found him there when I went to do it next morning. His boots and coat was off, and he was on the couch covered with rugs almost as if he'd meant to sleep there. He gave me half a crown. 'You needn't say anything,' he says, 'but I was that tired I dropt asleep.' And he took his coat and boots and slipped up to the spare room.

Honoured lord, it wasn't a week after when a young gent stopping here went to bed in the spare room – mistress couldn't bring herself to sleep there – as cheerful as might be, and in the morning he was dead – poisoned, the doctor said, with prussic acid. There he was, stretched out with his eyes staring horrible and his face blue and the room like an essence-of-almonds bottle. Mr Sinkin came down in an awful state. He got the papers to leave out the name of the house and paid us servants to keep it quiet. 'And, for Heaven's sake, don't leave the house,' he says to master, 'or I shall never let it again!' Master promised faithful. He had to settle it after with mistress. She begged him to take her away. She'd heard the noises that very night. 'I've promised uncle,' he says. So you see, honoured lord, I'm right in calling it an awful house. You don't know what a feel there is about it.

I wrote her one question. She replied, 'The middle front-room door opens in the passage just opposite the stairs. There's a little room at each end of the passage.'

I sought out Simpkins in his office.

'Simpkins, I shall be in suburbia this week. Can I leave a message from you at Edenhome?'

He finished the few lines of a letter he was writing and then looked up. What eyes he had! 'Pardon,' he said, 'I am anxious to catch this post. Now I am at your lordship's service.'

'Well, you heard what I said.'

He scanned me narrowly. 'My lord,' he returned, 'I fancied I could not have heard you aright.'

'I imagine you did.'

'I have let Edenhome,' he said evasively.

'To a nephew. I know. Can I leave a message from you?'

'Your lordship is pleased to jest. My nephew is not likely to be so favoured.'

'So, so. I must introduce myself.'

'There is not likely to be anything in common,' he said sneeringly, 'between Ted Lovell, the draper's son – I do not pretend to be a person of family – and your lordship.'

'I am interested in people,' I returned, observing him. 'I have heard of the suicide. I am interested in that haunted front room.'

I saw the watch-chain on his waistcoat lift high. Then he spread his hands with a deprecatory gesture.

'I regret that somebody has been playing on your lordship's . . . I will not say, credulity.'

'You have no message then?'

He followed me across the room with a curious cat-like tread. The air about him bristled with violence. 'You are pleased to be interested in my affairs,' he said with a suspicion of menace.

'I am interested in the construction of a certain room in the house I saw you building. You remember, I went over it once,' I added quickly, but not quickly enough. His eyebrows lifted.

'I was not aware it had been so honoured.' His manner changed.

'As you are so kind,' he said, smoothly, 'I will take the liberty of asking you to talk with Lovell. Since Rudderford's case he has spoken morbidly of suicide. It is idiocy in a man so well placed.'

'I will advise him to sleep in the large front room,' I said.

He turned as if I had struck him and went back to his work.

* * *

Hopkins opened the door. Her lids dropped on a gleam of recognition. It was the first rule of my institution that wheresoever or whensoever I should appear I was not to be identified. She took me into the drawing-room, and soon a pretty, fragile little creature in a tea-gown tripped into the room.

'I am pleased to know you,' I said, taking her hand. 'I am Lord Syfret. You will, perhaps, have heard of me. Mr Simpkins is my agent.'

She blushed and fluttered, smiling up at me. 'Uncle was good to speak of us, and your lordship is kinder to come and see us,' she said prettily.

Lovell had followed her into the room. He was a pale-faced, ill-grown cockney, proud of his lately acquired money, proud of all he had exchanged it for and genuinely proud of his little wife. 'She's a jewel I wouldn't change for the 'ighest lady in the land,' he confided to me. His watery eyes were full of tears. The statement was not likely to be put to the test, but I believe he honestly meant it.

'If you could put me up for the night I shall be infinitely obliged,' I said. They would be greatly honoured. I hinted to be allowed to occupy the front large room.

'Why, I'd just persuaded Milly we'd sleep there tonight –' he blurted.

Milly broke in, 'I will have a fire put there for you, Lord Syfret,' and tripped away.

We had finished dinner, and Milly had sung me her songs – sweet little ballads she sang in a sweet little unaffected way – when there came a knocking at the front door. After an interval Simpkins entered. His eyes were bloodshot, his air restless. As he came in he shot a look at Lovell. That look said plainly, 'I got your wire.' I received him coolly. I regarded his intrusion as an impertinence. With his entry a reserve fell upon us. Poor Mrs Lovell lost all her confidence and smiling gaiety. She watched him with a fascinated terror. She stole nearer to me as if for protection. Presently, she made her apologies. She was not well, and might she be excused? She was faint and trembling. I gave her my arm to the door. She sent one long shuddering look back at him. Then she drew a little agitated hand across he brow.

'O, my lord,' she moaned through her white lips, 'I am so afraid of him.'

I steadied her to a chair. Lovell came out. I went back to the drawing-room. Simpkins sat scowling there.

'Your lordship's and my visits were ill timed,' he said with a coarse laugh. 'This night, even, may make me a great uncle.'

After a few moments, professing anxiety about his niece, he left. Out in the hall an altercation sounded. I could hear his rough voice raised. I could hear the sob and pleading of a woman's voice and Lovell's cockney drawl. Once she cried out, 'O, Ned, I cannot, cannot sleep there.'

I went out. 'Is Mrs Lovell better?' I questioned.

She came to me with pleading hands. 'O, Lord Syfret . . .' she began.

Simpkins caught her by the arm. 'You are hysterical,' he said, roughly. 'You must not bother his lordship.'

I took her hand. 'Remember, my dear, that I am to have the haunted room.'

'Do you say it is haunted?' she asked with wild eyes.

'You frighten her,' Simpkins interposed, adding ceremoniously, 'I regret the room has not been prepared for you. It is Mr and Mrs Lovell's own room.'

She turned on him helplessly. She caught her breath with a sob. Lovell put his arm about her and persuaded her upstairs. At the top of the staircase she turned and swept one last terrified look down at us. Then she was gone. That look has never left me. To my death I shall regret that I did not act upon it and save her. I turned on Simpkins, who also stood looking up. There was in his face a singular malignant exultation.

'Why the deuce did you interfere?'

He looked me insolently in the eyes. 'Your lordship does not act with his accustomed breeding when he forces himself on an employee's affairs and even dictates the room his host shall put him in.'

He followed me into the drawing-room. There was an aggressive triumph about him.

'I sleep in town,' he said. 'Good-night.'

I bowed. At the door he turned back.

'My agreement with you ends next week,' he intimated airily.

* * *

In the middle of the night I was roused by a curious sound. It seemed to be a muffled rumbling close at hand. I threw on some clothes and slipped into the passage. In the dim light I could see a thin line of shadow sliding down the wall – almost as if the wall had been moving. From somewhere sounded a hollow ticking like that of an immense clock. Strange how the night develops sound. I had not seen nor previously heard a clock.

I was returning to my room, all noise but the sonorous tick having ceased, when I thought I heard a cry – a faint cry – in the same little voice that had sung me her ballads. It was followed by two deep groans. Heavens! What had happened? I stood listening with strained ears. But no other sound came, nothing but that ghostly ticking. I groped my way along the passage, feeling for a door. I missed it, but coming to the centre, where I had seen it earlier, I laid my ear against the wall. I was struck by a curious chillness. The wall was of iron! I did not stop to wonder, for now I could detect a deep-drawn breathing. It kept time intermittently with the clock. I knocked on the wall. It might be Lovell snoring, but I did not like the sound of it.

Suddenly I became aware of the same heavy odour I had before detected. It was no escape of gas. I remember Hopkins's words about the bitter almonds. This was just such a smell. Then I laughed at myself. I should be seeing Rudderford's ghost next. Yet so strongly were my senses worked upon that I grew presently faint with the overpowering odour. And it was unmistakeably a smell of bitter almonds. Again I groped for the door handle. I drew my hands along and up and down the wall, going over the whole expanse between the rooms at either end. I could find neither handle nor panel nor jamb. The whole extent was one smooth, iron-cold surface. The clock clacked – tick-tick-tick! – with sonorous beat. By this time the stentorious breathing had ceased. On the other side was silence.

Groping once more and finding no door I became alarmed. I ran back to my room – my head throbbing until I reeled – and lighted a candle. I dipped my handkerchief into water and bound it loosely across my mouth and nostrils. Then I carried my candle into the passage. It was as I had suspected. There was no door. As on that morning, so now the space between the rooms at either end of the corridor was one plain surface. Tapping and testing brought out the chill feel and hollow note of metal. An iron plate had been dropped over the door, barring egress and ingress. The horrible clock ticked on. For what purpose? I was now convinced of some catastrophe. I knocked and called. I pounded with my fists upon the iron plate. It sounded thunderously, reproducing in exaggeration the noise that had awaked me. But no other sound answered. I rushed upstairs and stood in the upper passage calling for help. I beat one or two doors. Soon a man appeared – the single manservant of the establishment. He thrust his head out sleepily.

'Come,' I insisted. 'Something has happened.'

As we descended, the same low, rumbling sound was audible. In the flickering light the wall was crossed again by a rapid line of shadow, a line that now ascended. Then all was silent. Even the clock stopped. By this time the almond smell was overpowering. I made the man protect his mouth and nostrils. The first thing my light flashed on was the door of Lovell's room, the door of which there had been no trace a minute earlier. Gracious, what devilry was this? And what the calamity? I knocked loudly on the panels. An ominous stillness reigned. I knocked again. Then I turned the handle and went in.

They were dead. They lay quiet as in sleep, only a curious blueness of skin and glassiness of the widely staring eyeballs showed the sleep final. Her hand was in his; her head lay on his shoulder. So they stared straight into eternity, a smile on their faces.

But this was not all. The pitifulness of it – the pitifulness! For at her side, curled up as if in slumber, lay a new-born babe – a tiny premature thing that nestled a darkly curling head against her arm.

* * *

Before it was day I had interviewed the magistrate and police. They pooh-poohed my version of the case, rejecting it as melodrama: such things were not out of romances. The case was manifestly one of concerted suicide. The sliding wall excited smiles. In the middle of the night, they said, one can be pardoned some fogginess of sense. They did not consider there was so much as a tittle of evidence on which to arrest Simpkins.

I sent for a London detective. I set an expert to explore the wall. It would be impossible, he said, to explain a singular construction without some preliminary and considerable damage which, pending the inquest, was not advisable. There were grooves in the door-jambs of the small rooms off the passage; there was space to contain such a sliding wall as I had indicated.

That night I secreted in the house my detective, two police officers and a friend. I knew Simpkins would come, and he came, as I likewise expected, with materials for a conflagration. Hopkins admitted him. He would remain the night, he said. He professed an overwhelming grief. He had already supped. He would go straight to that room where the dead had lain. Through a peep-hole punctured in the wall we watched him from one of the adjoining rooms. No sooner was the door shut than he dragged chairs, cushions, towel-rack, all else combustible towards the door. He even tore the curtains from the bed. Then he saturated the whole with oil he had with him. He had lighted a fuse and was making for the door when suddenly he stopped.

Tick-tick, began the clock. Tick-tick! It startled us with its suddenness and nearness. In a panic he flung his fuse. It fell short and lay smouldering on the floor. But he heeded nothing. He was beating frenziedly upon the door. However, we had seen into that. Tick! Tick! went the clock. He thundered with his fists and feet and shouted desperately.

A rumbling began. He flung himself upon the panels, but they held out bravely. Tick! Tick! went the clock; rumble, rumble rolled the descending wall. He sprang to the windows, but we had seen to those. Suddenly, I realized what was about to happen. The devilry planned by himself was on his track, hastened, it might be, by the explorations of my expert.

'Quick, quick!' I urged. 'Unlock the door. We must not take the law into our hands.'

But we were too late. Outside in the corridor the sliding wall came down – the door was sealed. The rumble ceased, but the clock ticked on, counting his moments. The almond smell rose strong.

'Where do the fumes come from?' I questioned.

The detective, with an impassive face, stepped aside from the peep-hole. I looked long enough to see that a soft spray, like tiny rain, was falling in the room. Already he lay on the floor with gasping breath and distended eyes. I left the peep-hole to more interested watchers. 'He's dead,' they said.

Still the clock ticked. We passed into the corridor. The wall slid presently up with its curious rumble. Then the clock stopped. We opened the door and went in. He was dead, truly. And death in his guise was not dignified. He had been caught in the trap of his own ingenuity – for the mechanism showed a devilish ingenuity. The clockwork regulating it – clockwork set by his own hand – had with a fine unerring justice timed away his life. I will wager that clockwork has rarely done the world greater service.

'LOOK,' HE WHISPERED. 'DO YOU SEE THAT IT
WILL NOT SHUT NOW?'
from 'The Warder of the Door' by L.T. Meade

L.T. Meade

THE WARDER OF THE DOOR

Elizabeth 'Lillie' Thomasina Meade (1844–1914) was a prolific Irish novelist once best known for her books for adolescent girls – of which she wrote close on 280 – plus many magazine essays and stories. She also edited the magazine Atalanta *from 1888 to 1893 and stepped down only because of the demands upon her time for writing. By 1893 she was becoming one of the most successful contributors to the popular magazines because of her ability to create story series in the style of Conan Doyle's Sherlock Holmes.*

*When Conan Doyle tired of Holmes and sent him and Moriarty plunging into the Reichenbach Falls in 'The Final Problem' (*The Strand, *December 1893) the editor and publisher of* The Strand *were at their wits' end as to how to replace him. They sought among their contributors for similar stories. Meade was already working in that vein, having started a series 'Stories from the Diary of a Doctor', which began in the* July 1893 *issue, but after the completion of the customary six episodes she was asked to the continue the series for another six, and a further series of twelve followed in 1895. These subsequently appeared in book form in 1894 and 1896 respectively, and other magazine series also issued in book form followed, including* The Brother-hood of the Seven Kings *(1899),* The Man Who Disappeared *(1901) and* The Sorceress of the Strand *(1903). Meade wrote all these stories herself, though she frequently called upon a medical and scientific expert for advice, and the stories were usually co-credited. Her first 'collaborator' was Clifford Halifax (real name Edgar Beaumont, 1860–1921), but her primary colleague was Robert Eustace (real name Eustace Barton, 1868–1943), and it was he who assisted on the story reprinted here.*

This was one of a series contributed to Cassell's Family Magazine *during 1897 that were published as* A Master of Mysteries *in 1898. The stories feature John Bell, an investigator into cases that appear to be of a supernatural origin but where he always finds the human agency.*

The Warder of the Door

'IF YOU DON'T believe it you can read it for yourself,' said Allen Clinton, climbing up the steps and searching among the volumes on the top shelf.

I lay back in my chair. The beams from the sinking sun shone through the stained glass of the windows of the old library and dyed the rows of black leather volumes with bands of red and yellow.

'Here, Bell!'

I took a musty volume from Allen Clinton, which he had unearthed from its resting place.

'It is about the middle of the book,' he continued eagerly. 'You will see it in big, black, Old English letters.'

I turned over the pages containing the family tree and other archives of the Clintons until I came to the one I was seeking. It contained the curse which had rested on the family since 1400. Slowly and with difficulty I deciphered the words of this terrible denunciation.

And in this cell its coffin lieth, the coffin which hath not human shape, for which reason no holy ground receiveth it. Here shall it rest to curse the family of ye Clyntons from generation to generation. And for this reason, as soon as the soul shall pass from the body of each first-born, which is the heir, it shall become the warder of the door by day and by night. Day and night shall his spirit stand by the door, to keep the door closed till the son shall release the spirit of the father from the watch and take his place, till his son in turn shall die. And whoso entereth into the cell shall be the prisoner of the soul that guardeth the door till it shall let him go.

'What a ghastly idea!' I said, glancing up at the young man who was watching me as I read. 'But you say this cell has never been found. I should say its existence was a myth, and, of course, the curse on the soul of the first-born to keep the door shut as warder is absurd. Matter does not obey witchcraft.'

'The odd part of it is,' replied Allen, 'that every other detail of the Abbey referred to in this record has been identified, but this cell with its horrible contents has never been found.'

It certainly was a curious legend, and I allow it made some impression on me. I fancied, too, that somewhere I had heard something similar, but my memory failed to trace it.

I had come down to Clinton Abbey three days before for some pheasant shooting.

It was now Sunday afternoon. The family, with the exception of old Sir Henry, Allen and myself, were at church. Sir Henry, now nearly eighty years of age and a chronic invalid, had retired to his room for his afternoon sleep. The younger Clinton and I had gone out for a stroll around the grounds, and since we returned our conversation had run upon the family history until it arrived at the legend of the family curse. Presently the door of the library was slowly opened, and Sir Henry, in his black velvet coat, which formed such a striking contrast to his snowy white beard and hair, entered the room. I rose from my chair, and, giving him my arm, assisted him to his favourite couch. He sank down into its luxurious depths with a sigh, but as he did so his eyes caught the old volume which I had laid on the table beside it. He started forward, took the book in his hand and looked across at his son.

'Did you take this book down?' he said sharply.

'Yes, father, I got it out to show it to Bell. He is interested in the history of the Abbey, and –'

'Then return it to its place at once,' interrupted the old man, his black eyes blazing with sudden passion. 'You know how I dislike having my books disarranged, and this one above all. Stay, give it to me.'

He struggled up from the couch, and, taking the volume, locked it up in one of the drawers of his writing-table and then sat back again on the sofa. His hands were trembling, as if some sudden fear had taken possession of him.

'Did you say that Phyllis Curzon is coming tomorrow?' asked the old man presently of his son in an irritable voice.

'Yes, father, of course. Don't you remember? Mrs Curzon and Phyllis are coming to stay for a fortnight. And, by the way,' he added, starting to his feet as he spoke, 'that reminds me I must go and tell Grace . . .'

The rest of the sentence was lost in the closing of the door. As soon as we were alone Sir Henry looked across at me for a few moments without speaking. Then he said, 'I am sorry I was so short just now. I am not myself. I do not know what is the matter with me. I feel all to pieces. I cannot sleep. I do not think my time is very long now, and I am worried about Allen. The fact is, I would give anything to stop this engagement. I wish he would not marry.'

'I am sorry to hear you say that, sir,' I answered. 'I should have thought you would have been anxious to see your son happily married.'

'Most men would,' was the reply, 'but I have my reasons for wishing things otherwise.'

'What do you mean?' I could not help asking.

'I cannot explain myself. I wish I could. It would be best for Allen to let the old family die out. There, perhaps I am foolish about it, and, of course, I cannot really stop the marriage, but I am worried and troubled about many things.'

'I wish I could help you, sir,' I said impulsively. 'If there is anything I can possibly do, you know you have only to ask me.'

'Thank you, Bell, I know you would, but I cannot tell you. Some day I may. But there, I am afraid, horribly afraid.'

The trembling again seized him, and he put his hands over his eyes as if to shut out some terrible sight.

'Don't repeat a word of what I have told you to Allen or anyone else,' he said suddenly. 'It is possible that some day I may ask you to help me. And remember, Bell, I trust you.'

He held out his hand, which I took. In another moment the butler entered with the lamps, and I took advantage of the interruption to make my way to the drawing-room.

The next day the Curzons arrived, and a hasty glance showed me that Phyllis was a charming girl. She was tall, slightly built, with a figure both upright and graceful and a handsome, somewhat proud face. When in perfect repose her expression was somewhat haughty, but the moment she spoke her face became vivacious, kindly, charming to an extraordinary degree. She had a gay laugh, a sweet smile, a sympathetic manner. I was certain she had the kindest of hearts and was sure that Allen had made an admirable choice.

A few days went by, and at last the evening before the day when I was to return to London arrived. Phyllis's mother had gone to bed a short time before, as she had complained of headache, and Allen suddenly proposed, as the night was a perfect one, that we should go out and enjoy a moonlight stroll.

Phyllis laughed with glee at the suggestion and ran at once into the hall to take a wrap from one of the pegs.

'Allen,' she said to her lover, who was following her, 'you and I will go first.'

'No, young lady, on this occasion you and I will have that privilege,' said Sir Henry. He had also come into the hall and, to our astonishment, announced his intention of accompanying us in our walk.

Phyllis bestowed upon him a startled glance, then she laid her hand lightly on his arm, nodded back at Allen with a smile and walked on in front somewhat rapidly. Allen and I followed in the rear.

'Now, what does my father mean by this?' said Allen to me. 'He never goes out at night, but he has not been well lately. I sometimes think he grows queerer every day.'

'He is very far from well, I am certain,' I answered.

We stayed out for about half an hour and returned home by a path which led into the house through a side entrance. Phyllis was waiting for us in the hall.

'Where is my father?' asked Allen, going up to her.

'He is tired and has gone to bed,' she answered. 'Good-night, Allen.'

'Won't you come into the drawing-room?' he asked in some astonishment.

'No, I am tired.'

She nodded to him without touching his hand; her eyes, I could not help noticing, had a queer expression. She ran upstairs.

I saw that Allen was startled by her manner, but, as he did not say anything, neither did I.

The next day at breakfast I was told that the Curzons had already left the Abbey. Allen was full of astonishment and, I could see, a good deal annoyed. He and I breakfasted alone in the old library. His father was too ill to come downstairs.

An hour later I was on my way back to London. Many things there engaged my immediate attention, and Allen, his engagement, Sir Henry and the old family curse, sank more or less into the background of my mind.

Three months afterwards, on 7 January, I saw to my sorrow in *The Times* the announcement of Sir Henry Clinton's death.

From time to time in the interim I had heard from the son, saying that his father was failing fast. He further mentioned that his own wedding was fixed for the twenty-first of the present month. Now, of course, it must be postponed. I felt truly sorry for Allen and wrote immediately a long letter of condolence.

On the following day I received a wire from him, imploring me to go down to the Abbey as soon as possible, saying that he was in great difficulty.

I packed a few things hastily and arrived at Clinton Abbey at six in the evening. The house was silent and subdued – the funeral was to take place the next day. Clinton came into the hall and gripped me warmly by the hand. I noticed at once how worn and worried he looked.

'This is good of you, Bell,' he said. 'I cannot tell you how grateful I am to you for coming. You are the one man who can help me, for I know you have had much experience in matters of this sort. Come into the library and I will tell you everything. We shall dine alone this evening, as my mother and the girls are keeping to their own apartments for tonight.'

As soon as we were seated, he plunged at once into his story.

'I must give you a sort of prelude to what has just occurred,' he began. 'You remember when you were last here how abruptly Phyllis and her mother left the Abbey?'

I nodded. I remembered well.

'On the morning after you had left us I had a long letter from Phyllis,' continued Allen. 'In it she told me of an extraordinary request my father had made to her during that moonlight walk – nothing more nor less than an earnest wish that she would herself terminate our engagement. She spoke quite frankly, as she always does, assuring me of her unalterable love and devotion but saying that under the circumstances it was absolutely necessary to have an explanation. Frantic with almost ungovernable rage I sought my father in his study. I laid Phyllis's letter before him and asked him what it meant. He looked at me with the most unutterable expression of weariness and pathos.

'"Yes, my boy, I did it," he said. "Phyllis is quite right. I did ask of her, as earnestly as a very old man could plead, that she would bring the engagement to an end."

'"But why?" I asked. "Why?"

'"That I am unable to tell you," he replied.

'I lost my temper and said some words to him which I now regret. He made no sort of reply.

'When I had done speaking he said slowly, "I make all allowance for your emotion, Allen. Your feelings are no more than natural."

'"You have done me a very sore injury," I retorted. "What can Phyllis think of this? She will never be the same again. I am going to see her today."

'He did not utter another word, and I left him. I was absent from home for about a week. It took me nearly that time to induce Phyllis to overlook my father's extraordinary request and to let matters go on exactly as they had done before.

'After fixing our engagement, if possible, more firmly than ever and also arranging the date of our wedding, I returned home. When I did so I told my father what I had done.

'"As you will," he replied, and then he sank into great gloom. From that moment, though I watched him day and night and did everything that love and tenderness could suggest, he never seemed to rally. He scarcely spoke and remained, whenever we were together, bowed in deep and painful reverie. A week ago he took to his bed.'

Here Allen paused.

'I now come to events up to date,' he said. 'Of course, as you may suppose, I was with my father to the last. A few hours before he passed away he called me to his bedside, and to my astonishment began once more talking about my engagement. He implored me with the utmost earnestness even now at the eleventh hour to break it off. It was not too late, he said, and added further that nothing would give him ease in dying but the knowledge that I would promise him to remain single. Of course, I tried to humour him. He took my hand, looked me in the eyes with an expression which I shall never forget and said, "Allen, make me a solemn promise that you will never marry."

'This I naturally had to refuse, and then he told me that, expecting my obstinacy, he had written me a letter which I should find in his safe, but I was not to open it till after his death. I found it this morning. Bell, it is the most extraordinary communication, and either it is entirely a figment of his imagination, for his brain powers were failing very much at the last, or else it is the most awful thing I ever heard of. Here is the letter. Read it for yourself.'

I took the paper from his hand and read the following matter in shaky, almost illegible writing:

MY DEAR BOY, – When you read this I shall have passed away. For the last six months my life has been a living death. The horror began in the following way. You know what a deep interest I have always taken in the family history of our house. I have spent the latter years of my life in verifying each detail, and my intention was, had health been given me, to publish a great deal of it in a suitable volume.

On the special night to which I am about to allude I sat up late in my study reading the book which I saw you show to Bell a short time ago. In particular, I was much attracted by the terrible curse which the old abbot in the fourteenth century had bestowed upon the family. I read the awful words again and again. I knew that all the other details in the volume had been verified but that the vault with the coffin had never yet been found. Presently I grew drowsy, and I suppose I must have fallen asleep. In my sleep I had a dream; I thought that someone came into the room, touched me on the shoulder and said 'Come.' I looked up. A tall figure beckoned to me. The voice and the figure belonged to my late father. In my dream I rose immediately, though I did not know why I went nor where I was going. The figure went on in front; it entered the hall. I took one of the candles from the table and the key of the chapel, unbolted the door and went out. Still the voice kept saying 'Come, come,' and the figure of my father walked in front of me. I went across the quadrangle, unlocked the chapel door and entered.

A death-like silence was around me. I crossed the nave to the north aisle; the figure still went in front of me; it entered the great pew which is said to be haunted and walked straight up to the effigy of the old abbot who had pronounced the curse. This, as you know, is built into the opposite wall. Bending forward, the figure pressed the eyes of the old monk, and immediately a stone started out of its place, revealing a staircase behind. I was about to hurry forward when I must have knocked against something. I felt a sensation of pain and suddenly awoke. What was my amazement to find that I had acted on my dream, had crossed the quadrangle and was in the chapel; in fact, was standing in the old pew! Of course, there was no figure of any sort visible, but the moonlight shed a cold radiance over all the place. I felt very much startled and impressed but was just about to return to the house in some wonder at the curious vision which I had experienced when, raising my startled eyes, I saw that part of it at least was real. The old monk seemed to grin at me from his marble effigy, and beside him was a *blank open space*. I hurried to it and saw a narrow flight of stairs. I cannot explain what my emotions were, but my keenest feeling at that moment was a strong and horrible curiosity. Holding the candle in my hand I went down the steps. They terminated at the beginning of a long passage. This I quickly traversed and at last found myself beside an iron door. It was not locked but hasped and was very hard to open; in fact, it required nearly all my strength. At last I pulled it open towards me, and there in a small cell lay the coffin, as the words of the curse said. I gazed at it in horror. I did not dare to enter. It was a wedge-shaped coffin studded with great nails. But as I looked my blood froze within me, for slowly, very slowly, as if pushed by some unseen hand, the great heavy door began to close, quicker and quicker until, with a crash that echoed and re-echoed through the empty vault, it shut.

Terror-stricken, I rushed from the vault and reached my room once more.

Now I know that this great curse is true, that my father's spirit is there to guard the door and close it, for I saw it with my own eyes, and while you read this know that I am there. I charge you, therefore, not to marry – bring no child into the world to perpetuate this terrible curse. Let the family die out if you have the courage. It is much, I know, to ask; but whether you do or not, come to me there, and if by sign or word I can communicate with you I will do so, but hold the secret safe. Meet me there before my body is laid to rest, when body and soul are still not far from each other. Farewell.

> – Your loving father,
> Henry Clinton

I read this strange letter over carefully twice and laid it down. For a moment I hardly knew what to say. It was certainly the most uncanny thing I had ever come across.

'What do you think of it?' asked Allen at last.

'Well, of course, there are only two possible solutions,' I answered. 'One is that your father not only dreamed the beginning of this story – which, remember, he allows himself – but the whole of it.'

'And the other?' asked Allen, seeing that I paused.

'The other,' I continued, 'I hardly know what to say yet. Of course, we will investigate the whole thing, that is our only chance of arriving at a solution. It is absurd to let matters rest as they are. We had better try tonight.'

Clinton winced and hesitated.

'Something must be done, of course,' he answered, 'but the worst of it is Phyllis and her mother are coming here early tomorrow in time for the funeral, and I cannot meet her – no, I cannot, poor girl! – while I feel as I do.'

'We will go to the vault tonight,' I said.

Clinton rose from his chair and looked at me.

'I don't like this thing at all, Bell,' he continued. 'I am not by nature in any sense of the word a superstitious man, but I tell you frankly nothing would induce me to go alone into that chapel tonight. If you come with me that, of course, alters matters. I know the pew my father refers to well; it is beneath the window of St Sebastian.'

Soon afterwards I went to my room and dressed, and Allen and I dined *tête-à-tête* in the great dining-room. The old butler waited on us with funereal solemnity, and I did all I could to lure Clinton's thoughts into a more cheerful and healthier channel.

I cannot say that I was very successful. I further noticed that he scarcely ate anything and seemed altogether to be in a state of nervous tension painful to witness.

After dinner we went into the smoking-room, and at eleven o'clock I proposed that we should make a start.

Clinton braced himself together, and we went out. He got the chapel keys, and then, going to the stables, we borrowed a lantern and a moment afterwards found ourselves in the sacred edifice. The moon was at her full, and by the pale light which was diffused through the south windows the architecture of the interior could be faintly seen. The Gothic arches that flanked the centre aisle with their quaint pillars, each with a carved figure of one of the saints, were quite visible, and further in the darkness of the chancel the dim outlines of the choir and altar-table with its white marble reredos could be just discerned.

We closed the door softly and, Clinton leading the way with the lantern, we walked up the centre aisle paved with the brasses of his dead ancestors. We trod gently on tiptoe as one instinctively does at night. Turning beneath the little pulpit we reached the north transept, and here Clinton stopped and turned around. He was very white, but his voice was quiet.

'This is the pew,' he whispered. 'It has always been called the haunted pew of Sir Hugh Clinton.'

I took the lantern from him, and we entered. I crossed the pew immediately and went up to the effigy of the old abbot.

'Let us examine him closely,' I said. I held up the lantern, getting it to shine on each part of the face, the vestments and the figure. The eyes, though vacant as in all statuary, seemed to me at that moment to be uncanny and peculiar. Giving Allen the lantern to hold I placed a finger firmly on each. The next moment I could not refrain from an exclamation; a stone at the side immediately rolled back, revealing the steps which were spoken of by the old man in his narrative.

'It is true! It is true!' cried Clinton excitedly.

'It certainly looks like it,' I remarked. 'But never mind, we have the chance now of investigating this matter thoroughly.'

'Are you going down?' asked Clinton.

'Certainly I am,' I replied. 'Let us go together.'

Immediately afterwards we crept through the opening and began to descend. There was only just room to do so in single file, and I went first with the lantern. In another moment we were in the long passage, and soon we were confronted by a door in an arched stone framework. Up until now Clinton had shown little sign of alarm, but here, at the trysting place to which his father's soul had summoned him, he seemed suddenly to lose his nerve. He leaned against the wall, and for a moment I thought he would have fallen. I held up the lantern and examined the door and walls carefully. Then, approaching, I lifted the iron latch of the heavy door. It was very hard to move, but at last by seizing the edge I dragged it open to its full against the wall of the passage. Having done so I peered inside, holding the lantern above my head. As I did so I heard Clinton cry out, 'Look, look,' he said, and turning I saw that the great door had swung back against me, almost shutting me within the cell.

Telling Clinton to hold it back by force I stepped inside and saw at my feet the ghastly coffin. The legend then so far was true. I bent down and examined the queer, misshapen thing with great care. Its shape was that of an enormous wedge, and it was apparently made of some dark old wood and was bound with iron at the corners. Having looked at it all around, I went out and, flinging back the door which Clinton had been holding open, stood aside to watch. Slowly, very slowly, as we both stood in the passage, slowly, as if pushed by some invisible hand, the door commenced to swing around and, increasing in velocity, shut with a noisy clang.

Seizing it once again, I dragged it open and, while Clinton held it in that position, made a careful examination. Up to the present I saw nothing to be much alarmed about. There were fifty ways in which a door might shut of its own accord. There might be a hidden spring or tilted hinges; draught, of course, was out of the question. I looked at the hinges, they were of iron and set in the solid masonry. Nor could I discover any spring or hidden contrivance, as when the door was wide open there was an interval of several inches between it and the wall. We tried it again and again with the same result, and at last, as it was closing, I seized it to prevent it.

I now experienced a very odd sensation; I certainly felt as if I were resisting an unseen person who was pressing hard against the door at the other side. Directly it was released it continued its course. I allow I was quite unable to understand the mystery. Suddenly an idea struck me.

'What does the legend say?' I asked, turning to Clinton. 'That the soul is to guard the door, to close it upon the coffin?'

'Those are the words,' answered Allen, speaking with some difficulty.

'Now, if that is true,' I continued, 'and we take the coffin out, the spirit won't shut the door; if it does shut it, it disproves the whole thing at once and shows it to be merely a clever mechanical contrivance. Come, Clinton, help me to get the coffin out.'

'I dare not, Bell,' he whispered hoarsely. 'I daren't go inside.'

'Nonsense, man,' I said, feeling now a little annoyed at the whole thing. 'Here, put the lantern down and hold the door back.' I stepped in and, getting behind the coffin, put out all my strength and shoved it into the passage.

'Now, then,' I cried, 'I'll bet you fifty pounds to five the door will shut just the same.' I dragged the coffin clear of the door and told him to let go. Clinton had scarcely done so before, stepping back, he clutched my arm.

'Look,' he whispered. 'Do you see that it will not shut now? My father is waiting for the coffin to be put back. This is awful!'

I gazed at the door in horror; it was perfectly true, it remained wide open and quite still. I sprang forward, seized it and now endeavoured to close it. It was as if someone was trying to hold it open; it required considerable force to stir it, and it was only with difficulty I could move it at all. At last I managed to shut it, but the moment I let go it swung back open of its own accord and struck against the wall where it remained just as before. In the dead silence that followed I could hear Clinton breathing quickly behind me, and I knew he was holding himself for all he was worth.

At that moment there suddenly came over me a sensation which I had once experienced before, and which I was twice destined to experience again. It is impossible to describe it, but it seized me, laying siege to my brain until I felt like a child in its power. It was as if I were slowly drowning in the great ocean of silence that enveloped us. Time itself seemed to have disappeared. At my feet lay the misshapen thing, and the lantern behind it cast a fantastic shadow of its distorted outline on the cell wall before me.

'Speak; say something,' I cried to Clinton. The sharp sound of my voice broke the spell. I felt myself again and smiled at the trick my nerves had played on me. I bent down and once more laid my hands on the coffin, but before I had time to push it back into its place Clinton had gone up the passage like a man who is flying to escape a hurled javelin.

Exerting all my force to prevent the door from swinging back by keeping my leg against it, I had just got the coffin into the cell and was going out when I heard a shrill cry, and Clinton came tearing back down the passage.

'I can't get out! The stone has sunk into its place! We are locked in!' he screamed, and, wild with fear, he plunged headlong into the cell, upsetting me in his career before I could check him. I sprang back to the door as it was closing. I was too late. Before I could reach it, it had shut with a loud clang in obedience to the infernal witch-craft.

'You have done it now,' I cried angrily. 'Do you see? Why, man, we are buried alive in this ghastly hole!'

The lantern I had placed just inside the door, and, by its dim light, as I looked at him I saw the terror of a madman creep into Clinton's eyes.

'Buried alive!' he shouted, with a peal of hysterical laughter. 'Yes, and, Bell, it's your doing; you are a devil in human shape!' With a wild paroxysm of fury he flung himself upon me. There was the ferocity of a wild beast in his spring. He upset the lantern and left us in total darkness.

The struggle was short. We might be buried alive, but I was not going to die by his hand, and seizing him by the throat I pinned him against the wall.

'Keep quiet,' I shouted. 'It is your thundering stupidity that has caused all this. Stay where you are until I strike a match.'

I luckily had some vestas in the little silver box which I always carry on my watch-chain, and striking one I relit the lantern. Clinton's paroxysm was over, and sinking to the floor he lay there shivering and cowering.

It was a terrible situation, and I knew that our only hope was for me to keep my presence of mind. With a great effort I forced myself to think calmly over what could be done. To shout for help would have been but a useless waste of breath.

Suddenly an idea struck me. 'Have you got your father's letter?' I cried eagerly.

'I have,' he answered. 'It is in my pocket.'

My last ray of hope vanished. Our only chance was that if he had left it at the house someone might discover the letter and come to our rescue by its instructions. It had been a faint hope, and it disappeared almost as quickly as it had come to me. Without it no one would ever find the way to the vault that had remained a secret for ages. I was determined, however, not to die without a struggle for freedom. Taking the lantern I examined every nook and cranny of the cell for some other exit. It was a fruitless search. No sign of any way out could I find, and we had absolutely no means to unfasten the door from the inner side. Taking a few short steps I flung myself again and again at the heavy door. It never budged an inch, and, bruised and sweating at every pore, I sat down on the coffin and tried to collect all my faculties.

Clinton was silent and seemed utterly stunned. He sat still, gazing with a vacant stare at the door.

The time dragged heavily, and there was nothing to do but to wait for a horrible death from starvation. It was more than likely, too, that Clinton would go mad; already his nerves were strained to the utmost. Altogether I had never found myself in a worse plight.

It seemed like an eternity that we sat there, neither of us speaking a word. Over and over again I repeated to myself the words of the terrible curse: 'And whoso entereth into the cell shall be the prisoner of the soul that guardeth the door till it shall let him go.' When would the shapeless form that was inside the coffin let us go? Doubtless when our bones were dry.

I looked at my watch. It was half-past eleven o'clock. Surely we had been more than ten minutes in this awful place! We had left the house at eleven, and I knew that must have been many hours ago. I glanced at the second hand. *The watch had stopped.*

'What is the time, Clinton?' I asked. 'My watch has stopped.'

'What does it matter?' he murmured. 'What is time to us now? The sooner we die the better.'

He pulled out his watch as he spoke and held it to the lantern.

'Twenty-five minutes past eleven,' he murmured dreamily.

'Good heavens!' I cried, starting up. 'Has your watch stopped, too?'

Then, like the leap of a lightning flash, an idea struck me.

'I have got it. I have got it! My God! I believe I have got it!' I cried, seizing him by the arm.

'Got what?' he replied, staring wildly at me.

'Why, the secret, the curse, the door. Don't you see?'

I pulled out the large knife I always carry by a chain and swivel in my trouser pocket and, telling Clinton to hold the lantern, opened the little blade-saw and attacked the coffin with it.

'I believe the secret of our deliverance lies in this,' I panted, working away furiously.

In ten minutes I had sawn half through the wooden edge, then, handing my tool to Clinton, I told him to continue the work while I rested. After a few minutes I took the knife again and, at last, after nearly half an hour had gone by, succeeded in making a small hole in the lid. Inserting my two fingers, I felt some rough, uneven masses. I was now fearfully excited. Tearing at the opening like a madman, I enlarged it and extracted what looked like a large piece of coal. I knew in an instant what it was. It was magnetic iron ore. Holding it down to my knife, the blade flew to it.

'Here is the mystery of the soul,' I cried. 'Now we can use it to open the door.'

I had known a great conjurer once who had deceived and puzzled his audience with a box trick on similar lines: the man opening the box from the inside by drawing down the lock with a magnet. Would this do the same? I felt that our lives hung on the next moment. Taking the mass, I pressed it against the door just opposite the hasp, and slid it up against the wood. My heart leaped as I heard the hasp fly up outside, and with a push the door opened.

'We are saved,' I shouted. 'We are saved by a miracle!'

'Bell, you are a genius,' gasped poor Clinton. 'But now, how about the stone at the end of the passage?'

'We will soon see about that,' I cried, taking the lantern. 'Half the danger is over, at any rate, and the worst half, too.'

We rushed along the passage and up the stair until we reached the top.

'Why, Clinton,' I cried, holding up the lantern, 'the place was not shut at all.'

Nor was it. In his terror he had imagined it.

'I could not see in the dark, and I was nearly dead with fright,' he said. 'Oh, Bell, let us get out of this as quickly as we can!'

We crushed through the aperture and once more stood in the chapel. I then pushed the stone back into its place.

Dawn was just breaking when we escaped from the chapel. We

hastened across to the house. In the hall the clock pointed to five.

'Well, we have had an awful time,' I said, as we stood in the hall together, 'but at least, Clinton, the end was worth the ghastly terror. I have knocked the bottom out of your family legend for ever.'

'I don't even now quite understand,' he said.

'Don't you? But it is so easy. That coffin never contained a body at all, but was filled, as you perceive, with fragments of magnetic iron ore. For what diabolical purposes the cell was intended, it is, of course, impossible to say, but that it must have been meant as a human trap there is little doubt. The inventor certainly exercised no small ingenuity when he devised his diabolical plot, for it was obvious that the door, which was made of iron, would swing towards the coffin wherever it happened to be placed. Thus the door would shut if the coffin were *inside the cell*, and would remain open if the coffin were *brought out*. A cleverer method for simulating a spiritual agency it would be hard to find. Of course, the monk must have known well that magnetic iron ore never loses its quality and would ensure the deception remaining potent for ages.'

'But how did you discover by means of our watches?' asked Clinton.

'Anyone who understands magnetism can reply to that,' I said. 'It is a well-known fact that a strong magnet plays havoc with watches. The fact of both our watches going wrong first gave me a clue to the mystery.'

Later in the day the whole of this strange affair was explained to Miss Curzon, and not long afterwards the passage and entrance to the chapel were bricked up.

It is needless to add that six months later the pair were married, and, I believe, are as happy as they deserve.

Lucy G. Moberly

THE TRAGEDY OF A DOLL

Lucy Gertrude Moberly (1860–1931) was a consistent writer, chiefly of romances, but often with a sensitive depth reflecting the hardships of life. She is barely remembered now and left little behind her. She was the daughter of a vicar and part of a large family, and she trained as a nurse. Her first book was Sick Nursing at Home *(1899), and nurses feature in several of her novels and stories. She also wrote poems, some of which were converted into songs. One of her poems, 'Commandeered', which recognized the role of horses in the First World War, was adopted by Our Dumb Friends' League. She never married, though she was betrothed to the cello player William E. Whitehouse in 1909, but sadly the engagement was cancelled. Her nursing knowledge is central to a series she contributed to* The Lady's Magazine *in 1903, 'Experiences of a Lady Doctor', as related by Cynthia Deane MD, from which the following story comes. So far as can be gleaned these were not collected into book form, and this story has not been reprinted until now.*

The Tragedy of a Doll

I WAS ONE of the resident medical officers in the hospital where what I am about to tell took place, and I have always looked upon the events as some of the strangest in my not altogether uneventful experiences as a medical woman.

I well remember the time of year – it was in June, a particularly fine and lovely June – and we were rejoicing over the beautiful weather and congratulating ourselves upon the probability of being able to hold our annual hospital fête in what was called, by courtesy, the garden of the institution.

Rather more than a week before the day arrived I stood at the window of my little sitting-room, planning a pretty arrangement of tables for the refreshments of our distinguished guests, when a hasty knock on the door was followed by the entrance of Sister Clara, whose wards (the women's and children's) were in my special charge.

'I have been planning a few flags,' I said absently. And, hardly looking at her, 'We must be extra gay this time. I hear the treasurer is bringing some rather important foreigner with him to the meeting and we must –'

'Could you come and see a new patient at once, Miss Deane?' Sister Clara broke in, and as I turned from the window I saw that her face looked worried and puzzled. 'I would not have troubled you just at tea-time, but the case doesn't seem quite straightforward, and I should like you to see it directly.'

I was my usual professional self instantly – flags and fêtes forgotten, the interest of a new case at once uppermost in my mind.

'Who admitted it?' I asked, as Sister and I passed down the stone passage to the ward. 'And what is it supposed to be?'

'The child was brought in by the police,' was the reply, 'and Mr

Higgins sent her straight upstairs. She is unconscious.'

A circle of screens in the farthest corner showed me where my new patient lay, and Sister and I were soon behind them looking down at the bed beside which a nurse stood silently.

'Has she moved since I left you?' Sister Clara asked.

'She turned a little and moaned once or twice, otherwise she has lain just as you see her,' the nurse answered.

The patient was a child of perhaps ten or eleven years, whose white face bore lines of suffering and anxiety strange in one so young. Her eyes were shut, but her brows were drawn together in a painful frown, and every now and then she moved her head uneasily. Gathered tightly into one of her arms, clasped closely against her breast, she held a great wax doll, whose rosy face presented a curious contrast to the white worn face upon the pillow.

'Poor little mite,' I cried. 'Was she brought in with her doll in her arms?'

'We can't get it away from her,' Sister Clara answered. 'Though she seemed quite unconscious she clung to that doll as tenaciously as though it were something very precious, and it evidently troubled and upset her so terribly when we tried to take it away that I thought it had better be left.'

'Certainly,' I answered with decision, 'nothing must be allowed to trouble or irritate her. She shows every sign of brain disturbance, and the quieter and calmer we keep her, the better.'

I examined her carefully, and everything I found pointed to the correctness of my first diagnosis: that some brain trouble was at the bottom of the child's condition, and, having given the necessary orders as to treatment, I moved from behind the screens with Sister Clara, leaving the nurse to watch the little sufferer, who seemed to grow increasingly uneasy at the sound of our voices.

When we were out of earshot of the bed I questioned Sister Clara about the child's admission. 'Who is she? Did no one come with her or give an account of her?'

'Only the policeman who brought her. He is waiting to speak to you.'

The policeman, a big man with shrewd eyes and a kindly face, gave business-like replies to my questions. It appeared that he was that day on duty inside King's Cross Station and that an hour or so earlier he had been summoned to the first-class waiting-room by the attendant. There he found our new patient crouching in a corner of one of the seats quite unconscious, her big doll hugged to her breast.

'But did the attendant say nothing of her?' was my next question. 'Someone must have left the poor child there. Was no one with her?'

'A man and woman brought her there sometime earlier, miss, so the attendant said, and they put her on the seat, and the man said to the attendant that they were going to look after their luggage and come back for her soon. She was conscious, then, looking about her sort of strange, the attendant thought, and then presently she seemed to drop asleep, and the attendant being busy forgot all about her till three hours had gone by. Then she found the child had fainted or something, and she called to mind that the people had never come back for her, so she fetched me in.'

'You looked for these people, I suppose?'

'High and low, miss, and couldn't find a trace of them. Case of desertion maybe. The attendant said the man was a queer-looking chap and spoke with a curious sort of accent. She thought maybe they were foreigners. But whether or no, that is so that they had disappeared, and the child seemed so ill that I brought her here.'

That was all that we could learn of the poor little thing, and, as without a doubt she was very ill, nothing remained but to keep her in the hospital and do our utmost for her.

There were no marks of identification upon her clothing, which was of a coarse and rough make, the garments oddly shaped and unusual in appearance. In her pocket was a shabby little purse, but it was empty, and nothing could be discovered anywhere about her that would give the faintest clue as to who she was or where she came from.

Our little patient lay day after day in that strange torpor of utter unconsciousness from which only one thing seemed to stir her. If anyone attempted to take from her the great doll she clasped in her arms she would rouse up into a kind of temporary wakefulness and an excitement that was very bad for her, only to sink back immediately into her former state of unconsciousness. Strict injunctions were issued to the nurses never to touch the waxen beauty, and so the strange couple remained silently in the corner bed – the white-faced unconscious child with the halo of dusky hair and the rosy, fair-haired doll, whose staring blue eyes were forever wide open, gazing vacantly into space.

'Acute brain disturbance following upon severe shock or strain' was the only diagnosis at which any of us were able to arrive, and beyond feeding the lonely little being thus cast into our midst, and keeping her as quiet and comfortable as possible, nothing more could be done for her. The people who had left her in the waiting-room at King's Cross had neither been seen nor heard of again. The child might have been dropped from the clouds for all connection she appeared to have with anybody.

A week went by, and, though my interest in the child was quite unabated, the coming hospital meeting, with its attendant festivities, absorbed a good deal of my time and thoughts – more especially as we were very anxious that our wards should show themselves at their best to the distinguished foreigner who was coming with the treasurer, Mr Darcy. Rumour had it that the visitor was a certain Russian lady of very high lineage and very great importance who was living in London for a time and was particularly desirous of learning all that she could of the methods and management of English hospitals with a view to improving those in her own land.

On the day before the meeting, when I went my morning rounds, the little patient who so much interested me was, as before, quite unconscious, but when I entered the ward in the evening for my second visit, Sister approached me with an odd look of excitement on her face.

'She is conscious,' was her eager exclamation – and it was not necessary for her to explain who was meant by 'she'.

'*Conscious!*' I answered with equal eagerness. 'Has she spoken? Has she said anything to give us a clue as to her identity?'

'She has spoken several times – in fact, she has said a good deal and seems to want to tell us something, but none of us can understand a word she says.'

I made no response, for by this time I was beside the child's bed, noting intently the change that had taken place in her since the morning. Her face had lost some of its deadly whiteness, there was a touch of colour in it now, and her eyes were wide open, great dark eyes that looked up into mine with a wistful, almost agonized expression, most pitiful in so young a child.

'What is it, dear?' I said, gently smoothing back her soft dark curls. 'Tell me what you feel – and what I can do for you.'

A still more distressing look shot into her eyes, her brows drew together, she shook her head vehemently and poured out a torrent of words in a language of which I could not understand a single syllable.

I shook my head and replied slowly that I could not understand her, repeating the same statement in French and German, but these languages were evidently as unintelligible to her as was English, and the trouble in her eyes deepened. I did my best to soothe her and spoke in reassuring accents, hoping that the very tones of my voice might have a calming effect, and I think they did quiet her, for her face grew less troubled, and, when I smiled at her, she smiled faintly in return.

Thinking I would try to establish a more friendly relation between us I laid my hand on the flaxen head of the doll that was still cuddled in her arms, and smiled encouragingly. But my action brought such an extraordinary change to the child's face that I was positively alarmed. She turned literally livid with what seemed like the most deadly fear. Her lips quivered, her eyes grew round and horror-stricken and she snatched the doll from my hand as if my touch were a defiling one, drawing her big waxen baby under the bedclothes and glaring at me with a glance in which defiance and fear were strangely mingled.

I spoke reassuringly again and smiled, but I saw a little shiver run through the small frame, and I thought I had better leave my little patient to sleep off her excitement, though I was puzzled to account for its cause.

I was puzzled also to imagine what language she had spoken, and I determined that as soon as possible I would ask a friend, who was an excellent linguist, to come and visit the ward and discover the nationality of our strange patient. But my friend's intervention was, after all, unnecessary, for the dénouement of the whole episode was not the least extraordinary part of it.

The day of our Annual Meeting was warm, clear and delicious – as perfect a June day as heart could desire – and even our scrubby patch of ground, dignified by the name of garden, looked bright and festive. Before three o'clock we were all ready to receive our grand company. The wards were gay with flowers, the patients lay smiling and happy under superlatively clean quilts, prepared to enjoy themselves to the full and to revel in criticizing the gowns of our lady visitors.

It so happened that an anxious case in one of our wards kept me away from the meeting, but as I was preparing to go downstairs to its conclusion and find some guests to escort over the building Sister Clara hurried up to me.

'Miss Deane,' she said quickly, 'please come and see poor little Twenty.' (This was our young patient who, being nameless, we were obliged to designate by the number of her bed.) 'She has been quiet all the morning, but now she is so restless and apparently delirious that we can do nothing with her.'

This was a confession seldom heard from the lips of so experienced and capable a nurse as our senior sister, and I instantly went with her into her ward. When I reached Twenty I saw at once that my patient was suffering, either from some fresh brain disturbance or from some severe recrudescence of the old one. She was sitting up in bed, her dark hair tossed wildly over her shoulders, her face flushed deeply, her eyes startlingly big and bright.

With one arm she clutched her big doll in a sort of feverish, desperate fashion; with the other she was gesticulating eagerly, almost, I should have said, despairingly, and all the time she talked, on and on and on, in a high clear voice perfectly audible all over the ward. Her words poured out with fearful rapidity, but they were, as before, perfectly unintelligible, and every moment her accents grew more emphatic, more excited and, if one could say so of so young a child, more full of some terrible despair. She looked at each of us in turn with a perfectly heart-rending appeal in her face.

No efforts of mine to calm the poor little girl had the slightest effect and, fearful lest actual and acute mania should be the result of her overwhelming excitement, I turned quickly from the bed to write a prescription for a soothing draught to be given her at once.

'All the extra stir and movement in the ward today will be very bad for her,' I said to Sister Clara. 'I think we must try to move her into a private ward, if –'

I had been going to say 'if there is time' when my sentence was interrupted by the opening of the ward door and the entrance of Mr Darcy, the treasurer, and his most distinguished guests.

'We rather pride ourselves on this ward, madam,' he was saying. 'There is nothing quite like it in London.'

A soft and singularly pleasant voice answered him, and, looking up, I saw by his side a tall and very beautiful woman whose stately height and graceful movements made one think of princesses in fiction. Behind her was a short dark lady whose face struck me as vaguely familiar and whose eyes held a wistful anguished look that reminded me of someone – someone – who was it they reminded me of? I wondered, while I listened to the treasurer's well-turned sentences.

'We shall hope to persuade Your Serene Highness,' he was saying suavely when, all at once, across the gracefully rounded periods of his sentence, there struck a torrent of words in a high, clear childish voice.

For a few seconds since the entrance of the visitors our little patient had been silent. Now, suddenly, that strange outpouring of words began again – the piteous, despairing sounds which, incomprehensible as they were to me, yet wrung my heart. The treasurer glanced around with a frown, but the distinguished stranger made a quick step forward and uttered a low exclamation.

'What is that?' she said in her pretty broken English. 'Who speaks? Why do they speak Russian?'

Russian! It was Russian the child was speaking, and this great lady was her fellow countrywoman. If only she would condescend to speak to the child, perhaps, I reflected, she would succeed in calming her, perhaps . . .

But while the thought had still barely flashed across my brain, the lady of whom I was thinking swept across the ward, her face alight and eager.

'May I see this patient?' she asked. 'It is so strange to hear my own tongue here in your English hospital. May I see her?'

Sister Clara drew back the screen, and the great lady passed through, followed by the other lady, who was evidently a lady-in-waiting or someone of that description. The child, as before, was sitting bolt upright in bed, gesticulating wildly and talking, talking, talking – and I saw a look of intense bewilderment flash over the great lady's face.

'She says strange things,' I heard her murmur, and then, as the other lady moved behind the screen and came into full view of the child, a most extraordinary thing happened. With a gasping, passionate cry she pressed past her mistress and flung herself on her knees beside the bed, her face aflame with indescribable emotion. She caught the child's hands and covered them with kisses, speaking to her in the low caressing accents of intense love.

The bewilderment of the great lady's face deepened. She put a hand on her companion's shoulder.

'Matushka,' she said almost sternly and in French, 'what is this? Is the little one your child?'

'My child – mine – mine,' the other cried in the same language. 'They sent her to me, and she never came. I lost her, my treasure, my heart's delight, my little Vera, whom I have not seen for two long years.'

And then she turned back to the child and drew her into her arms, kissing her and talking to her in soft cooing accents that seemed to soothe the poor little mite into a strange peace. But I noticed that the great lady's face was still curiously set and stern and that her eyes looked sadly down at the woman and the child, and presently she asked if she might hear all the story of the little one's submission to the hospital.

'We may go to your room, perhaps, Miss Deane?' the treasurer said courteously, his usual talkativeness and pomposity quite quelled by the odd events taking place about him.

'But I . . . I must stay here,' said the kneeling woman by the bed.

And her mistress answered quickly, 'Yes, you must stay there.' And her eyes flashed so strangely that I was startled.

She and the treasurer and I were soon in my room, and when the door was shut the Russian lady turned to me and said slowly, 'You do not know what the child said in her delirium?'

'No, madam,' I answered. 'Until today I did not even know what language she spoke.'

'And the doll she carries, you have noticed nothing remarkable about that?'

'Nothing, except that she is so devoted to it she will never let anyone touch it or take it from her.'

'Poor little child! Poor little child!' the lady said, her severity softening. 'To think that men and women should give their difficult tasks to the children. That little girl's brain is turned because of her doll.'

'Because of her doll?' I stammered.

'Yes. Do you know what she cried out in her delirium? She cried out that no one must touch the doll; no one must look at it; that the custom-house officers must let it pass; that the police must not *open its head*!'

'Open its head!' I exclaimed, feeling more mystified every moment.

'Ah, it is hard for you to understand such things in your free country, your happy country of freedom,' she said with a great sigh. 'In her doll's head that little girl carries important, all-important Nihilist papers. I know not yet to whom she was taking them nor with whom she travelled nor who left her here. This is yet to learn. But, I have learned,' her face grew very stern again, 'that Matushka, my own *dame de compagnie*, is the mother of a child who is employed to carry these documents. And I . . . I trusted her!'

The ending was so pathetic, the beautiful face grew suddenly so sorrowful, that I longed to say something comforting, but she drew herself up quickly and added, 'We must set to work now to learn the truth. My trust has been misplaced.'

Indeed, it had been greatly misplaced. Subsequent investigation brought strange facts to light – but though it took many weeks to unravel the whole of the strange story it all became clear at last. The parents of little Vera were Nihilists of a most advanced and dangerous type, and the poor little child had been used by them as a tool. Her father, having been involved in a most dastardly and terrible plot against the Tsar had, two years before this story opens, been sent to Siberia. Her mother fled precipitately from Russia and, being unable to take with her both her children, left Vera with friends in St Petersburg and took only her baby boy to Paris. There she contrived to pass as a friend and upholder of the Russian government and actually insinuated herself not only into the service but into the affection of the beautiful and distinguished lady who had visited the hospital.

Two years passed. She was now in England when tidings came to her that her little girl was being sent over from Russia bearing with her papers of the most supreme importance which she should take to the house of some Nihilists living in London.

Vera left Russia with a party of emigrants, the papers safely hidden in her doll's head, and what agonies of apprehension were endured by the child over the custom house and the police, her terrible illness showed only too plainly. She arrived at King's Cross with her conductors in safety, and they left her in the waiting-room while claiming their luggage.

And then the unexpected happened. They were arrested by the police on information given by Russian secret-service agents and, fearing for the safety of the papers little Vera carried, they abstained from mentioning the child at all, and by this means she came into our hands at the hospital. Her mother was found to be associated with the anarchical party in various more-or-less serious plots and was handed over to the police of her own country.

But little Vera has become one of the household of that distinguished and beautiful lady, who is goodness and tenderness itself to the plucky little soul.

Only one sign remains of the strain the child underwent: she has never been known to look at or touch a doll again.

Carolyn Wells

A POINT OF TESTIMONY

We end with Carolyn Wells (1862–1942), an American poet, anthologist and writer who, though an almost exact contemporary of Anna Katharine Green (whose work inspired Wells to turn from children's books to mysteries), has been almost completely forgotten. Some have attributed this to the fact that she was probably too prolific for her own good, having produced around 170 books, eighty-two of which were mysteries. The consequence of this output is that, though many of the novels contain ingenious plots and ideas, they suffer from being hastily written. Yet Wells knew her subject, and she was the first to write a 'how to' volume, The Technique of the Mystery Story *(1913). Her forte was really the short story, of which she didn't write enough. Though she had been almost totally deaf from the age of six after a bout of scarlet fever, she nevertheless developed a good rhythm in her work and a feel for language. She also had a sharp wit, which works better in her stories than novels. Most of her novels feature the bibliophilic detective Fleming Stone, but the story presented here (from the October 1911 edition of* Adventure*) features the shrewd and inspiring mind of socialite Bert Bayliss.*

A Point of Testimony

I

BERT BAYLISS WAS the funniest detective you ever saw. He wasn't the least like Vidocq, Lecoq or Sherlock either in personality or mentality. And perhaps the chief difference lay in the fact that he possessed a sense of humour, and that not merely an appreciative sense either. He had an original wit and a spontaneous repartee that made it well nigh impossible for him to be serious.

Not quite, though, for he had his thinking moments, and when he did think he did it so deeply yet so rapidly that he accomplished wonders.

And so he was a detective. Partly because it pleased his sense of humour to pursue a calling so incongruous with his birth and station, and partly because he couldn't help it, having been born one. He was a private detective, but none the less a professional, and he accepted cases only when they seemed especially difficult or in some way unusual.

As is often the case with those possessed of a strong sense of humour, Bayliss had no very intimate friends. A proneness to fun always seems to preclude close friendships, and fortunately precludes also the desire for them. But as every real detective needs a Dr Watson as a sort of mind-servant, Bert Bayliss invented one, and his Harris (he chose the name in sincere flattery of Sairey Gamp) proved competent and satisfactory. To Harris, Bayliss propounded his questions and expounded his theories, and, being merely a figment of Bayliss's brain, Harris was always able to give intelligent replies.

Physically, too, young Bayliss was far from the regulation type of the prevalent detective of fiction. No aquiline nose was his, no sinister eyebrows, no expression of omniscience and inscrutability. Instead, he was a stalwart, large-framed young man with a merry, even debonair face and a genial, magnetic glance. He was a man who inspired confidence by his frankness and whose twinkling eyes seemed to see the funny side of everything.

Though having no close friendships Bayliss had a wide circle of acquaintances and was in frequent demand as a week-end visitor or a dinner guest. Wherefore, not being an early riser, the telephone at his bedside frequently buzzed many times before he was up of a morning.

Every time that bell gave its rasping whir, Bayliss felt an involuntary hope that it might be a call to an interesting case of detective work, and he was distinctly disappointed if it proved to be a mere social message. One morning, just before nine o'clock, the bell wakened him from a light doze, and, taking the receiver, he heard the voice of his old friend Martin Hopkins.

'I want you at once,' the message came. 'I hope nothing will prevent your coming immediately. I am in Clearbrook. If you can catch the nine-thirty train from the city I will meet you here at the station at ten o'clock. There has been murder committed, and we want your help. Will you come?'

'Yes,' replied Bayliss. 'I will take the nine-thirty. Who is the victim?'

'Richard Hemmingway, my lifelong friend. I am a guest at his house. The tragedy occurred last night, and I want you to get here before anything is touched.'

'I'll be there! Goodbye,' and Bayliss proceeded to keep his word.

You see, Harris, he said silently to his impalpable friend, *Martin Hopkins is a gentleman of the old school and a man whom I greatly admire. If he calls me to a case requiring detective investigation, you may be sure it's an interesting affair and quite worthy of our attention. Eh, Harris?*

The imaginary companion having agreed to this, Bayliss went expectantly on his way.

At the Clearbrook station he was met by Mr Hopkins, who proposed that they walk to the house in order that he might tell Bayliss some of the circumstances.

'Mr Hemmingway was my oldest and best friend,' began Mr Hopkins, 'and, with my wife and daughter, I've been spending a few days at his home. He was a widower, and his household includes his ward, Miss Sheldon, his nephew, Everett Collins, a housekeeper, butler and several underservants. This morning at six o'clock the butler discovered the body of Mr Hemmingway in his library, where the poor man had been strangled to death. Clapham, that's the butler, raised an alarm at once, and ever since then the house has been full of doctors, detectives and neighbours. We are almost there now, so I'll tell you frankly, Bayliss, that I sent for you to look after my own interests. You and I are good friends, and you're the best detective I know. The evidence seems, so far, to point to someone in the house, and among those addle-pated, cocksure detectives now on the case it is not impossible that I may myself be suspected of the crime.'

'What!' cried Bayliss in amazement.

'Just that,' went on the old man, almost smiling. 'Hemmingway and I have had large business transactions of late, and as a big bundle of securities has disappeared from his safe it may look as if I had a hand in the matter.'

'I can't quite take that seriously, Hopkins, but I'll be glad to look into the case, and perhaps I can give justice a boost in the right direction. You've no further hints to give me?'

'No, the hints all point one way, and you'll discover that for yourself soon enough.' They walked together up the short path that led to the house of the late Richard Hemmingway.

Clearbrook was a small settlement of well-to-do society people who wished to live near but not in New York. The houses were rather pretentious, with well-kept grounds and picturesque flower beds, but Bert Bayliss paid little attention to the landscape as he hurried to the Hemmingway mansion. Once in the drawing-room Bayliss was presented by Mr Hopkins to his wife and daughter and to Miss Sheldon and Mr Collins.

It was surely a tribute to the young man that all these people, who were fully prepared to treat the detective with a supercilious hauteur, were won at once by his affable and easy demeanour and involuntarily greeted him as a man of their own class and standing.

Mrs Estey, the housekeeper, was also in the room, and at the moment of Bayliss's arrival Coroner Spearman was about to begin his preliminary queries of investigation. Quite content to gain his knowledge of the case in this way, Bayliss settled himself to listen.

Harris, he said silently to his faithful friend, *these are all refined and sensitive people, but, excepting Mr Hopkins, not one shows a deep or abiding grief at the death of this gentleman. Therefore I deduce that with most of them the loss is fully covered by inheritance.*

Marvellous, my dear Bayliss, marvellous! replied Harris correctly.

At the command of the coroner, Clapham the butler was summoned to give his account of the discovery of the body.

'I came downstairs at twenty to six, sir,' said the pompous but deferential Englishman, 'and it would be about six when I reached the master's library. The door was closed, and, when I opened it, I was surprised to find one of the lamps still burning, the one by the desk, sir. By its light I could see the master still sitting in his chair. At first I thought he had come downstairs early to do some work; then I thought he had been working there all night; and then I thought maybe something was wrong. These thoughts all flew through my mind in quick succession, sir, and even as I thought them I was raising the blinds. The daylight poured in, and I saw at once my master was dead, strangled, sir.'

'How did you know he was strangled?' asked the coroner.

'Because, sir, his head was thrown back, and I could see black marks on his throat.'

'What did you do then?'

'First, I called Mrs Estey, who was already in the dining-room, and then, at her advice, I went to Mr Collins's door and knocked him awake. He hurried downstairs, sir, and he said –'

'Never mind that. Mr Collins will be questioned later.'

Harris, said Bayliss silently to his friend, *that coroner is no fool.*

No, said Harris.

'If that is all the account of your finding of Mr Hemmingway's body,' continued Mr Spearman, 'tell us now what you know of Mr Hemmingway's movements of last evening.'

'He was in the library all the evening,' said Clapham. 'He went there directly after dinner and gave me orders to admit three gentlemen that he expected to call. He told me, sir, that I need not wait up to let them out as they would stay late, and he would see them to the door himself. The three gentlemen came, sir, between nine and ten o'clock. They came separately, and, after I had shown the last one into Mr Hemmingway's library, I did not go to the room again until this morning. I went to bed, sir, at about eleven o'clock, and at that time they were still there, as I heard them talking when I left the dining-room, sir.'

Good servant, Harris, commented Bayliss. *If this household is broken up he'll have no trouble in finding a new situation – and yet, is he just a trifle too fluent?*

Perhaps, said Harris agreeably.

Mrs Estey simply corroborated Clapham's story and was followed by Everett Collins, who had been the next to appear upon the scene of the tragedy.

Bayliss looked upon this young man with interest. He was not of an attractive personality, though handsome and well set up. He had the physical effects of an athlete, but his face was weak and his glance was not straightforward.

He impresses me as untrustworthy, Bayliss confided to Harris, *and yet, confound the fellow, there's something about him I like.*

Yes, said Harris.

Mr Collins had little to say. He had been wakened by Clapham from a sound sleep and had hastily run downstairs to find his uncle dead, evidently strangled. As to his own movements the night before, he had spent the evening out, had returned at about half-past eleven, had let himself in with his latchkey and had gone to bed. He had noticed that the library door was closed, and he could not say whether anyone was in the room or not.

Miss Ruth Sheldon testified to the effect that she had played bridge with Mr and Mrs Hopkins and Miss Ethel Hopkins until about eleven, when they had all retired. The Hopkins family corroborated this and all agreed that they had heard no sound of any sort downstairs after reaching their rooms.

'It was Mr Hemmingway's habit,' volunteered Miss Sheldon, 'if he had late callers to let them out himself, to close the front door quietly after them and then to go up to his room with great care in order not to disturb any of us who might be asleep. He was most thoughtful of others' comfort, always.'

The members of the household having been heard, Mr Spearman turned his attention to some others who sat in a group at a small table. One of these was the lawyer, Mr Dunbar. He simply stated that he had full charge of Mr Hemmingway's legal affairs and was prepared to make an accounting when required. But he added that his client's business with him was not extensive, as the late financier was accustomed personally to look after all such matters as did not require actual legal offices.

Mr Hemmingway's private secretary, George Fiske, testified that he was in the habit of coming to Mr Hemmingway's home every day from ten o'clock to four. He had left as usual the day before at four o'clock and knew of nothing unusual regarding his employer or his business matters at that time. Fiske had been sent for earlier than usual on this particular morning but could throw no light on the affair. He knew the three men who called, and they were three of the richest and most influential citizens of Clearbrook, who were more or less associated with Mr Hemmingway in some large financial interests. As a confidential secretary, Mr Fiske courteously but firmly declined to go into details of these matters at present.

There seemed to be no reason to suspect anyone whose name had been mentioned so far, and the coroner next turned his attention to the possibility of an intruder from outside who had forced an entrance after the three gentlemen had departed and before Mr Hemmingway could have left his library. But investigation proved that the windows were all securely fastened and that the front door shut with a spring lock which could be opened only from the outside by a latchkey. No one, save those who were already accounted for, possessed a latchkey, and, as no doors or windows had been forced, it began to look to the coroner as if the evidence pointed to someone inside the house as the criminal.

The doctor declared that Mr Hemmingway had died between twelve and one o'clock, and the three men who had called, being asked over the telephone, asserted that they left the house about midnight. One of these, Mr Carston, had tarried after the others and had talked a few moments with Mr Hemmingway at his door, but, though this would seem to make Mr Carston the last person known to have had speech with the dead man, nobody dreamed for a moment of suspecting him. Bayliss's eyes travelled over the assembled listeners.

Pshaw, he said silently to Harris, *there are too many suspects. Granting the criminal was in the house, it might have been any of the servants, any of the guests, the ward or the nephew. Every one of them had opportunity, for, apparently, after midnight the callers were gone and everyone in the house was sound asleep except the victim and the criminal. But the fact of strangulation lets out Mrs and Miss Hopkins, who are too slender and delicate for such a deed. That big, athletic Miss Sheldon might have done it had she been inclined; that gaunt, muscular housekeeper could have accomplished it; and, as to the men, young Collins, old Mr Hopkins and that complacent butler are all capable of the deed physically. So, Harris, as we've heard the facts of the case we'll now hunt for clues and theories.*

Marvellous, Bayliss, marvellous! breathed Harris with deep admiration.

II

Reaching the library, Bayliss found the precinct inspector busily going through the papers in Mr Hemmingway's desk. Inspector Garson had heard of clever Bert Bayliss and was glad to meet him, though a little embarrassed lest the city detective should look upon his own methods as crude.

With the coroner's permission, the body of the dead man had been removed, but otherwise no changes had been made in the room. Bayliss glanced interestedly about. There were no signs of a struggle. The position of several chairs showed the presence of callers who had evidently sat around in conversation with their host. The desk, though not especially tidy, showed only the usual paraphernalia of a man of business.

By themselves, in an open box, had been laid the articles taken from the dead man's pockets. Bayliss looked at, without touching, the watch, the bunch of keys, the knife, the pencil, the pile of small coins and the handkerchiefs which, together with a few papers, comprised the contents of the box.

Then Bayliss looked swiftly but minutely at the desk. The fittings of handsome bronze were of uniform design and rather numerous. Every convenience was there, from pen rack to paste pot. There were a great variety of pens, pencils and paper cutters, while many racks and files held a profusion of stationery, cards and letters.

Yet everything was methodical: the plainly labelled packets of letters, the carefully sorted bills and the neat memoranda here and there, all betokened a systematic mind and a sense of orderly classification.

'The motive was, of course, robbery,' said the inspector as several others followed Bayliss into the library, 'for though everything else seems intact, a large bundle of securities, which Mr Dunbar knows were in Mr Hemmingway's safe last Friday, are now gone.'

'Oh, those,' said George Fiske. 'I didn't know you looked on those as missing. I have them at my own rooms.'

'You have?' said the surprised inspector. 'Why did you not state that fact when interviewed by Mr Spearman?'

'Because,' said the young man frankly, 'I didn't consider that the time or place to discuss Mr Hemmingway's finances. I was his confidential secretary and, though prepared to render an account at any time, I am careful not to do so prematurely. The bonds in question are at my home because Mr Hemmingway gave them to me last Saturday to keep for him temporarily. Here is a list of them.'

Fiske took a card of figures from his pocket-book and handed it to the inspector, who glanced at it with satisfaction and approval.

'You did quite right, Mr Fiske,' he said, 'and I'm glad the securities are safe. But then what, in your opinion, could have been the motive for the deed last night?'

Fiske made no reply, but the expression on his face seemed to imply, against his will, that he could say something pertinent if he chose.

Might it not be, Harris, whispered Bayliss, *that that young man overestimates the confidentialness of his secretaryship at this crisis?*

Hm, said Harris.

Meanwhile, the inspector was rapidly looking over a sheaf of opened letters, each of which bore at its top the rubber-stamped date of receipt.

'Whew!' he whistled as he read one of these documents. He then looked furtively at George Fiske, who was occupied with some clerical work which had to be done at once. Without a word, Inspector Garson handed the letter to Bert Bayliss, signifying by a gesture that he was to read it.

After a glance at signature and date, Bayliss read the whole letter:

Sunday afternoon,
September 9th

My Dear Mr Hemmingway,

After our talk of yesterday morning, I feel that I must express more fully my appreciation of your declaration of confidence in me and my gratitude therefor. I was so surprised when you asked me to act as executor of your will that I fear I was awkward and disappointing in my response. But, believe me, dear sir, I am deeply grateful for your trust in me, and I want to assure you that I shall perform all the duties of which you told me to the very best of my ability, though I hope and pray the day is far off when such need shall arise. I am not a fluent talker and so take this means of telling you that a chord of my nature was deeply touched when you asked me to assume such a grave responsibility. I am, of course, at your service for further discussion of these matters, but I felt I must formally assure you of my gratitude for your kindness and of my loyalty to your interests.

As to the revelation you made to me, it was so sudden and such a surprise I cannot bear to think your suspicions are founded on the truth; but, as you requested, I will observe all I can without seeming intrusive or curious. I have in safe keeping the papers you entrusted to my care, and I hope our present relations may continue for many happy years.

Faithfully yours,
George Fiske

With his usual quick eye for details, Bayliss noted that the letter was dated two days before (that is, the day before the murder, which occurred Monday night); it was postmarked at the Clearbrook post office Sunday evening and had therefore been delivered to Mr Hemmingway by the first post Monday morning. This was corroborated by the rubber-stamped line at the top of the first page, which read: 'Received, September 10'. This letter was among a lot labelled 'To be answered', and it seemed to Bayliss a very important document.

'I think,' he said aloud to the inspector, 'that we would be glad to have Mr Fiske tell us the circumstances that led to the writing of this manly and straightforward letter.'

George Fiske looked up at the sound of his name. 'Has that come to light?' he said, blushing a little at being thus suddenly brought into prominence. 'I supposed it would, but somehow I didn't want to refer to it until someone else discovered it.'

'Tell us all about it,' said Bayliss in his pleasant, chummy way, and at once Fiske began.

'Last Saturday morning,' he said, 'Mr Hemmingway had a long talk with me. He expressed his satisfaction with my work as his secretary and kindly avowed his complete trust and confidence in my integrity. He then asked me if I would be willing to act as executor of his estate when the time should come that such a service was necessary. He said it was his intention to bring the whole matter before his lawyer in a few days but first wished to be assured of my willingness to act as executor. He told me, too, that he would add a codicil to his will leaving me a moderate sum of money. All of this was on Saturday morning, and when I left at noon, as I always do on Saturdays, he gave me a large bundle of securities and also his will, asking me to keep them for him for a few days.'

'You have his will then?' asked Inspector Garson quickly.

'I have, and also the bonds of which I have given you a memorandum. They are all at your disposal at any time.'

'Then Mr Hemmingway died without adding the codicil to his will in your favour,' observed Bayliss.

'Yes,' replied Fiske, 'but that is a minor matter in the face of the present tragedy.' Bayliss felt slightly rebuked, but he couldn't help admiring the manly way in which Fiske had spoken.

'And this conversation occurred on Saturday,' went on Mr Garson. 'You took occasion to write to Mr Hemmingway on Sunday?'

'I did,' agreed Fiske. 'I was so surprised at the whole thing that I was unable to express myself at our interview. I am always tongue-tied under stress of great pressure or excitement. So I sat down Saturday afternoon and wrote to Mr Hemmingway. I mailed the letter Sunday evening, and he had already received it when I reached here on Monday morning at ten o'clock as usual.'

'Did he refer to your letter?' asked Bayliss.

'Yes. He said he was glad I wrote it and that he would answer it on paper that I might also have his sentiments in black and white. Then he said we would discuss the matter more fully after a day or two, and we then turned our attention to other matters.'

'And this revelation he made to you?' queried Inspector Garson, running his eyes over the letter.

Mr Fiske hesitated and looked not only embarrassed but genuinely disturbed. 'That, Mr Garson, I want to be excused from telling.'

'Excused from telling! Why, man, it may help to elucidate the mystery of Mr Hemmingway's death!'

'Oh, I hope not, I hope not!' said Fiske so earnestly that both Bayliss and the inspector looked at him in surprise.

'You *do* know something,' said Mr Garson quickly, 'that may have a bearing on the mystery, and I must insist that you tell it.'

'It is because it may *seem* to have a bearing that I hesitate,' said Mr Fiske gravely. 'But, to put it boldly, as I told you I am not fluent under stress of excitement; in a word, then, Mr Hemmingway implied to me that . . . that he had a half-defined fear that some time his life might . . . might end suddenly.'

'In the way it did?'

'Yes, in that way. He feared that someone desired his death and that was the reason he asked me to care for his will and his valuable securities for a few days.'

'Why were these things not in a safe deposit vault?' asked Bert Bayliss.

'They have been, but a few days ago Mr Hemmingway had them brought home to make some records and changes, and as it was Saturday he could not send them back then, so he gave them to me. I have a small safe at home, and, of course, I was willing to keep them for him.'

'Then Mr Hemmingway feared both robbery and murder,' said Bayliss, and Mr Fiske shuddered at this cold-blooded way of putting it.

'Yes, he did,' said the secretary frankly.

'And whom did he suspect as his enemy?'

'That I hope you will allow me not to answer.'

'I'm sorry, Mr Fiske,' broke in the inspector, 'but you have knowledge possessed by no one else. You must, therefore, in the interests of justice, tell us the name of the man whom Hemmingway feared.'

'The man,' said George Fiske slowly, 'is the one who inherits the bulk of Mr Hemmingway's fortune.'

'Everett Collins, his nephew?'

'His wife's nephew,' corrected George Fiske. 'Yes, since I am forced to tell it, Mr Hemmingway feared that Mr Collins was in haste to come into his inheritance, and . . . and . . .'

'You have done your duty, Mr Fiske,' said Inspector Garson, 'and I thank you. I quite appreciate your hesitancy, but crime must be punished if possible, and you need not appear further in the matter. After your evidence the law can take the whole affair into its own hands.'

III

The law took its course. Though circumstantial evidence was lacking, the statement of George Fiske and the undoubted opportunity and evident motive combined caused the arrest of Everett Collins. The will, when produced, left nearly all the estate to him, and as he was known to be a thriftless, improvident young man the majority of those interested felt convinced that he was indeed the villain.

The property of the late Mr Hemmingway, however, was of far less amount than was generally supposed, and also the large fortune which he had in trust for his ward, Miss Sheldon, had dwindled surprisingly. But this, of course, was in no way the fault of the nephew, and it was thought that Mr Hemmingway had perhaps been unfortunate in his investments. George Fiske became executor, as desired by the late millionaire, but probate of the will was deferred until after Everett Collins should have been tried at the bar of justice.

Collins himself was stubbornly quiet. He seemed rather dazed at the position in which he found himself but had nothing to say except a simple assertion of his innocence.

And he is *innocent, Harris!* declared Bert Bayliss soundlessly. *No villain ever possessed that simple straightforward gaze. Villains are complex. That man may be a spendthrift and a ne'er-do-well, but I'll sear he's no murderer, and I'll prove it!*

Marvellous, Bayliss, marvellous! said Harris.

Bayliss had come to Clearbrook on Tuesday, and on Wednesday Collins was arrested. On Wednesday afternoon Bayliss shut himself up alone in the library to clue-hunt, as he called it. Acting on his conviction that Collins was innocent he eagerly sought for evidence in some other direction. Seating himself at Mr Hemmingway's desk, he jotted down a few notes, using for the purpose a pencil from the pen tray in front of him. He looked at the pencil abstractedly and then he suddenly stared at it intently.

A clue! he said mentally to Harris. *Hush, don't speak*, though Harris hadn't. *I sure have a clue, but such a dinky one.*

He looked at the pencil as at a valuable curio. He glanced about the desk for others and found several. In a drawer he found many more. They were all of the same make and same number, and while those on the desk were all more or less well sharpened, those in the drawer had never yet been cut.

'Oh!' said Bayliss, and, putting carefully into his pocket the pencil he had used in making his notes, he began scrutinizing the wastebasket. There were not many torn papers in it, but the top ones were letters, envelopes or circulars, each torn once across. On top of these were some chips of pencil cedar and a trifle of black dust.

As if collecting precious treasure Bayliss, with extreme care, listed out the top layer of torn envelopes and, without disarranging the tiny wooden chips and black lead scrapings, laid all in a box, which he then put in a small cupboard and, locking its door, put the key in his pocket. Then he returned to the desk and picked up the packet of letters which had been received on Monday and from which Mr Fiske's letter had been taken. There were about a dozen of them, and he looked with interest at each one. Every one was cut open the same way, not by a letter-opener but with shears – a quick, clean cut which took off a tiny edge along the right-hand end. Each was stamped at the top with the rubber 'Received' stamp in red ink.

Clever, clever villain! mused Bayliss. *I say, Harris, he's the slickest ever! And nobody could have found him but Yours Truly.*

Marvellous, murmured Harris.

Then straight to Inspector Garson Bayliss marched and asked to see the letter that Mr Fiske wrote to Mr Hemmingway. Receiving it, he stared at it steadily for a moment then, going to the window, scrutinized it through a lens.

Moved by an excitement which he strove not to show he returned it to Mr Garson, saying, 'You've no doubt, I suppose, as to the genuineness of that letter and all that it means and implies?'

'No, I haven't,' said Mr Garson, looking straight at the young man. 'I have wondered whether there could be anything wrong about Fiske, but that letter is incontrovertible evidence of his veracity.'

'Why couldn't it be faked?' persisted Bayliss.

'I've thought of that,' said Mr Garson patiently, 'but it's too real. Whether it was written Sunday or not, it was positively posted Sunday evening, and it was positively delivered to Mr Hemmingway Monday morning. The postmark proves that. Then Mr Hemmingway opened it, for it is cut open precisely the way he cuts open all his letters, and he dated it with his own dating-stamp and put it with his lot 'To be answered'. Can anything be more convincing of Fiske's good faith?'

'And yet,' said Bert Bayliss, 'it *is* a faked letter, and George Fiske's the murderer of Richard Hemmingway!'

'My dear sir, what *do* you mean?'

'Just what I say. Richard Hemmingway never saw this letter!'

'Can you prove that?'

'I can. Look at the envelope closely with this lens in a strong light. What do you see between the letters of Mr Hemmingway's name?'

'I see . . .' the inspector peered closer '. . . I see faint pencil marks.'

'Can you make out what they spell?'

'No . . . yes . . . "G-e-o" . . . *is* it "George Fiske"?'

'It is, though not all the letters are discernible. Fiske wrote this letter on Sunday and mailed it on Sunday, *but* – he addresses it to himself, *not* to his employer.'

'Why?' exclaimed Mr Garson in amazement.

'Listen. He addressed it with a very soft pencil to himself, and traced the address very lightly. It reached his boarding-house Monday morning, of course, and then he erased the pencil marks and boldly wrote Mr Hemmingway's name in ink. Then he cut off the end in precisely the way Mr Hemmingway opens his letters and put the whole thing in his pocket. All day he carried it in his pocket (I am reconstructing this affair as it must have happened), and at four o'clock he went home with the missive still there.

'Late Monday night he returned. After the three visitors had left he strangled Mr Hemmingway. He knows he's an athlete, and his employer was a frail man.

'And *then* he used the rubber stamp on his own letter and tucked it into the bunch of 'To be answered'. Then he rifled the safe with Mr Hemmingway's own keys, turned off all the lights but one and swiftly and silently went home to bed. The rest you know.'

'Mr Bayliss, I can scarcely believe this!' said Inspector Garson, fairly gasping for breath.

'What, you can't believe it when the villain has written his own name as damning evidence against himself?'

'It must be,' said the inspector, again scrutinizing the faint trace of pencil marks. 'But why did he do it?'

'Because he wanted to be executor and thus be able to convert into cash the securities he has stolen.'

'He returned those.'

'Only a few. Oh, it was a clever and deep-laid scheme. Fiske has quantities of bonds and other valuable papers entirely unaccounted for and which, as sole executor, he can cash at his leisure, all unknown to anyone.'

'How did you discover this?'

'By the simplest clue. I chanced to notice on Mr Hemmingway's desk a pencil, freshly sharpened, but sharpened in a totally different way from those sharpened by the man himself. I looked at all the other pencils on his desk, at the one taken from his pocket and at one in his bedroom – they are all sharpened in exactly the same way with numerous long careful shaves, producing a whittled pyramid. The pencil I spoke of – here it is – is sharpened by only five strong, clean cuts, making a short exposure of cut wood quite different from the long point of wood in the others. Then I looked in the wastebasket – which at your orders had not been touched since the discovery of the crime – and *on top* I found the chips and lead dust of this very pencil. They were *on top* of some torn envelopes whose postmarks proved they had come in Monday evening's mail, which reaches the Hemmingway house about six-thirty. Hence, whoever sharpened that pencil did it *after* six-thirty o'clock Monday night and *before* the discovery of Mr Hemmingway's dead body.'

Mr Garson listened breathlessly. 'And then?' he said.

'And then,' went on Bayliss, 'I looked around for some pencils sharpened like that and found several on and in Fiske's desk in the library. The pencil might have been borrowed from Fiske's desk, but it was sharpened right there at Mr Hemmingway's desk after half-past six. Fiske, as you know, testified that he left at four and did not return until Tuesday morning.'

Bayliss's deductions were true. Confronted suddenly with the story and with the traced envelope, Fiske broke down completely and confessed all. He had been planning it for weeks and had the decoy letter ready to use when Mr Hemmingway should have a large amount of bonds in his own home safe. The whole story of the Saturday-morning interview was a figment of Fiske's fertile brain, and, of course, Mr Hemmingway had no suspicions of his nephew. Fiske had known of the expected callers, had watched outside the house until the last one went away and then, running up the steps, had stopped Mr Hemmingway just as he was closing the door and requested a short interview. Innocently enough, Mr Hemmingway took his secretary into the library and, while waiting for his fell opportunity, Fiske talked over some business matters. While making a memorandum Mr Hemmingway broke his pencil point and, unthinkingly, Fiske obligingly sharpened it.

And to think, murmured Bayliss to Harris, *that little act of ordinary courtesy proved his undoing!*

Marvellous, Bayliss, marvellous! said Harris.

Companion volumes to *Sisters in Crime*

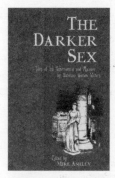

THE DARKER SEX
Tales of the Supernatural and Macabre by Victorian Women Writers
Mike Ashley (Ed.)

Ghosts, precognition, suicide and the afterlife are all themes to be found in these thrilling stories by some of the greatest Victorian women writers. It was three women who popularized the Gothic-fiction movement – Clara Reeve, Mary Shelley and Anne Radcliffe – and Victorian women proved they had a talent for creating dark, sensational and horrifying tales. This anthology showcases some of the best work by female writers of the time, including Emily Brontë, Mary Braddon, George Eliot and Edith Nesbit. Mike Ashley contextualizes each story and shows how Victorian women perfected and developed the Gothic genre.

PB 978-0-7206-1335-3 • 248pp • £9.99 / EPUB 978-0-7206-1438-1
KINDLE 978-0-7206-1468-8 / PDF 978-0-7206-1467-1

'A magnificent and terribly readable collection' – BBC Radio 4
'Editor Ashley does his usual fine job in selecting and introducing the eleven entries in a reprint anthology sure to appeal to fans of both Victorian fiction and ghost stories.' – *Publishers Weekly*

THE DREAMING SEX
Early Tales of Scientific Imagination by Women
Mike Ashley (Ed.)

It is a common perception that science fiction is largely the domain of men. Yet the contribution of women should never be underestimated. This book brings together a selection of early science-fiction stories by British and American writers – including Mary Shelley, Harriet Prescott Spofford, Adeline Knapp, Mary E. Braddon, L.T. Meade, Mary Wilkins Freeman, G.M. Barrows, Roquia Sakhawat Hossein, Edith Nesbit, Clotilde Graves, Muriel Pollexfen, Greye La Spina and Clare Winger Harris – and highlights their significance in the early development of the genre and shows the very different angle they cast on the wonders and fears that technological and scientific advances may bring.

PB 978-0-7206-1354-4 • 248pp • £9.99 / EPUB 978-0-7206-1405-3
KINDLE 978-0-7206-1406-0 / PDF 978-0-7206-1407-7

'Tales by some of the most imaginative female genre writers of the Victorian era' – *Sci-Fi* magazine
'A very interesting collection . . . a useful and entertaining addition to the library of the genre's prehistory . . . deserves some considerable attention' – *Foundation*, the journal of the Science-Fiction Foundation

Also published by Peter Owen

Edith Wharton
The Demanding Dead
Second collection of the author's finest ghost stories, a companion volume to *The Ghost-Feeler*. Selected and introduced by Peter Haining.
978-0-7206-1272-1 / PB / £10.95
'The selection here is an excellent one.' – *Scotland on Sunday*

Wilkie Collins
Sensation Stories
Tales of mystery and suspense by the author of *The Woman in White*. Selected and introduced by Peter Haining.
978-0-7206-1220-2 / PB / £12.50
'Collins is the one man of genius who has an affinity with Dickens . . . no two men could touch them at a ghost story.' – *G.K. Chesterton*

Vernon Lee
Supernatural Tales
Chilling collection of eerie tales written between 1881 and 1913 when the genre was at its most popular. Edited by I. Cooper Willis.
978-0-7206-1194-6 / PB / £9.95
'Seductively dangerous ghosts and exquisite evocation of place.' – *Times Literary Supplement*

Charles Dickens
Hunted Down: The Detective Stories of Charles Dickens
Dickens's detective stories – many informed by his time as a court reporter – are some of the earliest of the genre. Selected and introduced by Peter Haining.
978-0-7206-1265-3 / PB / £9.95
'A fascinating anthology. Dickens's tone is brisk and the details are unembellished.' – *Independent on Sunday*

Peter Owen Publishers
81 Ridge Road, London N8 9NP, UK
+44 (0)20 8350 1775
info@peterowen.com
www.peterowen.com

SOME AUTHORS WE HAVE PUBLISHED

James Agee • Bella Akhmadulina • Tariq Ali • Kenneth Allsop • Alfred Andersch
Guillaume Apollinaire • Machado de Assis • Miguel Angel Asturias • Duke of Bedford
Oliver Bernard • Thomas Blackburn • Jane Bowles • Paul Bowles • Richard Bradford
Ilse, Countess von Bredow • Lenny Bruce • Finn Carling • Blaise Cendrars • Marc Chagall
Giorgio de Chirico • Uno Chiyo • Hugo Claus • Jean Cocteau • Albert Cohen
Colette • Ithell Colquhoun • Richard Corson • Benedetto Croce • Margaret Crosland
e.e. cummings • Stig Dalager • Salvador Dalí • Osamu Dazai • Anita Desai
Charles Dickens • Bernard Diederich • Fabián Dobles • William Donaldson
Autran Dourado • Yuri Druzhnikov • Lawrence Durrell • Isabelle Eberhardt
Sergei Eisenstein • Shusaku Endo • Erté • Knut Faldbakken • Ida Fink
Wolfgang George Fischer • Nicholas Freeling • Philip Freund • Carlo Emilio Gadda
Rhea Galanaki • Salvador Garmendia • Michel Gauquelin • André Gide
Natalia Ginzburg • Jean Giono • Geoffrey Gorer • William Goyen • Julien Gracq
Sue Grafton • Robert Graves • Angela Green • Julien Green • George Grosz
Barbara Hardy • H.D. • Rayner Heppenstall • David Herbert • Gustaw Herling
Hermann Hesse • Shere Hite • Stewart Home • Abdullah Hussein • King Hussein of Jordan
Ruth Inglis • Grace Ingoldby • Yasushi Inoue • Hans Henny Jahnn • Karl Jaspers
Takeshi Kaiko • Jaan Kaplinski • Anna Kavan • Yasunuri Kawabata • Nikos Kazantzakis
Orhan Kemal • Christer Kihlman • James Kirkup • Paul Klee • James Laughlin
Patricia Laurent • Violette Leduc • Lee Seung-U • Vernon Lee • József Lengyel
Robert Liddell • Francisco García Lorca • Moura Lympany • Dacia Maraini
Marcel Marceau • André Maurois • Henri Michaux • Henry Miller • Miranda Miller
Marga Minco • Yukio Mishima • Quim Monzó • Margaret Morris • Angus Wolfe Murray
Atle Næss • Gérard de Nerval • Anaïs Nin • Yoko Ono • Uri Orlev • Wendy Owen
Arto Paasilinna • Marco Pallis • Oscar Parland • Boris Pasternak • Cesare Pavese
Milorad Pavic • Octavio Paz • Mervyn Peake • Carlos Pedretti • Dame Margery Perham
Graciliano Ramos • Jeremy Reed • Rodrigo Rey Rosa • Joseph Roth • Ken Russell
Marquis de Sade • Cora Sandel • George Santayana • May Sarton • Jean-Paul Sartre
Ferdinand de Saussure • Gerald Scarfe • Albert Schweitzer • George Bernard Shaw
Isaac Bashevis Singer • Patwant Singh • Edith Sitwell • Suzanne St Albans • Stevie Smith
C.P. Snow • Bengt Söderbergh • Vladimir Soloukhin • Natsume Soseki • Muriel Spark
Gertrude Stein • Bram Stoker • August Strindberg • Rabindranath Tagore
Tambimuttu • Elisabeth Russell Taylor • Emma Tennant • Anne Tibble • Roland Topor
Miloš Urban • Anne Valery • Peter Vansittart • José J. Veiga • Tarjei Vesaas
Noel Virtue • Max Weber • Edith Wharton • William Carlos Williams • Phyllis Willmott
G. Peter Winnington • Monique Wittig • A.B. Yehoshua • Marguerite Young
Fakhar Zaman • Alexander Zinoviev • Emile Zola